FINDING CRISTINA

TREASURES ON EARTH

FINDING CRISTINA

TREASURES ON EARTH

Emilia Rosa

ISBN: 979-8-9869635-2-5
ISBN Ebook: 979-8-9869635-3-2
Library of Congress Control Number: 2024925067

Editor: Flora Church
Cover design by: MystWorks, LLC; Rosa Simencio Otero
Author picture: Rosa Simencio Otero

MystWorks, LLC

To the memory of my grandparents Higino Rosa and Rita Urdangarin Rosa.

Love is a fire that burns unseen,
a wound that aches yet isn't felt,
an always discontent contentment,
a pain that rages without hurting.
—Rimas, Luis Vaz de Camões. 1585.

En cel an qu'ai dist orendroit,
Je ne sai à tort ou à droit,
Furent li Templiers sans doutance
Tous pris par le royaume de France.
Ou mois d'ocembre, ou point du jour,
A un vendredi, fust le jour
Que furent pris, si com j'ai dict,
Au jor de Diex en crois pendist.
—Chronique Métrique de Godefroy de Paris, 1313.

TABLE OF CONTENTS

FINDING CRISTINA: TRESURES ON EARTH

PREFACE

When you read this story keep in mind that these fictional events happened in the early XX Century, and mores were different from today's. I tried to stay truth to that as much as possible.

Rio Grande do Sul, the setting of this story, is the southernmost state of Brazil. It borders Uruguay on the south and Argentina on the west. It is the land of the proud Gaúchos, tough cowboys honed by the wild coxilhas and the freezing Minuano wind.

We take for granted words with which we grow up, and so did I with Gaúcho (Gaucho in Spanish). As I started my research for this novel, I realized I had no idea of that word's origin. According to a study by Uruguayan author Buenaventura Caviglia Hijo there are thirty-six possible origins of the word! Portuguese, Tupi, Guarani, Arabic, Spanish, Araucanian, Charrua, Latin, Gypsy, Fench, and Hebrew are just a few.

Since the 1600s Rio Grande do Sul has witnessed bloody skirmishes and even a war that, for ten years, turned the state into a country: the Guerra dos Farrapos, the Ragamuffins War. The ragamuffins counted among their ranks with Indians and freed Black slaves. Subjugated, the state was returned to the Brazilian empire in 1845. Later on, came a civil war, lasting from 1893 to 1895. It is considered one of the most barbaric revolutions in Brazilian history, for the brutality of the conflict that included the elimination of most prisoners, who were beheaded, and sometimes previously castrated.

When this story starts—1933—Cristina is living in Rio Grande do Sul for a few years. Revolt was rampant around the country and the state. With the worldwide Depression the price of Brazilian coffee, which represented almost 70 per cent of national exports, had fallen more than 50 percent. Brazil was highly indebted and in 1932 a terrible drought ravaged the country's northeast region. As the President, the Carioca Washington Luis, insisted in pouring money into the coffee industry, states like Rio Grande do Sul rebelled and started to hold strong influence in the country's politics. Upon losing the 1930 presidential election, Getúlio Vargas, a native of that state and its former governor, led a coup d'état and ruled provisionally until 1934, when a new constitution was written and he was elected president. Vargas, who originally believed in the autonomy of the states, later became an advocate of centralized government. And for nineteen years (between 1930 and 1954) he held power—until his suicide.

Among the changes in Brazil at that time, one of the most significant, perhaps, was that in 1932 Brazilian feminists saw their dream become reality: women were allowed to vote. But not without some restrictions; these were removed in the 1934 Constitution, at the influence of biologist Berta Lutz, appointed for that task by the government in 1933.

The city in which this story develops is called Bagé, very near the border with Uruguay, where my father was born. The fictional Fazenda Minuano (Minuano Farm) is located several miles from the city of Bagé, in an area called Arvoleto (Arvolito, or Arbolito), where my paternal grandfather's small farm still is. It has a little cemetery surrounded by whitewashed walls that sits on a gentle slope I remember visiting when I was a child. It is the last resting place of my grandfather, Higinio Rosa, and my grandmother, Rita Urdangarin—who died when my father was born. The views Cristina sees from her windows live in my memory. Describing them brings back loved ones long gone.

Emilia Rosa
Ohio, November, 2025

ACKNOWLEDGMENTS

Once more, I had to rely on the knowledge of some very smart people to learn more about historical facts of the era I wrote about. If I omit to cite anyone it is due to my memory, not their importance in my research.

Helen Uffner (Helen Uffner Vintage Clothing, LLC) for fashion advice. Luciano Botelho de Lucas (Nossa Senhora Auxiliadora School, principal's office), for information and photographs about the school, and its administration. Yuri Cougo Dias (Universidade da Região da Campanha, Communications & Marketing Adviser) and Doris Borges Franz (Museu e Arquivo Histórico da Escola de Engenharia/UFRGS) for information about the creation of the Agronomy and Veterinary Science Institute at the School of Engineering in Porto Alegre. Jon Brausch and Hugh Northup, with everything related to airplanes. Kleia Pagoni, a pretty Greek young lady who helped me with that language. Ricardo Chaves for information about the airport in Porto Alegre and hydroplanes. Ana Luiza Koehler with information about the Confeitaria/Café Colombo in Porto Alegre. Ismael Maynard Bernini, (Biblioteca FABICO, librarian) who directed me to a thesis by Iris Graciela Germano about Carnaval in 1930's Porto Alegre. Roger Gundlach for his knowledge of horses. Claudio de Leão Lemieszek, Marcia Duro Mello, and my cousins Beth Rosa de Andrade, Zezé Urdangarin and Julio Urgandarin for information about Bagé. Abel Domenech for information and pictures of Gaúcho knives. Inge Coad helped me with German. Art Mirtes drove me in his 1921 Model T and helped me with technical information. Ina Scherbaum (Veterinary College at the University of Leipzig, secretary) with information about veterinary course. Museu Júlio de Castilhos (Porto Alegre, Rio Grande do Sul) for allowing me to use Vicente Gervasio's picture Gaúcho Rio-Grandense on this book's cover.

Emilia Rosa

FIRST IMPRESSIONS

Life with its narrow round
Day after day
Widened and perfected
By one sweet ray.
—In Linnæa; The Story of a Friendship, Girl's Own Paper Vol. XX,
No. 999, February 18, 1899.

Dear Diary:

Mommy told me to start riting when I got to the farm in Brazil. We arrived today. It is a city called Bajay or something, and there are no asphalt roads to the farm but I liked the ride in Uncle Robbie truck. Auntie Cris drove the truck and I sat in the front wid mommy, Cousin Donny and Bacon, his dog that I like very much. Papa and Uncle Robbie drove the two seeter that belongs to Auntie Cris because our luggage and mommy trunks was sent in advance so they didn need the big car. They put the two bags mommy brot in the back of our truck, and it all jumped up and down wid all the holes in the road. Mommy said they are pot holes. Donny was mad because he wanted to ride wid the men, because he is a man. His mommy said your just a baby and we all laughed at him and Bacon barked weech I believe is laughing too. Everybody is sleeping now. I am riting under the sheet wid my flashlight. I mean I am writing wid my pen, holding my flashlight so I can see wat I am riting. I hear noises and wonder if these are animals or wind outside. Maybe I can see the animals from the window. Wait, Ill look and come back. I saw no animals and I am sure the noise is from the wind in the windows. Donny

5

took Bacon to his bedroom and I got mad because I wanted the dog to stay here in my bedroom! He said he is going to find another dog for me. If he does I will call him Picolo like the little monkey I saw in a circus once and Ill take him to the school wid me. Tomorrow Im going to ride a horse! I cant wait until it is morning. I dont think I can sleep tonight, because I am so ekcited aldow Im so sleepy and. . .

Here a long scratch from the pen marked the page: eight-year-old Anne Marie had fallen asleep.

CHAPTER ONE

Gaucho, cha (of uncertain origin) – 5. m. A mestizo who, in the 18th and 19th centuries, lived in Argentina, Uruguay, and Rio Grande do Sul, in Brazil, was a nomadic horseman and skilled in livestock work.
—Diccionario de la Lengua Española, Real Academia Española.

It was early morning, still dark. The surrounding darkness delineated a farmhouse, on top of one of many undulating hills. Its solitary, long bulk was like a brushstroke of white paint on a dark canvas. Invisible roof tiles mated with the obscurity, while the stained-glass windows and blood-red front door were like colorful interruptions against the whitewashed walls. The Corinthian columns that flanked the windows and door were not visible yet. A balustrade encircled the tiled roof and held twelve urns that matched each column below. The trees at the back of the house and the tall umbú[1], that formed the orchard, had not yet awakened their color to the morning. In daylight the house would reveal the many shades of its rosy tones, like the cheeks of a shy lady of times past.

Slowly, as if reluctantly, the starless sky started to waver and pale, as dawn pushed its way through. Things started to take shape. A line of narrow, short pillars became visible: these ghosts are concrete supports that held iron rails and formed a fence that surrounds the house. The arch atop the entrance gate—where no gate existed—held, with fancy ironwork, the name of the farm and the date of the house's construction:

---

[1] Umbú, *Phytolacca dioica*, is not actually a tree, but an herb that can grow up to sixty feet.

7

Fazenda Minuano[2] - 1790

Daylight would reveal a path made with large slabs of stone leading to the front door, culminating on three steps, flanked by two exquisitely-elaborate benches of the same material. Above the door, on the fanlight, the same delicate ironwork of the gate, that held pieces of stained-glass, awaited the sun to be brought back to life. A profusion of flowers and vegetation populated the house's front yard. In the back was the walled kitchen garden—or as the Laughton's friend, Spigot, would call it, the jardin potager.

There vegetables, tubers and herbs grew together with an ornamental orchard. Plum, apple, pear and peach trees grew against the brick walls, in the espalier method brought from France by Mlle. Héloïse Jacquet, the first owner's wife, creating decorative designs that were even more appealing when the trees were in bloom. A fig tree proudly held the center of the kitchen garden's attention, stretching almost twenty feet tall, as if proclaiming its independence to her fructiferous rivals crucified on the garden brick walls.

Cristina was responsible for three additions to the first chatelaine's vegetable menagerie. From a neighboring farm she obtained seedlings of three banana trees. The guava tree came from one of the farm hands and was placed among the herbs, to benefit from many hours of sun. But her pet was the maracujá roxo[3]. She placed that vine with the climbing roses that ornamented a little white gazebo, where she enjoyed sitting with her husband on warm evenings.

Inside, the house was silent, except for the noises that houses make, even when no one is there to hear them. Cristina loved this time of the day. Now at thirty, she had three children and was as much in love with her husband as when she first met him in her early twenties. She opened

---

[2] Minuano: cold, dry wind that blows from the Southwest during winter in Rio Grande do Sul. Also an Indian tribe from that state.

[3] *Passiflora edulis*, passion fruit, native of Brazil. From from Tupi *mboruku'ya*, "food in the gourd."

the kitchen door at the back of the house, and stepped outside. A somnolent Bacon had sneaked out of Donny's room and walked past her. He sat down on his back haunches and yawned mightily before going out to his favorite spot to do his matutinal business. From inside the kitchen, the light of the electric bulb filtered through the window and painted golden parallelograms on the ground.

Cristina heard a shrill keek-keek somewhere nearby, the call of the Quero-Quero[4]; probably a mother defending her nest from some predator. Why the silly birds built their nests on bare ground she could never understand. They kept finding vestiges of destroyed nests and little mangled bodies, and it pained her.

Slowly, as if reluctantly, the starless sky started to waver and pale, as dawn pushed its way through. In the East she could see a ribbon of light slowly widening. Closing her eyes, she took a deep breath. It had rained a good part of the night, and the scent of the wet soil and vegetation was invigorating. Then she opened her eyes and, turning to the right, beheld the rough beauty of her surroundings. The ground rolled smoothly down, a soft, green sea, to then rise up to the next hill and repeat that undulating movement a thousand times. These grass-covered undulations were called coxilhas by the Gaúchos and formed the campanha, the Pampas region near the border with Uruguay. Here and there clusters of trees could be seen, cutting the monotony of the landscape; they looked like silhouettes of people huddled up close together. It would be several months until July, when winter and its companion, the Minuano wind, would lay frigid hands upon the coxilhas. The humid night air had left behind a hint of fog, that looked like tightly woven spider webs, lying low on the ground. All the plants were still covered with a patina of last night's rain, and seemed to gleam under the aurora's light touch.

Robert found his wife doing what he called her 'daily devotional' and stood back watching. She was still wearing a light cotton house coat. During winter, when she went out to work on the farm, she adopted the

---

[4] *Vanellus chilensis*, the southern lapwing is called Quero-Quero in Brazil.

farmhands' bombachas: trousers with baggy legs gathered at the ankle by cuffs, that were tucked into leather boots. Instead of the Gaúcho's broad-brimmed hat, she preferred a beret. When horse-riding, Cristina wore a very large poncho, that covered her to her feet, as protection against the cold. It was made with wool from the farm's sheep that she washed, carded, and spun. It matched thick gloves of the same material.

Summer would find her leaping from bed before daybreak, when she bloomed like an exotic flower, while the cold weather kept her longer in bed. Cristina missed the sea. There was never a more pleasant time than a perfect day at the beach. Her body abandoned itself to the flow of the waves, gently cradled in a rhythmic to and fro. Then slathered in tanning oil, she would lie unmoving, stretched on the beach towel, the soft warm sand under her. And as the sun rays made her skin tingle, she would rush to the water, and plunged into it with open eyes, marveling at the blue sea and the multitude of foamy bubbles exploding all around her.

CHAPTER TWO

Every sword that is drawn against Germany now is a sword for peace.
—The War to End War, H. G. Wells. 1914.

But Cristina had no regrets. Her love for her husband and children was such that it compensated the loss of her beloved Copacabana. Her family filled that void so perfectly that she seldom thought of those days. And it was her husband's voice she heard, greeting her in German.

"Guten Morgen, mein Liebling."

"Good morning, to you too. Don't let your cousin hear you!" she admonished him.

The cousin was Desiree, Robert's childhood companion, who he used to call 'Little Scourge of God' when they were children. She acquired a visceral hatred of anything related to Germany after her parents and brother died during the bombing of the Lusitania by a German U-boat in 1915—the cause of the United States joining in that 'war that will end war'[5]. The German-descendent Maria, who helped raise Cristina, was an inexplicable exception.

Robert gave his wife an impish grin and turned his cheek to her for the expected kiss. She patted his closely shaved face, but kissed his lips instead, and nestled in his arms while Bacon tried to get his attention by jumping on his leg. Robert and Cristina stood there for a few minutes, watching the day slowly chasing the darkness away. The dog turned away from them and left the kitchen in search of a cozy nook; after a whole

---

[5] Title of H. G. Wells 1914 book.

night slumbering in Donny's bedroom, he felt refreshed and ready for another nap. Bacon would be waiting for the call to join the children in their daily exploits around the farm.

"Love you, babe," Robert whispered in his wife's ear while holding her tighter in his arms.

She snuggled a bit longer, then started to disengage herself, telling him that coffee was ready.

"I'll make breakfast for you."

She turned to get to the kitchen when her husband stopped her.

"Oh, you ain't getting away so easily. One last kiss, frau," and he followed his words with action. "Where's Alcina?" he asked, as Cristina busied herself in front of the stove.

Alcina and Alcino Christensen, twenty-eight-year-old twins, had been living on the farm and stayed when Robert and Cristina acquired the property, a few years ago, in 1929. Alcino worked with the horses and managed the farm, and his sister Alcina assisted in household duties. The high cheekbones and slightly slanted eyes betrayed the young man's Indian[6] descendance. And while his sister also had a similar bone structure, she inherited her looks from her Danish father. She was much taller than her twin, had deep blue eyes and light blond hair. Alcino lived in a little house on the farm, with their widowed mother, Alice, and Claes, his teen brother. Alcina lived in the main house. Together with young Claes, the twins were the younger and last of Alice's children, that lady having begotten two pairs of twins before. Alberto and Alberta, and Adélio and Adélia perished with their father, Claes, in a train wreck several years ago.

Young Claes was the apple of his grieving mother's eye, who spoiled him rotten. The boy seemed to have a grievance with everyone. Other than his mother—who had concentrated all her love on him—and his sister—who had sense enough not to waste it on such undeserving brother—he adored "Miss" Cristina. The boy simply refused to address her properly. The rest of the world, and particularly Robert (who ignored

---

[6] The grassy plains of south of Rio Grande do Sul were inhabited by the Pampeano Indians. It is said that they invented the boleadeiras and the lasso. The Gaúcho custom of meeting in the galpão (working shed) for a mate and chat is also said to derive from these Indians.

his existence, a high offence in the boy's eyes), were a constant target of his scorn.

"Alcina went to Cine Coliseu with Bunky and Maria last night," Cristina reminded him.

"Bunky went to the theater with them? O-ho, I see! The Coliseu is right at the Jardim. I bet he went to the Sorocabana for some giggle juice!"

Sorocabana was a bar where, traditionally in the morning, men congregated for a daily coffee, smoke and gossip, and, later in the day, for something stronger. It was within shouting distance of Praça do Jardim, a square in downtown Bagé, that a few years later—in 1938—would be renamed Silveira Martins.

"Nope. He went to watch that new film, The Miracle Woman." And at his surprise she explained with a meaningful expression, "With Barbara Stanwyck."

"Of course. I must make sure I'll tease him," and a merry glint lit his blue eyes.

"When we got home from the train station they were not home yet, so I left them a note telling them to stay longer in bed."

At that moment Mr. Valentino, the rooster, let out his morning call. Cristina thought of the irony of the skinniest, ugliest cockerel she had ever seen, named after the handsome Rudolph Valentino. Donny's idea, of course. He had wanted to tease Alcina, who idolized the deceased actor. She never referred to the animal by her idol's name. Many a time she had threatened to have "that scrawny lizard" stuffed into a large pan for a rice and chicken dinner. But that never materialized, since the bird was under the patronage—and close surveillance—of his champion and godfather, Donny.

What a sense of humor her child had, Cristina mused, thinking of his dog, who he had named Bacon. Their boy had inherited not only the looks, but also his father's mindset.

"A bit late, that gentleman gives us his warning that the day is starting. Maybe I'll put an alarm clock in the chicken coop for Mr. Valentino," Robert suggested.

"Come inside, kid, and close the door after you."

As he came in, Cristina kissed his cheek as he stood behind her, and stuck his head past her shoulder, inhaling the air.

"Since you're a good boy I'm also making pancakes. And we have maple syrup your cousin brought from the States," she motioned with her hand to a cupboard to her left. "Can you get it to the table? Right there, second door on the left."

They had been there for several minutes when they heard a light scratch on the outside door.

"Probably Donny's friend," Cristina said. Robert's eyebrows went up a fraction while he watched her. "Don't just stand there, hon, open the door."

Robert was not prepared for this visitor.

"What the…"

"It's your son's latest acquisition."

Standing outside, his muzzle turned up, a strange little animal analyzed Robert with little round eyes. He had the face of a large squirrel with tiny ears and long whiskers. The body and its thick fur were those of a beaver, but ended on a thin mouse tail. He stood up on incongruent duck feet, while the front paws resembled those of a squirrel. Brazilians call it ratão do banhado[7], swamp rat.

"You ain't coming in, you freak," Robert admonished the animal and got a bizarre, wavy whistle for answer.

"He won't. He's Donny's new friend. Your son feeds him; that's why he's here. Close the door," she told her husband. "He just wanted to let us know he is here."

"What does he eat?"

"Oh, little peels and scraps from veggies and fruits we use during the day and keep there," she pointed out to a corner of the counter where sat a glazed bowl covered with a napkin. "The next day Donny gives it to him; it's his breakfast."

"Nice of him to show up bright n' early."

"The farmhands told me that they stay tucked away in their houses by the river when it's light out. They make holes at water level and live there."

"I've seen those from afar and they look just like a beaver, but on closer inspection it's more like a fat, hairy rat."

"That's why we call them rato," his wife told him.

---

[7] *Myocastor coypus*, also known as nutria.

Cristina finished her breakfast.

"Well, since the kids are still in bed, I'm going to fix our bedroom," she told her husband and started to get up.

"No need, princess," he stopped her, between two mouthfuls of bacon and scrambled eggs, "I've already done it."

"You know, I don't care what everybody else says, you're a swell guy," and she tousled his hair. "I'm going to check on the twins." She turned to him, eyes sparkling: "Or have you already seen to them too?"

"God forbid! Dr. Jekyll and Miss Hyde are still sleeping. I tiptoed when I passed that den of iniquity! Let sleeping children lie! But don't go yet, young lady. Come to papa," he patted his lap, "and tell me what you're up to today, you gorgeous li'l armful." And he went back to working on his food.

At that moment their first-born burst into the kitchen, cutting short his father's romantic intentions. He was followed by his cousin; both looked very sleepy.

"Mom, where's Leonidas' food?"

"And a good morn to you too, young master," his father chided him, then turned to Anne Marie, "Did you sleep well, young mistress?"

"Like a log, Uncle Robbie," the girl muttered then yawned.

"'Morning," said a contrite Donny to his father; then turning to his mother, "'Morning, Mom."

"There's Leonidas' bowl, darling," Cristina indicated the container while giving both children an affectionate peck on the top of their heads.

Donny got hold of the bowl and Robert watched as the boy and his cousin left through the kitchen door. "And who in blazes is Leonidas?" he asked his wife.

"You met him not long ago."

"The soggy rat? Named after a Spartan warrior! I must see that," and Robert went to the door. The two children were squatting outside.

"Hello, Leo," Robert heard Donny say. The little animal answered with a series of grunting sounds. "This is my cousin Anne Marie," and he gestured to the girl. "We call her Annie."

"What a darling," she said. "Can I pet him?"

15

"I think not," said Robert, coming out from the kitchen.

"Yeah," his son ignored the command, "he's quite tame."

Robert watched, bemused, while the kids lavished the little creature with awkward little pats on his back. The beast's little eyes closed and he seemed to enjoy the attention.

"Here's your breakfast, Leo," and Donny put the dish in front of the little animal.

After a few little grunts the kids took as expressions of thanks, it started to quickly eat.

Robert went back into the kitchen to see his wife putting their dishes in the sink.

"They are on nickname basis already—it's Leo," he chuckled. "I bet our son will want a lion next," he mused.

"If he does," that lady answered with a humorous glint in her eyes while pouring Quaker Oats in a pan containing milk, "the lion better watch out for the ferocious Leonidas."

CHAPTER THREE

BAGÉ, a town and municipality of the state of Rio Grande do Sul, Brazil, about 176 m. by rail W.N.W. of the city of Rio Grande do Sul. Pop. of the municipality (1890) 22,692. It is situated in a hilly region 774 ft. above sea-level, and is the commercial centre of a large district on the Uruguayan border in which pastoral occupations are largely predominant. This region is the watershed for southern Rio Grande do Sul, from which streams flow E. and S.E. to the Atlantic coast, and N.W. and S.W. to the Uruguay river. The town dates from colonial times, and has always been considered a place of military importance because of its nearness to the Uruguay frontier, only 25 m. distant. It was captured by the Argentine general Lavalle in 1827, and figured conspicuously in most of the civil wars of Argentina. It is also much frequented by Uruguayan revolutionists.
—In 1911 Encyclopædia Britannica.

The city of Bagé in Brazil's southernmost state, Rio Grande do Sul, was several miles away from the Minuano Farm on dirt road. At the beginning that change had seemed too radical to Cristina, accustomed as she was to asphalted thoroughfares, cable cars, and big cities. Life on a farm is filled with hard work, but she quickly fell in love with it, the hands, the animals. Even Donny enjoyed it and, despite his young years, helped in the stables—which actually meant he spent most of the time chatting with the men when he was not pampering his horse Bucyrus.

Robert also seemed at ease, although never having been on a farm before. He worked as a consulting engineer for the town of Bagé, but most of his day was absorbed by farm chores. He had quickly mastered the art of lassoing. He also became so fast at shearing sheep, that he

17

gained the admiration of the hands, who already respected his drive. But the honor of the fastest shearer was still held by the skinny, redheaded Mercúrio, who got his nickname from the Brazilian spelling of mercurochrome—Mercúrio Cromo.

The regularity of nature and farm chores, the tending and feeding of animals, everything that involved farm life, Cristina found it all stimulating, challenging at times, but enjoyable. And then, there were her very active children, Donny and the twins, Alex and Loulou. With them she had no time for boredom: they made sure one day was never like the prior!

Cristina's life story was unusual. From an infant she had been raised by Vasili and Sonya Abramov. She was born in France in 1903, the daughter of Helena Sergeievna Dobrinsky, then a widowed Russian countess. The Abramovs had been the countess' playmates in Russia and accompanied her in her travels when she retired from the world after being widowed. Cristina's real father, Alexandre Rebelo de Oliveira, belonged to a traditional and wealthy Brazilian family. He and Helena were not yet married when urgent family business called Alexandre back to Brazil. While he was gone, Cristina was born, and not long afterwards life gave Helena a harsh blow: Alexandre died in a car accident in Brazil. The news devastated her and she fell ill. While recovering, her mother, an overwhelming personality who directed the young woman's life, convinced Helena to travel to Brazil to find Alexandre's family and get them to recognize the child. It was decided Cristina would be sent to Brazil ahead, while her mother convalesced.

So, the trusted Abramovs took baby Cristina to Brazil, while Helena and her mother remained in France. They were to contact Alexandre's family, ahead of Helena's arrival, and introduce the infant. The Abramovs arrived in Brazil safely, but were unsuccessful on their mission. Meanwhile in France catastrophe struck: Helena's mother died in a shipwreck while on a pleasure trip on the river Seine. Utterly alone, inexperienced, and almost mad with grief, the young woman fell ill again. By the time she recovered, she had lost contact with the Abramovs.

Twenty years later, with the help of John Laughton, Robert's father, the ex-countess found her daughter as well as her friend Sonya, Vasili Abramov having passed away. Cristina was told of her parentage, and reunited with her real mother. At that time Helena, who had married a second time to a friend of John Laughton, was once more a widow.

Upon her marriage to Robert, Cristina moved to New York, but frequently visited Sonya in Rio de Janeiro, accompanied by her mother. On one of these trips, Cristina found Sonya out of sorts. She and Robert decided to move to Rio de Janeiro to be closer to her. Helena, who had married John Laughton, did not rest until she moved near her daughter and her dear, childhood friend. So, early in 1929 father and son decided to sell all their property in New York, converting it to gold, and move to Brazil. Theirs was a lucky move because at the end of October of that fatal year the world took a terrible economic blow that would be known as the Wall Street Crash, that caused a worldwide depression.

John Laughton had extensively visited south of Brazil and Robert had also been in that area[8]. Learning of a farm for sale, they bought it. At first, they had not intended to move in, but as they spent a few weeks in their new state, the desire to move grew. Sonya insisted that she would be fine staying in Rio, promising to visit them soon—a promise she never fulfilled—and so their move to the farm was accomplished. With electricity in the farm, Robert equipped the rooms with electric fans for the sweltering months of summer. And in the kitchen, a ceiling fan, a very costly contraption, was installed.

The Laughtons did not change anything in the house, except for the addition of a generator, an exception in the area, which, initially, made their neighbors think of them as excentric. With acquaintance, they realized the benefits of electricity and some farmers decided to follow suit.

---

[8] Finding Cristina: A New Life

CHAPTER FOUR

Article 1: From the date of this law, slavery is declared extinct in Brazil.
Article 2: All dispositions to the contrary are revoked.
—Lei Áurea, May 13, 1888.

The little cottage stood at the end of a small slope, under the protection of a very tall and wide-spread umbú tree. The location was advantageous on hot days, but as winters in south of Brazil are wet, a potbelly stove had to constantly work to compensate for the tree shade during the cold season. Unlike the houses of workers in other farms, with roofs covered with corrugated metal, this one—like all the houses in the Minuano Farm—had ceramic tiles. The front door was painted a dark red, almost brown, repeated on the window shutters, that, now open, let one see gauzy white curtains—one of the many little touches Cristina had bestowed upon this little dwelling.

The low walls were made of stones that had been recently whitewashed. The rustic appearance of the little house was softened by flowers. Rows of tall daisies, rosemary and lilies lined up all along the front of the house, flanking the door. When the weather was too dry, Cristina would come by to water them, carrying water from the little pond that stood in the backyard, that was also used for bathing. Today the water was so still it resembled a mirror, perfectly reflecting the tufts of furry clouds lazily navigating the sky. Nature seemed to be asleep. Even the leaves on the umbú were silent, unmoving. All animals seemed to be taking a siesta that day. Only a lone turtledove calling in the distance broke the feeling of solitude.

FINDING CRISTINA: TREASURES ON EARTH

Uncle Benedito opened the door to find Donny and Annie waiting for him. As he got outside, he took a little branch from the rue planted in a vase near the door, lightly rubbed it in his hands and tucked it behind the left ear. According to the African religions brought to Brazil by the slaves, this herb represented an African deity—Eshú—and would keep him and the ones around him safe. He then lowered himself to a little stool made from a wood stump that stood near the front door, that he left wide open. After the greetings, he started his story, which was one of the reasons why the children frequently visited him.

"At the time of my story, the fields were still open. No borders, no fences and you could catch wild cattle, and deer and ostriches ran free."

He took a long puff from his new corn cob pipe, a gift from Desiree. He wore an immaculate white cotton shirt with soft collar, and a pair of pristine white linen pants, also her gifts. But on his feet, he had his old espadrilles—the alpargatas, or alpercatas, made of canvas fabric sewn on soles of twisted cord Gaúchos liked to wear informally. His abundant white, crinkly hair was cut short, parted on one side so straight it seemed done with a ruler. Benedito had been born on September 28 of 1861. Or, as he liked to joke, ten years too early, referring to the Rio Branco Law, the Law of Free Birth, enacted exactly ten years later.

The Lei do Ventre Livre—as it is called in Portuguese—established that children born from slave mothers would be free. The final chapter of slavery in Brazil was written on May 13 of 1888. With just a few words, by a Princess with a long name—Isabel Cristina Leopoldina Augusta Micaela Gabriela Rafaela Gonzaga—daughter of the last Brazilian Emperor, Pedro II. Isabel, the Redeemer. She died at seventy-one in France, where she and her family lived since November 17 of 1889, having that day been exiled by a military coup.

On the right side of seventy, Benedito still carried traces of the tall, handsome man, with a powerful carriage he was in his youth. A few little creases around the eyes and the constant wide smile attested his mild disposition. Yet, throughout his youth, he was thought of as a bit of a Don Juan. Gossip had imputed to him the parentage of some children born with skin a shade too dark, or hair curlier than their forefathers'. All gossip, of course.

Donny and Annie sat on the ground, facing Uncle Benedito. Their childish faces raised to the old man, drinking each word he enunciated in his strong, yet suave baritone voice, between puffs from the pipe. His little pet fox, Peludo, made a sudden appearance. He was a Pampas' Fox, what Gaúchos call graxaim. He came from behind the house, where he had probably been hunting. He had been raised with Benedito's fowl—chickens, pigeons, and geese—since he was found hurt as a cub, becoming their fierce defender.

Little did Peludo know, but Max, ignorant of the customs of the place, had brought a copper hunting horn, hoping to put it to use hunting foxes; he was quickly undeceived: no such thing as a British hunt took place in those parts. Besides, the robust pet took care of any intruders of his or any other species that dared disturb his fowl friends.

But the little fox had a champion: Desiree, who abhorred the hunt, was overjoyed. "A bunch of grown men on horses, and blood-thirsty, crazed dogs running after a defenseless little animal. I'm glad it won't happen here!"

"But foxes are vermin," her husband argued, "that's what they are, vermin!"

"No matter. It's not fair!"

"What, you want us to give it a horse to ride, old gal?" And that question went unanswered.

Peludo sniffed the children who greeted and petted him, and walked to his master, at whose feet he laid down and curled up. Following on his steps came Demosthenes, a duckling who the fox had saved and followed his benefactor everywhere. The name was a courtesy of Donny—who had never read the Greek's orations, but hearing his name, immediately thought of the duck.

"There was a rancher, very rich, but he was bad, oh, very bad," the old man continued, shaking his head in disapproval. "The door of his house would not open to anyone in need, even with the frosty Minuano blowing outside. One day he asked one of his slaves, a li'l boy, to take some hosses to pasture. He told him to watch them hosses careful like, but one of them escaped."

A stressed 'oh' came from the girl.

"That night," uncle Benê continued, "the rancher saw the bay hoss was missin'. Furious, he sent the little slave to find the hoss. The li'l boy prayed to his godmother, the Virgin Mary. With a li'l candle stub to help 'im see, he started the search, all alone. It was pitch black. The whole night he searched and found nothing. Tired, he fell asleep and the rancher found him like that in the mornin'. He thrashed the boy till he was almost dead then threw him on an anthill!"

Here both his listeners gasped in horror.

"But the next mornin' the rancher came across the boy, and the child had no injuries on his body." Donny and Annie cheered with joy. "And the boy was ridin' the lost bay hoss, and the Virgin Mary was with him! The farmer dropped to his knees and asked for forgiveness while the boy galloped the bay hoss to heaven. That's why they say that when you lose something, if you light a candle near an anthill and ask for help, the Li'l Black Shepherd will help."

"Tell us another story, Uncle Benedito," Annie asked him. Her Portuguese was without fault and she was proud to show off to her cousin.

"Tomorrow Uncle Benê will tell you one I never did before to Master Donny. About some soldiers in France, a very, very long time ago. They were warrior monks," a statement that surprised the children. "They were called Templars and their order was created to defend pilgrims in the Holly Land—where our Lord Jesus Christ was born. They say there is a treasure from these Templars in these parts."

"Here?" the children exclaimed in unison.

"Seems so. Miss Tória's grandpa tole me stories of them Templars when I was a kid. He event went overseas to visit their places," Uncle Benê explained. "And Master Bernardo inherited that angst to find the treasure," the old man shook his head deprecatingly at that memory. "But not so Miss Tória. She jess liked roaming these hills with her hosses. Didn't care 'bout treasures."

The old man always enjoyed his chats with the two children, but he realized how stiff his joints were, from sitting too long in that position. He decided it was time to let the kids go back home. "'Tis a long story. Come back some other day and I'll tell ya." And as they started to protest, he added, smiling, "This ol' man needs his rest, children."

After Annie kissed Uncle Benedito and Donny shook hands with him, they were preparing to leave when he told Donny the library in the house had books about the Templars. "From the old master and Miss Tória's father too. Both the father and the son was keen interested in them Templars."

Excited, the children started to take off, running, when the old man stopped them. "Master Donny, go to the kitchen and get a jar of butiá⁹ jelly I made for your mom."

It was a recipe his mother had learned in the big house's kitchen, and Benedito had committed to a notebook where he kept all her recipes. His mother always had some back home, for the young Benedito who loved to eat it with bread at breakfast. He watched them go, followed by Princesa, the fourteen-year-old pigeon, matriarch and queen of Benedito's dovecote. This venerable snow-white bird was large enough not to tempt the farm cat, Mr. Felix. She would let the children pet and caress her—and Annie was even allowed the right to kiss Princesa's little head. Then she would follow them to the kitchen garden where they would feed her her favorite thing: seeds from the sunflowers that bloomed in the walled garden. When satiated, the little animal would fly back to hold court over her subjects.

---

⁹ *Butia eriospatha*, also known as coquinho in Rio Grande do Sul.

CHAPTER FIVE

But the Knights of Christ may safely fight the battles of their Lord, fearing neither sin if they smite the enemy, nor danger at their own death; since to inflict death or to die for Christ is no sin, but rather, an abundant claim to glory.
—In Praise of the New Knighthood, St. Bernard of Clairvaux. 1136.

That evening Donny and Annie were barely able to sit through dinner. They gobbled their food, and paid scant attention to the conversation.

Robert reached to a book his son had placed on the table, beside his plate.

"The Republic. Plato," Robert eyed Donny quizzically, then turned to his wife. "We've gotta do something about this, wife." His wife stopped a forkful of food halfway to her lips, merely lifting her eyebrows questioningly, so he explained, "Otherwise our child will grow up to be one of those pedantic intellectuals who grew up reading Latin and Greek literature."

"Like yourself?"

"You've got my point. Besides, what example to those two mites," he motioned to the twins, who were following the exchange with attentive eyes.

At that Donny, fidgety, asked permission to leave the table, seconded by Annie.

"What's the hurry?" Robert asked them. "What mischief are you two planning?"

"Nothing, sir, we're just going to the library to read," Donny answered.

25

And after obtaining permission, he and Annie left under the gaze of the stunned Robert.

"Such eagerness to go to the library makes me a bit uncomfortable, wife. What's next?" Robert asked Cristina, who shrugged.

"He likes to read. Annie likes to read too. So, what's so unusual?"

"I don't know… Every time this boy does something that seems harmless, he causes trouble. Better watch him."

"Oh, hon, don't be so hard on him. He's a good boy."

Cristina's comment elicited a guffaw from her husband.

"I'm with you, Robert," Max agreed. "We better keep an eye on these two."

A statement that got him a healthy kick from his wife.

As they opened the library door, the light from the corridor illuminated a large picture hanging above the fireplace, dominating the room. Donny turned the switch on. From the frame the liquid blue eyes of Héloïse Jacquet watched them.

The painter, Madame Vigée Le Brun, had recreated a similar ambience of the 1783 portrait of the French queen: 'Marie-Antoinette with a Rose'—not the infamous one, in a chemise dress, but the formal picture. Young Mlle. Jacquet was portrayed as one of the Muses—Erato, who represented music, song and dance. She dressed a white taffeta robe à la française, in the fashion of the Eighteenth Century, in a more subdued, less Rococo style. Intricate silver lace embellished the neckline and sleeves and the center of her stomacher was decorated with a row of small silver ribbons. Unlike her queen, the young Frenchwoman held a little harp in her left hand, while delicately plucking it with long, delicate fingers. As was the fashion at the time, her skin was pearl-white and her cheeks a bright pink. Her powdered hair, tousled, with curls arranged over the shoulder, balanced a large straw hat, a concoction made with interlaced silk and organza, garlanded with colorful flowers and pink feathers; an incongruous choice of dressing, that of the beautiful Héloïse, for behind her was a cerulean sky above a luxuriant forest.

"She was so pretty." Annie could not take her fascinated eyes away from the beautiful picture.

Donny, who did not give the picture a second look, had concentrated on the bookshelves.

"You don't think she's pretty?" his cousin asked him, surprised at the boy's lack of interest.

"Don't know." He gave a brief, dispassionate look to the painting. "Guess if you say so. She looks a bit odd, though."

"Odd?" the girl exclaimed, outraged, then pointed at the depiction of loveliness with a dramatic gesture of the hand. "How can you be so insensitive? Oh, men!" she shook her head, and gave him a commiserating look, wondering about men's lack of empathy for beauty that women naturally possess. Seeing that her cousin only had eyes for the books, she turned hers to the shelves, and could not help admiring the neatly packed rows.

Since their arrival on the farm, Donny had perused several shelves, but there were still many more waiting to be explored. They lined the room from top to bottom and, behind glass doors, shelf upon shelf held hundreds of volumes.

Annie approached the displays. "Gosh, look at all these books."

Her amazed eyes travelled through the lined titles, until they fell upon her favorite subject—Ancient Egypt. There was a 1923 copy of Peet and Woolley 'The City of Akhenaten'; one Davies' 'Rock Tombs of El Amarna'; and several copies of Flinders Petrie's books. Issues of the Journal of Egyptian Archaeology were neatly stacked on one of the shelves.

Meanwhile Donny had clambered on the ladder and carefully replaced Plato between two of his peers—Marcus Aurelius and Seneca. They were in good company with Roman scholars, like historians Livy and Cassius Dio. Neighboring these were Homer poems, the tragedies of Euripides and Sophocles' plays.

He came down and inspected the shelves. "I saw something about Templars, but thought it was religious stuff," he told his cousin. "There," he pointed to a high shelf. Climbing the rolling ladder that connected with higher shelves, he reached the books and started tossing them to Annie.

"'The History of the Knights Templars', Charles G. Addison," she read. Then opening the book and turning the pages, "From 1842! This one is more recent—1925," she said, holding another book, "'A Story of the Life and Times of Jacques de Molay', by H. H. Haywood."

"This is in French," Donny said and was about to replace the book when Annie asked him to hand it to her, since she read French.

"'La Règle du Temple'. The author is a Henri de Curzon." She turned the pages until she found the edition: 1886.

"And another from the same author."

"'La Maison du Temple de Paris: Histoire et Description avec Deux Planches'." She looked up at her cousin, still perched on the ladder, analyzing the books. "I think we have enough to read here, Donny."

"Just wait till you see this." He jumped down holding a book. "This I think might be very interesting. Check it out," and he turned the cover to face her, so she could read it.

"'Templários na América do Sul?' by Dr. Elisete da Silva Costa."

She grabbed the book and looked at her cousin. "Templars in South America," she translated, excited. "This might be *the* book to read, Donny!"

CHAPTER SIX

Beauty is the shimmering, high answer to the deep hunger of mortals; beauty of living, beauty that is mystery and poetry and faith, beauty of line and color.
—The Quest of Beautiful, Elizabeth Arden advertisement booklet.
1923.

D esiree had handed out almost all the gifts she had brought. Several jars of Jumbo Peanut Butter were already stored in the larder, bringing peace to Cristina's household. (The contents of the last jar had been the cause of many disputes between Robert, his son, and Bunky.) Boxes of cigars were shared between Bunky and Robert. Maria had received a large stack of American magazines, of which she had become keen after learning English when living in New York; there were a couple of years-worth of Picture Play, Better Homes and Gardens, McCall's, and Ladies' Home Journal. She also got the most beautiful pincushion: the top was a lady holding a fan made of frail porcelain, and a wide, gathered satin skirt that could hold pins and needles. Donny got boxes of his favorite candy bars: Hershey's with almonds, and Baby Ruth, with the addition of the new kids' sensation, 3 Musketeers.

Desiree told him that each little package had one piece with three flavors—chocolate, vanilla and strawberry. "So, you can share it with two friends."

He thought for a few seconds then told her that since there was only Annie, he would share one with her and eat the other two. Before he scurried away with his treasures, Desiree rescued the boxes of Reese's Peanut Butter Cups from his clutches. "The penny cups are for your dad.

29

And these are for you," turning to Cristina, she bent over the trunk and handed her two small boxes.

"Herbal Mask, Helena Rubinstein," Cristina read the labels, while opening the packages. "Iridescent Eye Shadow," then turning the little container upside down read: "Violet-Gold."

"It will match your eyes," Desiree explained. "Oh, I had the most marvelous treatment at Mme. Arden's! At her Fifth Avenue salon. They call it a five-point-plan—or something like that. They give you a face treatment, then you do some exercise. Next the Ardena Bath. They put you in a tub lined with waxed paper, then pour deliciously warm paraffin on you. The paraffin hardens and I felt all nice and warm, and they gave me a nice massage afterwards. Oh, and I just remembered," she straightened up and turned to Cristina, "I brought several jars of Hellmann's for my Waldorf Salad."

Cristina sat patiently while Desiree chattered contentedly and tucked her dainty underwear and nightgowns in the drawers of a tall chest of drawers.

"I kept this for last, because it is my special gift for you," Desiree told her, removing a large cardboard box from the bottom of her steamer trunk. Placing it on the bed, she stood watching Cristina remove the lid.

As she lifted the sheets of tissue paper that hid the contents of the box, she uttered a muffled 'oh.' Under the silken sheets was the most beautiful mink capelet. Desiree placed it over Cristina's shoulders, adjusting the high collar around her slender neck.

Cristina turned to the mirror and looked at her image, speechless. The immaculate fur shone like snow on a sunny day, creating a dramatic contrast with Cristina's black hair. "For me? You can't possibly—"

"I can and that's the end of it," Desiree interrupted. "Now, let's get you out of this before you suffocate with the heat," and she followed word with action, placing the capelet back in the box.

"But, why?"

"Because I haven't been to your birthday for a few years. It's for all the ones I missed! And to make the local females purple with envy. I wonder if they ever heard of mink," and Desiree gave her friend a naughty look.

"Jeez, Desiree! I'll have you know some of these females went to finishing schools in Europe," Cristina chided. "Just because they live in the countryside doesn't mean they're a bunch of rustics!"

"Do you like it?" Desiree asked her, taking no notice of the other's indignation.

"Like it? I love it," Cristina answered with a fervent expression. She adoringly caressed the capelet's soft surface, and decided that she must accept the gift. She hugged Desire and kissed both her cheeks. "You're a darling!" Then, changing the subject: "I just remembered that we need to visit the school sometime soon."

"Oh, the school," and Desiree gave a weary sigh. "What a bore! Well, I guess it can't be helped," she said, turning weary eyes to Cristina.

"No, it can't. We'll go to Espirito Santo, the girls' boarding school first. And since it's near Nossa Senhora Auxiliadora, the boys' boarding school, we'll go there afterwards. I need to see the principal, Father Valentim. He organized the school orchestra and the band. And last year he founded the Coral Auxiliadora. Donny plays the piano really well; I'd like to ask about him joining the orchestra. But I hope I can also introduce you to Father Roberto Germano when we're there. He's chaplain at the girls' school."

Germanito, as his close friends and former students affectionately called him, was a very active man, full of energy, whose joy in life was communicated to all who came in contact with him. He taught geography and history at the boys' school. Born in Uruguay he came to the school in February of 1904, "and it was Carnaval," as he liked to recall. Together with a group of Salesian priests they founded the boys', then the girls' boarding school, the latter being run by Franciscan nuns.

"He's a dear, very popular," Cristina continued. "Students love him. He even plays soccer with the boys during recess."

Desiree did not seem impressed. "He sounds like a softie. Wonder if he can control our little monsters."

"Oh, no! He's very strict, but also fair. You'll understand as soon as you meet him."

"Well, I expect the nuns are gonna take Annie—since you told me they're good with misbehaving children. The question is: how long are they gonna keep her?"

31

During Annie's stay at the school in Switzerland, she was the source of much trouble. On her first day she set fire to a girl's tresses during mess. On one especially chilly night she sounded the fire alarm in the middle of the night. On another occasion she filled the Math teacher's inkwell with disappearing ink; the next day, when Mlle. Bertier started to hand the tests to the girls, the corrections and notes had vanished. When one of the servers found a frog in the water jar she was about to take to the headmistress' table, Annie was suspected, but no one ever proved she had a hand in it. Her last act, that got her expelled, was breaking a girl's nose—when she also broke a couple of her own fingers in the process. On that occasion she told her parents that Donny had taught her the move.

"And that Jennifer was a pest. She bullied the younger girls. Someone had to do something," she justified herself. "So, I saved a little girl from being turned into pulp and got expelled. That's gratitude for you! The world is not fair," she told her bemused parents.

And that is when both her genitors decided to send their little darling to the same school Robert and Cristina were sending their too lively son.

"Don't worry, the two schools are used to getting troublesome children."

Robert had just entered the room, and was opening a box of Peanut Butter Cups. Hearing that, he added, with a comical expression, for his cousin's benefit, "They even accepted Donny." Next, he unwrapped another candy and popped it into his mouth. And seeing the box with the fur on the bed, asked them, "Who skinned all the rats? Max?"

CHAPTER SEVEN

If a woman is poorly dressed, you notice her dress, but if she's impeccably
dressed, you notice the woman.
—Coco Chanel.

The four women beheld a dress laying on a bed—Cristina, Desiree, Maria and Alcina. They were in the latter's bedroom. The little chamber had light pink walls, the same tone of the chenille bedspread and the lace curtains. The dress had been ironed to perfection, but the wide sash that held it to the hips revealed it to be passé, as waists had been going back to their proper places since 1930.

"Oh, but that won't do, Alcina. You are not going to a ball at Clube Comercial with your young man wearing this." The scandalized Cristina had put into words the other two women's thoughts. And as Alcina tried to argue, she added, "We'll get something else. Wait here. Don't move," she ordered and left the room, followed by Desiree.

They were back in a couple of minutes, each holding a dress.

"This will fit you, as we're the same build," Cristina held an airy confection of pink organdy, very similar to the Letty Lynton dress[10], just with a few less frills. "And you'll wear my pink evening shoes that go perfectly with it."

And before Alcina could protest, Cristina quickly turned the girl around and started undoing the buttons on the back of her dress.

---

[10] Wore by Joan Crawford in the 1932 film Letty Lynton; it was created by Hollywood designer Gilbert Adrian.

"We'll just need to adjust the hem," Desiree said, as she held her dress up so Alcina could see it.

The women's fascinated eyes said all they felt about it, for no words came from their lips. When Desiree turned it to show the dress' back, a unison, low gasp expressed their admiration.

The fabric was silk crepe satin in shell pink, cut on a bias, and sleeveless. One could imagine it gliding down over the body, as on a Greek statue. On the back two wide columns of magenta velvet plunged down with the deep V, coming from the shoulders, and ending in a wide bow on the waist, that held a gathered train.

"Where did you get this marvel?" Cristina spoke reverently, the first to come out of the silent spell in which the silky apparition had held them. "It is. . . It is absolutely amazing," she added, fondling the soft fabric.

"Oh, it's something from Augusta that I just got," Desiree answered.

The nonchalantly referred to as Augusta, was none other than the famous Augusta Bernard, the French couturière whose exclusive salon was on the also exclusive Rue de Faubourg Saint-Honoré in Paris.

"Oh, dear, this is way too daring for me," Alcina was finally able to articulate, although her eyes seemed to tell a different tale.

"Besides, we wouldn't have time to shorten it. All this fabric," Maria held the hem, shaking her head, while Cristina translated Alcina's comment to Desiree and added, "Not even the four of us together would be able to shorten the hem in time for the ball."

Cristina's dress fitted Alcina perfectly. Desiree, helped by Maria, had worked the young woman's hair, with the help of the magic Presto-Matic bob pin curlers she had brought from New York. As they finished, the three women stepped back to see the effect.

"She looks lovely," was Maria's comment, while she fluffed the ruffles around the dress' hem. Desiree and Cristina agreed.

Alcina beheld her reflection on the cheval mirror and the women admiring her thought that Joan Crawford would not hold a candle to this beauty. She looked like a picture out of a fairy tale, with little golden curls framing her high forehead, and the long hair tucked on the nape of her lovely neck. Now, they thought, she was ready to join her young man. And not too early, for they heard the chug-chug of a motor approaching the house.

Cristina ran to the window, opened it and, sticking her head out, was just able to see a car disappearing at the corner of the house. "Your beau just arrived, Alcina."

Said beau was Joaquim Feliciano de Araujo Valentim, better known as Jô Valentim. Only son of a wealthy farmer who lived in the neighborhood, Fidêncio Enildo de Araujo Valentim, and nephew of vicar José Luiz de Araujo Valentim, the popular, much-loved Father Valentim. By taking Alcina to the party, the young man—who Robert deemed was not the sharpest knife in the drawer—had, for the first time in his life, gone against his mama's wishes. He had to amass much needed courage to defy that lady, who ruled her family with an iron fist.

The proud Mrs. Joaquina Perpétua da Silva Gama Valentim was not much to look at. She was a little bit over five feet, thin, with a foreboding expression. Bunky, who had disliked her from their first meeting, called her a desiccated stick with an attitude. But the lady had a pedigree as long as her name, and if that was not enough to command respect, her haughty demeanor did the rest. The illustrious ancestor whose name she constantly referred to was Admiral Paulo José da Silva Gama. He was a cousin, albeit a distant one, of Portuguese extraction. For six years Gama was the governor of the Captaincy of São Pedro do Rio Grande do Sul, which had gained its administrative independence from the Captaincy of São Paulo. In 1818 he became minister of Brazil's Supreme Military Court. He was created Baron of Bagé in 1823 by Emperor Pedro I. The Baron did not live much longer to enjoy the title, which was left to a son of his same name, with whom the title went extinct. That aristocratic line, she felt, should not be besmirched by being mixed with such a mongrel as Alcina. She would see to it!

CHAPTER EIGHT

A pretty young woman whose men friends come in occasionally and play cards with the others, or dance to a small and not loud phonograph in the kitchen, is merely being treated humanly.
—The Maids' Men Friends in Etiquette, Emily Post, 1922.

Cristina had stayed up. She lay on the sofa in the living room. Were it winter, she would have been in the kitchen, curled up in one of the arm chairs near the wood cook stove; at that time of the year, it was her favorite place to read, with the lit stove making the place so cozy.

The heat of the day had considerably abated and the wide-open French windows filtered the cool night air in through the meshes of fine screens that kept the mosquitoes out. She had been reading one of the books Desiree had brought her—Stuart Palmer's Murder on Wheels—when, around ten o'clock, she fell asleep.

She woke up with a start to the sound of a car approaching the house. There was silence for a while as the engine was shut off. She sat up and listened. They must have been making their adieux, she thought. She tried to imagine that serious young lady, Alcina, and her shy young man with the starry sky and a soft breeze as witnesses of that romantic moment. Then the engine resumed and the sound was drowned by the distance. The kitchen door opened and steps resonated on the tiled floor. Cristina got to the kitchen to find Alcina opening the refrigerator.

The girl had her back to her, so she did not immediately see her face. "How was it?"

"Very nice," Alcina answered, turning to face Cristina, holding a glass with water.

The girl was bright-eyed and somewhat disheveled after being wooed by Jô Valentim.

"And parting is such sweet sorrow, that I shall say good night till it be morrow," Cristina dramatically quoted Romeo, making the other blush deeper. "C'mon, my girl, no pussyfooting. 'Very nice' doesn't even begin to explain your sparkling eyes and pink cheeks. I want an account of everything," she insisted and, pulling a couple of chairs around the table, sat down and patted the one beside her. "First things first: where did you have dinner?"

Alcina joined her and after taking a few sips from the glass, started talking.

"He took me to the Hotel do Comércio. He had reserved a table in the inside patio."

"He reserved a table! Are you talking about Jô Valentim?"

"And there was a large vase jammed with three dozen red carnations on our table," Alcina continued, not minding Cristina's joke.

"Red carnations mean he's deeply in love, my girl. How romantic!"

"So much for romance: the scent was so strong they had to be removed," she smiled then added with a pained expression, "And they were too cumbersome to take to the ball, so we had to leave them..."

"Never mind, you can have all the carnations you want from our garden. Now, what about the ball? Give me the details."

"The place was packed. It was a pity you didn't go," she lamented. "From Gervasio Rodrigues and his wife—"

"I can't stand that little woman!" Cristina added dismissively, referring to the mayor's wife.

"—to Mr. Ribas of the Correio do Sul," Alcina continued, mentioning the local newsman. "Everyone who's someone around here was present. And, of course, also the no-ones—like me," she smiled at her own witticism, which got her lightly slapped on the shoulder by Cristina. "Oh, you know how it is! They all looked down their noses at me. And some didn't even look."

"You know why they did that: because all those ugly inbred females were jealous of you."

"Now, I bet you'll never guess who was the first to dance with me."

"Who?" And as Alcina demurred, Cristina insisted, "C'mon, stop this teasing and blurt it out!"

"Mr. Valentim."

"Jô's father? I can imagine Mrs. Valentim's sour face watching her so laboriously kept status being ruined by her own husband," Cristina said with tragic inflections in her voice. "Oh, but it's too delicious," she added, delighted. "So, who was next?"

"Well, even before the first song was over, guess who was pushing Mr. Valentim out of the way?" And without waiting, "The mayor himself," Alcina giggled. "I imagine the gossip going on behind our backs. Dr. Adaucto Pires was there," she continued. He was the doctor who treated Donny last year when he fell from a tree and broke an arm. "He danced with his wife the whole time, but had one with me. Does he cut a rug!"

"Mariazinha's already going to balls?"

"Did you forget their kid is already one?"

"My, how time flies and you don't realize."

Alcina described a few more people, their clothes and behavior, the drinks, the decorations, and the music.

"But I didn't tell you the most incredible thing that happened. And before we even left here."

Cristina looked mystified. "Before you left? What d'you mean?"

"As I entered the car, I noticed something very large, covered with a tarpaulin, on the back seat. Jô was already on the road when he finally answered my question. You won't believe what it was…"

"Try me!"

"A body."

"A… A body?"

Alcina nodded.

"You mean, as in a dead body?"

"Yes, a body. Corpse, cadaver," and she couldn't help laughing at Cristina's amazed expression.

"You're kidding me."

"No, I'm serious as halitosis, as Mr. Bunky likes to say. It was one of their farmhands—can't remember his name. Anyway, Jô was taking the body to the funeral home in Bagé. At his mother's insistence…"

"Oh, now it makes sense. The old witch thought that would stop you from riding in the car. She must have been surprised when you entered the room on her son's arm."

"Boy, was she?"

"And what about the body?"

"We stopped at the funeral home. They got it done so quickly I barely saw it happen."

They gossiped for a few more minutes, until Cristina yawned and, checking the kitchen clock, realized morning was not long in arriving.

"Well, me dear, now that we badmouthed the entirety of Bagé's haute société, we can go to bed and rest on the certainty that we did our duty! Nite. Pleasant dreams," and she accompanied her last words with a wink.

The roadster sped through, its headlights illuminating the path ahead, revealing a rough dirt road. The young driver bounced up and down at every pothole the wheels met. There were too many, but he did not seem to notice or, at least, did not mind. His hair that had been kept in place with brilliantine, with the car roof down, was being ruffled by the wind. But that did not bother him either. Jô Valentim had been dreaming of Alcina's lip. He still did not believe she let him kiss her. It had been a chaste, merely touch of the lips, but to him it was the most wondrous thing.

So, he drove in amazed contentment, alternately whistling and singing Richard Rodger's song 'Isn't It Romantic.' He was no Maurice Chevalier, but had a good voice nevertheless. Yet the sounds out of his throat came out choppy, as the car jostled the singer madly. It was more like hiccupping the melody in little jets of sounds.

Isn't it romantic?
Music in the night, a dream that can be heard
Isn't it romantic?

All of a sudden, he jammed his foot on the brake pedal. The tires skidded several feet, making a deeply rasping sound. As the car came to a halt, a cloud of dust gathered behind it. Very slowly it started to creep forward and surround the car.

"I know what I'm gonna do," he slammed the steering wheel, with joy. "I'm going to serenade her!" And as he voiced his decision, he had a coughing fit as the dust had finally reached him.

But that did not interfere with his happiness. He put the car in gear again and, still coughing, sped up to a white night, peopled with thoughts of his beloved.

CHAPTER NINE

We generically [sic] term the different types of edged weapons used by gauchos in the past as cuchillos criollos (creole knives). We employ this generic name as the gauchos didn't use just one class of knife, but would employ different ones depending upon their personal tastes, customs, or what they could find or acquire.
—Del Facon al Bowie, Abel A. Domenech, 1988.

Sunday afternoon. Slowly the hands started to congregate in the galpão, the big wooden shed of the Minuano Farm that also kept working tools. Above the wide door hung a large cow skull. When he first beheld the desiccated monstrosity, Robert turned to his wife and quoted Shakespeare—"I knew him, Horatio: a fellow of infinite jest, of most excellent fancy." From then on, the skull became known to his family as Yorick. There was where the hands gathered before work started, and in the evening, after work, for a charla[11] and chimarrão[12]. And on their free days they were there for the eagerly awaited churrasco[13].

Not far from the shed, old João Silvano was starting the fire under a cluster of angicos[14]. He whistled through his teeth, moving economically,

---

[11] Spanish, chat.

[12] The Gaúcho's quintessential beverage, chimarrão (also called amargo, or mate) is made with the dried leaves of herva mate, the *Ilex Paraguariensis*. The leaves are packed inside a dried gourd (cuia), and hot water is slowly poured over it. The liquid is sipped through a bomba, a metal straw with a filter at the rounded end.

[13] Barbacue

[14] *Anadenanthera colubrina*. Anadenanthera: Visionary Plant of Ancient South America. Constantino Manuel Torres and David B Repke. 2006.

as was his habit. The men liked to tease him, saying that he was slower than a lame turtle, as the sayings went in those parts.

When he was a toddler, Silvano's family had come from Melo, a city on the border with Uruguay and Rio Grande do Sul. He spoke Portuguese, but like most Gaúchos who lived near the border, he incorporated many Spanish words into his vocabulary.

The sun, starting its dying trajectory, splashed the sky with bloody gashes, lighting evanescing fires. It was still hot and steamy, but under the tall angicos it felt cool. It was like stepping into a cathedral, one with a large central pillar holding a cupola of embroidered green leaves. Here and there uncovered roots broke through the soil, like stiff tendons, gigantic claws, to then return to their place of origin. The ground was a soft rug of flimsy grass and dry leaves. Golden sunlight, sliding down the tangle of leaves that covered the branches, filtered down, forming little shining puddles. Smoke lazily rose to the tree top, a straight column, twining through the mass of green and chasing the birds away. Silvano put the kettle over the fire, readying it for the preprandial amargo.

He pulled a long knife from the leather sheath tucked on his guaiaca[15]. It was not something fancy, like the ones belonging to rich ranch owners, whose knives and sheaths were made of silver. But it was not any ordinary knife either; it was an excellent Broqua & Scholberg, with carved wooden handle. He remembered when, upon his tenth birthday, his father gave it to him. It had been with him all these years, cutting the flesh of animals, but on a couple of occasions, imbibed in human blood, saving its master.

He took his time, methodically honing this daily serviceable companion of many years. When he decided it was sharp enough, he pierced each piece of meat in three places. Weaving the skewers through these tiny holes, he proceeded to stand the skewers vertically over the embers. That done, he turned his face up to observe the sky. In the steely blue floated large white clouds. Seeing some crows flying very high, he thought to himself: rain. Far away, flocks of sheep painted the meadows and slopes with white spots, like balls of wool drying in the setting sun.

Just before the water boiled, Silvano took the kettle off the fire and poured the liquid on the gourd—the cuia—over the herb he had

---

[15] Wide belt made of leather, that may also have pockets to keep money, etc.

previously put in it. Sucking the bomba, he started to drink the first mate, which is the strongest and bitterest, but with one eye on the meat. He sat himself on one of these crude little seats—mochos—arranged around the fire, not too close to the heat. As the hands arrived and sat on the little mochos, the chimarrão started making its rounds through the circle they formed. Some chopped tobacco and rolled cigarettes, smoking while waiting for their turn to sip mate. Like the Indians who inhabited that area, Gaúchos like to sit low, crouching, near the soil.

The last one to arrive was Lobo. He was the seventh boy in a family of six girls. His father was so ecstatic at his wife's finally complying with the need of an heir, that he named him Sétimo Filho do Nascimento. Who first started calling him Lobo is not known; what is certain is the reference to the myth that the seventh son in a family of girls becomes a werewolf—lobisomen in Portuguese. Lobo took pleasure in enforcing the legend by vanishing on nights of full moon, when many reported hearing the howling of a wolf. As he grew older, his wavy hair, darker skin and full lips, coupled with his great strength and stature, started to cause people to wonder. And the name of Uncle Benê, who at the time was only Benê and a strapping man in his early forties, was on people's minds. His indignant father's knife silenced many an impudent tongue who dared question his wife's honor. Mrs. Nascimento was a descendent of the Pampeano Indians—most had been massacred by Uruguayan troops in 1830—which, insisted her husband, explained the boy's looks.

The meat changed color, wrinkled, and then slight crackling sounds were heard. Drops of grease trickled slowly from the lower edges of the meat onto the embers, raising smoke and spreading a strong scent. Silvano removed the pieces of meat from the fire, and slashed it here and there. He sprinkled brine with the help of a little brush made of gorse—which abounded on the farm—and returned it to the fire. Not long after that he thought it was ready. Removing the skewers from the fire and sticking them on the ground, he invited the men: "Come closer, 'cause this is good barbecue and some more."

They approached, silently, like religious devotees on their way to church and reverently cut chunks of the sizzling meat, which they chewed with the hunger that always preceded their Sunday barbecue. Drops of bloody fat sometimes dripped from the corners of their lips or hung on a moustache, to be reclaimed by a tongue.

"Muy bueno, no doubt, che!" praised Alpídio Rodriguez, helping himself to another slice.

He was a skinny youth whose fuzzy moustache he passionately cultivated, to little success.

Even Lobo, a man of few words, felt the need to express his unconditional approval of what he considered was another of Silvano's gastronomic prowess. "Mas bah, che!"

Silvano, who was as parsimonious in his eating as he was in his behavior, had already finished and was preparing a cigarette. With a little penknife he cut a piece of tobacco and chopped it into tiny pieces on the palm of his calloused hand. Selecting a corn husk from a pocket on his guaiaca, he poured the tobacco on it, rolled it into a cigarette, lighting it with an ember, then sat on one of the mochos.

"What about some music?" Alpídio suggested.

Young Adonis Bello, who they called Belo[16], and despite his sobriquet shared no beauty with that Greek god, needed no encouragement, having brought his accordion for that very purpose. He sat on the thickest tree root and started adjusting the straps of the instrument to his shoulders. He toyed a bit with the keyboard and the buttons, working the bellows, then started playing a plaintive tune. Poor Belo was mercilessly described by his peers as being uglier than priest's shoes—as the saying went in those parts.

During the first break Belo took, Fulgencio Ribas, the official story-teller—who, as in all circles where farmhands met, told mostly lies or grossly exaggerated accounts—picked up from his last account of his favorite hero, Candinho. He did it as was his habit, as if a whole day had not elapsed. Ribas was a thickset, short, middle-aged man with a weather-beaten face, crisscrossed with many wrinkles, like an old crumpled parchment. A huge mustache that rivaled his bushy eyebrows gave him an involuntary ferocious appearance, which disagreed with his real nature, for he was the mildest of men.

"Pues, as I was sayin', Candinho once told me he had a foster son. On one occasion he took the brat to help them bring the cattle back from wintering. Pues, the kid, still inexperienced, was pushing his horse, dangerous like, among the animals. Candinho shouted at the boy, but

---

[16] Portuguese, handsome.

44

the scamp didn't care, so Candinho lowered the whip good on his back," and Ribas proceeded to whip the air, as he imagined his hero had done. "That whip, hombres, was sometink special." He looked at each man, taking his time, then explained: "Thick as my wrist, made of the toughest hide. Strong man that he was, the whip wound itself tight around the boy's body, and when Candinho gave the tug, it untwisted the boy with such force that he went whizzing away, like a human whirlwind, and plumb disappeared!"

The men, used to Riba's hyperboles, eyed each other and smiled: they knew something even more improbable was coming.

"But that is nothink," he assured the group. "Fifteen years passed. Candinho was travelling, far away, near Uruguaiana[17], when he saw this very tall, strong young man. 'But I knows this one,' he think to hiself. And the young man approached him, and 'bless me, my father,' he say to Candinho! 'But who are you,' Candinho arsked the young man. 'Don't doubt father, 'tis me.' And saying that the young man pulled his shirt open, and exposing a wide chest said: 'Pues, behold the scars from your whip!' And what is most amazing is that the scars were still healing," Ribas finished with a straight face, unabashed by the men's guffaws.

Alcino sat a little apart from the group, absorbed in thought, watching the darkening sky. In the silence of the arriving night the crackling of the fire, the sound of the men's voices seemed not to reach him. The hoot of an owl, close by, startled him back to the present. Not too far away, in the farm house, he saw the lights in the dining room turn on. And as he watched, he noticed two little silhouettes outlined against the dying lights in the sky, approaching. Donny and Annie were bringing dessert. Every Sunday it was sent to the hands; the same the Laughtons and their guests would have. He took the basket from the children and thanked them. He stood there watching them run back to the house while behind him the men's voices were just a hum.

Alcino opened the basket and peeked into its contents: the dessert—some fancy, creamy stuff—napkins (that the men invariably returned untouched), dishes and spoons. Cristina always prepared the basket, Alcina had once told him. Her lovely hands had touched everything. Somehow it was as if he could feel their contact in the handles of the

---

[17] City on the border with Argentina, about 230 miles west of Bagé.

basket. He loved her. Since the first moment he saw her. When his eyes opened to the morning light, his first thought was of her, and she was the last thing in his mind before he fell asleep. Every smile she had ever addressed him was carefully stored in his precious memories of her, like pictures you keep in a photo album. Her mysterious eyes possessed the infinity and softness of the coxilhas—sometimes sunny, singing with life, sometimes a languorous moonlit night. She was an idol to be worshiped from afar. He knew his love had no future, and carried no past, but it filled the emptiness where before was a lonely desert. Life was worth living because she existed.

"Hey, Alcino, you keeping the dessert all to yourself, che?" It was Alpídio, whose words brought forth a symphony of lighthearted complaints from the other men.

Alcino smiled, took hold of the basket handles, and started walking back to join them.

(But old Silvano knew better. Alcino, he thought to himself, was suffering more than a nun's knees during Holy Week. A suffering that had no cure.)

CHAPTER TEN

Whoever spares the rod hates their children, but the one who loves their children is careful to discipline them.
—Proverbs 13:24.

Dinner was well on the way when trouble started to brew.
Robert sat at the head of the table. To his right was his cousin Desiree. Beside her Annie, glumly eyeing Donny across the table. Her father, Max sat next to her. Across from Robert, on the opposite side of the table, sat Cristina, with the twins to her left, and next to them, Bunky. Sitting between Bunky and Maria, Donny was busy with a steak when he caught his cousin's eye.

"I won't take you next time!"

For an answer, Anne Marie grimaced and turned her head away.

Robert looked inquiringly at Cristina.

"They went fishing in the stream this afternoon. That's all I know," she answered and continued to attend to the twins.

"She talked like a parrot and scared the fish away!" Donny accused.

"I did not!"

"Did so!"

"Your dog is called Bacon, because he looks like an ugly, smelly pig," Anne Marie parried.

The victim of this terrible slander, oblivious that his looks were being berated, placidly continued to gnaw on a bone under the table.

Swoosh and plop—and a flying glob of mashed potatoes, expertly catapulted from Donny's spoon, landed on Annie's chest, splashing some of it on her face. A couple of splashes also decorated her father's elegant, well-cut suit.

"Donald!" was the cry from the culprit's mother. Then silence fell in the room like a blanket.

"That's no way to treat a lady." Robert's voice was calm. Too calm.

"Is she a lady?" was Donny's defiant answer.

"Outside. Now." Robert told his son while getting up from his chair.

"Hon—" Cristina pleaded, but when her eyes met her husband's, she decided to say naught else.

Bunky gave a low growl, but before he could even express a word, Robert was on his feet.

"This is between men."

It was dark outside, but the light from the dining room filtering through the windows made father and son discernible to each other.

"Should I smear this in your face?" Robert had brought a spoon full of mashed potatoes that he showed his son.

"No, Sir," the child answered, contrite. "I rather get a spanking."

"OK. You know what to do. Go pick your switch."

"You didn't spank the child!" Bunky half rose from his chair when Robert and Donny returned to the dining room.

"Spare the rod, spoil the child. That's what you used to tell me before you spanked me, remember? Then you'd take me to Central Park to pick my switch, and we'd go back home and…"

"I remember, I remember," protested that worthy, "but you deserved it!"

"Oh, and your new charge doesn't?" Robert turned to his son: "Now, what should you do?"

Donny walked around the table to where his cousin sat. Annie's blouse and face had been wiped clean, but stains remained. Her eyes, where welled tears had been forced back, were very serious as she watched him stand in front of her.

"Sorry 'bout the mashed potatoes," he told her, his head held down.

He then walked sedately back to his place at the table. All around him the adults were praising him. That, they were saying, that is how a gentleman acted—he admitted his mistakes. Bravo, Donny. Dinner resumed and the sound of silverware on porcelain rang through the room.

"He stuck his tongue at me!" Anne Marie whined.

"Did not!"

"Did so!"

Wishing they could also take part in that contest, the twins started a racket, drumming on their high chairs and rising on chubby legs. They screamed in unison, giggling, elated with the opportunity of showing their verbal prowess: "Did so! Did so!" they kept repeating. It was some time before all the children were quiet and order returned. By then the food was almost cold and the adults decided it was time to put their respective tots in bed.

CHAPTER ELEVEN

But still, even in these, nobleness shines through when a man bears contentedly many and great mischances not from insensibility to pain but because he is noble and high-spirited.
—The Nicomachean Ethics of Aristotle.

The 1924 Ford Model T came out of the large garage where it was kept with a1915 Model T, a Model A Rumble Seat Deluxe Roadster, an old truck, several tools and farm implements. There was also parked a brand-new tractor, viewed suspiciously by the farmhands, which Robert intended for the future plantation—corn and alfalfa. The Ford Roadster had been John Laughton's gift to Cristina, his dear daughter-in-law, on her birthday two years ago.

It was a hot, humid day and Robert kept the roof of the old Model T up to protect them from the scorching sun and the dust while driving the many miles to the city of Bagé. Both Model T and the truck came with the farm and had been kept remarkably well.

"Remember to buy the threads, hon," Cristina reminded her husband.

"Bunky has the list, princess. I'm sure he won't let me forget."

"You bet I won't, 'cause if I do it'll be my fault he forgot!" the large man squeezed in the little seat snapped at Robert.

"See what I mean?" Robert winked at her, threw a kiss, pushed in the left pedal and advanced the throttle. The car started to slowly clatter down the path.

"Drive carefully," she yelled as an afterthought, although they were too far to hear.

Cristina stood there watching. A fall from Simoom, Robert's horse, that resulted on a twisted ankle, had been keeping her at home for several days. Alcino had tried to dissuade her from getting on the horse, insisting that Robert had requested it be saddled for a round on the farm. Maybe he had foreseen the accident—his mother had visions, it was believed, so maybe he inherited her gift. As soon as Cristina settled on the horse, the animal bucked. Despite the name, Simoom[18] was a reliable animal, so caught by surprise, Cristina had fallen. She could not recover from the shock of finding three little thorny mamona[19] seed pods under Simoom's saddle blanket. Donny, who owned a small collection of slingshots of his own manufacture, had been called to account; looking steadily into his mother's eyes he swore—on his Scout's honor—that it was not his doing.

Although her ankle was almost mended, Robert insisted on leaving her on the farm and doing the shopping for her, since he had to drive to Bagé. As the car advanced, from the occasional shrubs that flanked the pathway flushed out a few partridges that flew around, like leaves rushed by gusts of wind. The car passed through the entrance gates, far away. Right before the road dipped down and hid them, Robert stuck his arm through the window and waved a goodbye. Then the car was gone, leaving behind a cloud of dust, like a dirty bride's veil. Cristina watched it float in the still air until it vanished.

Her eyes stayed a little longer on the landscape. How different from Rio de Janeiro or New York. Yet, she had learned to love these undulating distances as if she had sprouted from the loins of that rough land. The sun baked the meadow, dressing the countryside with dazzling light. In the distance, with the hot air that rose from the ground, they seemed to undulate in a sea of vibrations. A few birds cut through the skies in short flights, most of them having probably decided to find refuge among the cool foliage of the trees. Following their example, she directed her steps—now no longer in need of a cane—to the house, in search of coolness. As she approached it, Donny and Annie rushed out, laughing, with Bacon bouncing at their heels. The three disappeared

---

[18] Simoom: a hot dry violent dust-laden wind from Asian and African deserts. Merriam-Webster dictionary.

[19] *Ricinus communis L.*, castor oil plant, mamona in Portuguese. From the Quimbundo, mumono.

behind the house. She wondered what misdeeds the two were planning. They had suddenly developed a taste for camping. Their haversacks filled with what they considered bare necessities, they disappeared for a couple of days, coming back dirty and hungry, but their cheeks rosy and their eyes shining with excitement. Bacon always made a much earlier appearance, the children's provisions not catering to his taste.

They had been driving for just a few minutes.

"Do you always have to drive at breakneck speed on this bumpy cow path?" Bunky complained.

"Thirty miles an hour is hardly breakneck speed, Bunky," Robert answered, turning to Bunky's scowling face and slapping the other's shoulder with a grin.

When he turned his attention back to the road, it was too late: he could not avoid a crater-like hole that was hidden by the curve. The car bumped wildly, and both occupants would have been thrown out had the roof been down. Robert lost control of the brakes and the steering wheel, and by a miracle missed a boy on horseback, who had been galloping in their direction. The front wheel on his side broke loose, and the car leaned over to the left. Then it took a nosedive, skidding several feet, carving a long gash into the dirt of the road, shaking the two occupants inside like dolls. The sound of twisted metal and broken glass was deafening. The car tumbled and rolled a few times, then came to rest upside down, its nose facing the wire fence of the Minuano Farm. The dust that formed, enveloped the car in a brownish cloud.

The boy had brought his nervous steed to a sudden halt, and was almost thrown from the saddle with the momentum. He was petrified for a few seconds, but suddenly came back to life and jumped down from the horse with the agility of an acrobat. He was a fifteen-year-old, lean and tall and ran towards the car in wide strides of his long legs. But as he got nearer, no sound came from the occupants. The boy gingerly walked to the road's shoulder. With the last tumble, that side of the car—the passenger's—was more exposed. Slowly he went around to that side, afraid to look and find mangled bodies inside.

CHAPTER TWELVE

Since human wisdom cannot secure us from accidents, it is the greatest effort of reason to bear them well.
—John Paul Jones letter to Robert Morris, September 4, 1776. In The Life and Character of John Paul Jones, John Henry Sherburne, second edition. 1851.

S uddenly the door on the other side was pushed open from inside. In two strides the boy crouched beside Bunky who had managed to partly extricate himself from the wreckage. Bunky was trying to drag himself through the door with the help of one good arm, while the other laid on an odd angle across his chest and wavered at each of his movements, imprinting a rictus of pain on his face. A bruise was already forming on his forehead. Not able to go farther, he rested his head against the battered metal of the door and sighed, waiting for the swoon to dissipate.

"Robert?"

After the tremendous racket of noise, Bunky's worried voice sounded strange, cutting through the silence that descended upon them as the dust settled.

Receiving no answer, he grew frantic and tried to get up. Sharp pain in his shoulder, like a knife stab, stopped him. He bit his lip to silence a moan.

"Robert! Are you OK?" he called again. This time pain had forced his voice down.

"Not sure," came the answer from the opposite side of the car, after a few seconds.

Bunky shut his eyes and took a deep breath. At least the boy was alive, he thought, relieved.

"I think my shoulder is dislocated." A slight movement brought the confirmation. "Ouch!"

"What's that?"

"I'm trying to remove the adornments on my face. Don't think it goes well with my complexion." And at Bunky's mumbled 'what?', Robert explained, "Pieces of the windshield glass stuck in my forehead. And my right hand." A few more muttered curses and expressions of pain, then in a dejected tone, "What about you?"

"Elbow."

"I'll go look for help," the boy was poised to run to the horse and was stopped by Bunky.

"Não, não," he urged, and with his good arm pointed the other way. "Fazenda Minuano," he pronounced the words slowly, making sure his Portuguese was understood.

The boy nodded understanding, adroitly jumped on the saddle and took off with a clatter of hoofs.

"Who's that?"

"Gildo Rosa," Bunky answered.

"Who are they?" Robert questioned.

"Boy, did you lose your hearing?" growled Bunky. "It is one person: Gildo Rosa. Gildo is his name—or nickname, I think—and Rosa is the boy's last name. His father is Higino, who lives on a little farm not far from here. But Gildo lives with his granny, near town. You know, the old lady who makes the jams you like."

"Oh, yes, Emilia, isn't it?" asked Robert, fondly recalling the old lady's delicious preserves and jams. "Well, I wish help won't take long."

"Why? Are you in much pain?" A moan from Robert had caused this concerned question from Bunky.

"No, it's just that I'm not looking at your best angle…"

Turning his head backwards with difficulty Bunky was able to see Robert's face: his eyes were dancing while he held himself in check not to burst out laughing.

CHAPTER THIRTEEN

Double, double toil and trouble,
Fire burn, and cauldron bubble.
—The Witches Song in Macbeth, William Shakespeare

"I came as soon as I heard about your accident. I was having coffee at the Sorocabana—picking up the latest gossip from the regulars," Rafael Souza[20] grinned. "The town is abuzz with it."

"Beats me how quickly news gets around," Robert shook his head, perplexed. "Bunky and I are fine. Only Bunky's getting a bit hard of hearing," he explained, while they walked through the corridor on the way to Bunky and Maria's bedroom. "You'll have to speak up."

They stopped in front of a door. Robert opened it and looked inside. Bunky was on the bed, propped up by some pillows, eyes closed, his arm held by a sling. A nasty, purple bruise crowned his shaved head.

"So, how're you feeling today, old man?" he asked loudly.

"It hurts from eve till the next day!" the other answered without opening his eyes.

"At least it was just one elbow and a tiny bump on that hard skull of yours," Robert added in a loud tone of voice.

"What d'you want? Why can't you just let me rest? And why aren't you resting?" His eyes opened a fraction. "I was having a nice dream: you were gone to the Petogonee…"

---

[20] Finding Cristina: A New Life.

"Patagonia," Robert corrected, amused. "Never mind that. Someone's here to see you."

Robert stepped aside and into the room to reveal the tall, handsome figure of Rafael Souza framed by the threshold. He was impeccably dressed, as always, in an off-white bespoke suit from Frederick Scholte—tailor for the Prince of Wales. On one hand he held a Panama hat and the ivory cane that was Donny's coveted prize. As he entered the room Bunky growled in the back of his throat and shut his eyes.

"Double, double trouble and trouble," the recumbent man intentionally misquoted Macbeth's witches.

"It's a pleasure to see you too, Mr. Bunky." Rafael flashed one of his dashing smiles. "Glad to see the damage was not too extensive." Like Robert, he also spoke in a loud voice.

"You should see the other guy," Bunky muttered. He disliked when people called him mister

"The car didn't come out of the accident so well," Rafael continued, ignoring Bunky's little joke.

Robert indicated a chair to Rafael and sat himself on the bed, wincing as his arm, also held in a sling, bounced with the move. While Bunky had twisted his elbow, Robert had dislocated his shoulder.

"Fortunately, being hardheaded has its benefits!" Robert jokingly stroked Bunky's leg, getting a grunt in response. "Rafael has been sniffing around the area where the accident happened."

"You don't say," Bunky turned to Robert, smirked then shut his eyes.

At that moment Bacon entered the room. Not immediately recognizing Rafael, the hair on his back rose and he growled menacingly.

"I will never hear another word against Bacon: the dog has taste," Bunky muttered.

Rafael hid a smile when Bacon approached him to be patted, tail wagging.

"Well, he has an interesting story you'll wanna hear. Pay attention," and he shook Bunky's leg, this time bringing out a grunt of pain.

"Why are you two yelling? I'm not deaf—yet," he stared at both men, annoyed.

"Sorry, didn't mean to yell," and Rafael turned to Robert to find him looking suspiciously innocent. "I searched every inch of that ground— where the accident happened—and found nothing of note." Bunky showed no interest in the news. "Then I took a look at the wheels." Still no reaction from the recumbent man. "The one on the driver's side had two lug nuts." Now he had Bunky's attention. "Yes, my very thoughts: where did the other two go?"

CHAPTER FOURTEEN

Offensive acts come back upon the evil doer, like dust that is thrown against the
wind.
—Buddha

They were in the garage. A half hour had elapsed.

"The car was in a garage in Bagé a couple of weeks ago and they put on new tires. I know the owner; a reliable man who's worked with our cars since we moved here. Everyone in this area use him."

Rafael listened to Robert's explanation in silence as they walked through the garage. It was a large building that once had kept carriages, horses and their tack and fittings. When they moved to the farm, Robert had the coach house turned into a garage. The horse stalls were removed so they could fit the two cars, the truck and the tractor. All the way to the back, in the left corner, was a tiny apartment, where the coachman used to live. That had been kept and was now a deposit for rags, grease and oil, gasoline cans, rugs and various tools.

"Look here, Rafael, clearly there's nothing really suspicious. Accidents happen." Robert had done a desultory search, convinced it was a waste of time. He viewed what happened as a mere accident. He attributed Rafael's eagerness for a search to the fact that he was a private investigator, and as such, was always suspicious.

"I wouldn't be so sure." The other's voice sounded muffled from inside the coachman's den.

He stepped out through the door back into the garage and, stopping in front of Robert, stretched his arm, his hand balled in a fist. Turning it upwards, he opened it to reveal two lug nuts.

"They were badly concealed behind an empty gasoline can. I found them by accident: I toppled the can when I pulled some rags piled beside it. Whoever did this was not very clever when concealing these things. He should have found a better hiding place. The river would have done a better job."

The two men looked at each other—Robert perturbed; Rafael exultant at being proven right.

"I don't want my wife to know about this," to which Rafael agreed. "This dies here," he looked intently at the other man. "I'll be in charge of this situation."

Rafael answered with a shrug of his shoulders.

Robert, in turn, stretched his opened hand to Rafael, who, without a word, handed him the lug nuts. Robert put them away in a box sitting on one of the shelves that lined one side of the garage. They walked back to the house in silence.

Unbeknownst to Robert, Rafael had also found a wrench, which he carefully handled with the help of a handkerchief, and concealed in his pocket. He decided to do some covert investigating. Whoever caused the accident was trying to harm either Robert or Cristina. Although he felt upset by Robert's accident, his biggest concern was Cristina's safety. He had never stopped loving her. In silence, from far away, but as intensely as the first time he saw her years ago.

Rafael Souza worked for his father, who owned Quick Detectives in New York. He avoided letting people know his relationship to the agency owner, and omitted his father's last name, signing only his Brazilian mother's, Souza. The son of an American father and a Brazilian mother, he spoke both his parents' languages fluently, without accent. The agency was very successful and had branches in Rio de Janeiro, Milan and Paris. A few years ago, at his suggestion, a branch was opened in the south of Brazil, in a city southeast of Bagé, Rio Grande. Rafael had not been in that city since the agency's inception, knowing he would not be able to resist the urge to travel to Bagé to see Cristina. During this last trip the desire to see her had been overwhelming.

CHAPTER FIFTEEN

It was kind of lazy and jolly, laying off comfortable all day, smoking and
fishing, and no books nor study.
—Adventures of Huckleberry Finn, Mark Twain, 1885.

After a late lunch. Robert, Max and Rafael went outside to enjoy some cigars, while Bunky was left in the dining room, snoring, unaware that everyone had left. They had gone out through the front door and were soon walking on the road that led to the farm's gate. Their shoes made a crunching noise on the gravel, like the crinkling of cellophane. A gust of breeze—a mere whisper—went through the branches of the trees nearby, barely upsetting the quiet leaves. The little clouds of smoke the men exhaled floated lazily above their heads then slowly vanished. The world was very quiet and the shrill screech of a bird broke the spell of that perfect afternoon.

"How long are you staying in Bagé?" Robert asked Rafael.

"Probably a couple more weeks."

"Make sure you'll stay until our party. We'll have dinner with a few people from the neighboring farms, two weeks from now, Sunday. We'll have some local talented musicians come to play and we'll follow with what Bunky likes to call a shindig."

"It'll be a pleasure," Rafael agreed, happy with another excellent excuse to see Cristina. He would make sure he would dance with her.

"I'm looking forward to it," said Max, whose first time was in that part of the world, and was eager to learn more about their people.

"So, when are you going to get hitched?" Robert asked.

The unusual question startled Rafael out of his reverie.

"The lady of my dreams is taken," he said very quietly.

"I think the Fates are sending you a message." And as the other turned a quizzical look his way, Robert explained, "It's time to move on."

Rafael had arrived in the morning and, after accepting lunch, had stayed at Cristina and Robert's invitation. Later on, telling the couple that he would be perfectly fine visiting the farm alone, he went to the stables and procured a horse. His intention was actually to meet the farmhands, which he did. Casual conversation with each of them elicited nothing new. They were all aware of Robert and Bunky's accident and seemed genuinely glad both came out of it almost completely unharmed. Mrs. Cristina, as they all referred to her, seemed to be a favorite. That, instead of facilitating, made his task more difficult: who, among these men who seemed so sincere, might hate the Laughtons so much that he would go so far as to try to cause an accident that might have been fatal?

Deep in thought, he directed the horse away from the farm buildings. Approaching the stream to water the horse he met Claes—Alcina's teenage brother. Rafael judged him to be in his late teens, an understandable mistake as the thirteen-year-old was very tall and well-developed for his age. Rafael immediately recognized this handsome youth's parentage with Alcina. Like his sister, Claes had also inherited his father's Nordic looks. But unlike her, his habit of pulling down the corners of his mouth and constant frowning, marred the regularity of his traits. He was not a pleasant youth, barely answering Rafael's friendly greeting, which the detective excused as an attitude not uncommon to adolescents.

"Catching fish?" he asked, dismounting and leading the horse to the water.

"Nope, birds," Claes said without turning his eyes away from the water. If his intent with such a truculent answer was to ruffle Rafael and make him go away, he failed.

"I'd think a young man would be interested in cars, especially since the farm has two."

"I prefer horses," was the curt answer.

"Cars are more interesting, more complicated and unpredictable than horses. Is that why you prefer horses?"

"And what's that to you that I prefer horses to cars?" the boy snapped, turning a glaring face to Rafael. "You're scaring the fish with this babbling." He turned back to the water, making it clear Rafael's presence was not welcome.

The young detective hid a smile. "What did you think about the car accident—Robert and Bunky's?" he asked. He tucked his hands deep into his pockets, undaunted by the other's rudeness.

"That I was glad it was not Miss Cristina," he answered and, again, turned murderous eyes to the other man.

"So, you like Mrs. Laughton?"

"Yes," he muttered after a few seconds.

"And dislike her husband."

"Yes—I mean, no! I don't particularly like or dislike him."

Claes stood up abruptly. Reeling the line in, he rested the fishing pole on his shoulder, and grabbed his tackle. Without a word or a glance, he turned and was gone, before the surprised Rafael could ask another question.

"What temper," he told himself, shaking his head and wondering at such a trick of Mother Nature as to have bestowed a deformed foot on this handsome specimen of the human race.

An object on the ground, reflecting the sun, attracted his attention: a fishing lure. It must have fallen from Claes' tackle box when he hastily collected his things to leave. It had the shape of a stylized fish, no more than three inches long, with red beaded eyes, with a double hook on one end and a triple hook on the other. Rafael bent and, as it was second nature to him, picked it with a handkerchief, and put it in his jacket pocket.

He mounted the horse and went back to the stable. There he removed the saddle and gave the animal a good brushing.

"You know a bit bout hosses, mistah," said Dionisio Bello, the young man who tended them. He was Adonis' younger brother. The two were the antithesis of their appellations: Adonis was no beauty to look at, and Dionisio had no Bacchic inclinations.

"I have a horse in New York, where I live most of the year." Rafael reminisced fondly of his early morning gallops in Central Park with his fiery Andalusian, Don Juan Cartujano.

The horse had been smuggled out of Spain on a boat, while very young, a little more than a foal. It was a risky scheme, against the law, as that breed of horse was not exported. But at the time Rafael, also quite young, did not heed the danger and only thought of it as the adventure of a lifetime. And by many twisted ways, the animal was hidden on a small farm, in a quiet corner of Portugal. A year after his arrival, Don Juan travelled to New York via a tramp ship privately commandeered by Rafael, arrived safely and was kept in the stables near Central Park. The gods, it seems, watched over Rafael.

CHAPTER SIXTEEN

I could dance with you till the cows come home. On second thought, I'd rather dance with the cows till you came home.
—Groucho Marx in Duck Soup, 1933.

In the living room the gramophone was blasting Red Nichols and His Five Pennies' 'Fan It' while Desiree taught the latest steps to Cristina and Alcina. Robert, who had been watching and amusing himself with criticism, was finally shooed out of the room. He was happy to give his ears a rest and went out to the porch to find Bunky lying in a hammock, and Rafael and Max each sprawled on a lounging chair, smoking cigars in congenial silence. A jar of butiá liqueur and small glasses sat on a frail little table, at easy reach of the men.

It had been a sweltering day. The high humidity increased the discomfort, making one feel clammy and ill tempered. But as dusk started to settle, heavy clouds unleashed a brief but quite intense storm that cooled the air. The parched soil had gorged on that present from the sky. On the roads and paths, recently filled potholes opened again and jealously kept the precious liquid in pools, waiting for the next passing axel to break. Everywhere there was that pungent, earthy scent that comes after the rain, when life itself, washed, seems to start anew.

On the horizon the sleepy hills draw sinuous profiles. Deceivingly small from the distance, wooded spots resembled islands. Moving patches of shadows, changing the color of the fields, played a race with the clouds moving across the sky. From the porch you could see everything around, a sea of rolling plains. Beyond the hills, to the left, the twilight started to amass large inky clumps, getting ready for its ghostly show. The late afternoon breeze was not cool enough to give anyone shivers, but it was trying hard.

"I saw Donny and Annie leaving when there was still light out. Know where they're gone?" Robert asked Bunky while sitting down on a lounge chair. He stretched his long legs, then selected a cigar from the box of Henry Clay sitting on the floor near Max.

Bunky let out a thick cloud of smoke before answering, eyes narrowed and a pleased expression on his face: "Went cow tipping."

Robert, who had just taken a long puff from his cigar, choked. Bunky leaned over and slapped his back several times, while Max watched, eyes dancing. Beside him Rafael smoked with his eyes closed.

"Did you instruct them well?" Robert was finally able to ask.

"Oh," Bunky chortled, "did I!" And to Robert's delight he explained with a crooked smile, "First, to make sure they are downwind and to be very quiet so not to alert the animal. Sneak up on the beast and then both should push as hard as they can." He took another puff of the cigar, a contented expression on his face. "Wish I was there to see," he said longingly.

The four men chuckled quietly and continued to smoke in contented silence.

Several minutes passed in peaceful companionship when they heard hurried steps approaching. It was the two partners in crime, Donny and Annie. The children were out of breath, hot and covered in mud. Dripping from their disheveled hair, lines of sweat opened clean paths on their flushed, muddy faces. As they approached, they saw the men and slowed down, conscious of their unbecoming appearance.

"So, how was the enterprise, young Master?" Bunky asked then added, keeping a straight face with much effort, "You look a bit out of sorts."

Donny rubbed a hand on a muddy nose, and scraped an even muddier boot on the edge of the porch's floor, intending to clean it, unsuccessfully.

"Not so good," the boy answered evasively.

"The cow won't tip! You must have left something out, Uncle Bunky," Annie complained. And as the men laughed, she asked, "What's that?"

"You couldn't possibly know, but Donny lives on a farm long enough to know why you can't tip cows," and Bunky looked at the boy expectantly. Getting no answer he continued, "They don't lock their legs like horses do!"

The children turned to each other, bright eyed. In an excited voice Annie expressed their thoughts: "That means we can go horse-tipping!"

"Absolutely not," Robert cut their enthusiasm short. They immediately dropped the smiles and adopted injured pouts.

"Oh, Dad, don't be a killjoy," Donny pleaded and started approaching his father.

"Oh, Papa," Annie turned puppy eyes to her father, who, unmoved, merely shook his head.

"Wow," Robert stretched both arms, warding off the children as they started to approach him. "Stop right there! You seem to be drenched in some very strong cow pie perfume, you brats. Get yourselves inside and wash. Not that way," and Robert pointed to the opposite direction, "through the kitchen door!"

"And use the faucet outside, before you enter, or Maria will skin you alive," cried Bunky as an afterthought.

The men watched the children walk away dejectedly.

"Horse tipping," Bunky exclaimed, shaking his head. "What next? Sheep tipping?" He considered the possibility for a few seconds while examining his cigar, then added, "I might suggest that tomorrow."

CHAPTER SEVENTEEN

I loved thee, though I told thee not,
Right earlily and long,
Thou wert my joy in every spot,
My theme in every song.

And when I saw a stranger face
Where beauty held the claim,
I gave it like a secret grace
The being of thy name.

And all the charms of face or voice
Which I in others see
Are but the recollected choice
Of what I felt for thee.
—The Secret, in Major Works, John Clare.

Cristina looked at the clock: almost one in the morning. She could not sleep. It was probably the several little cups of coffee she had after dinner. As a result, she now lay tossing and turning in bed. So as not to wake up Robert, she put on a housecoat over the cotton pajamas, grabbed her tiny satin slippers, and tiptoed on bare feet to the door that connected with the twin's bedroom.

She went through the door, her soft footfalls not making a sound, and stood there for a few moments, watching the children. In their abandon, their little faces seemed a subject good enough to adorn a painting by Raphael Sanzio. She chuckled inwardly thinking how Robert called them Dr. Jekyll and Miss Hyde. They were her little angels. Their chubby little bodies, relaxed, reflected the innocence of their childish dreams. She kissed both curly little heads and quietly left the room.

Right across from Alex and Loulou's was Donny's bedroom. The corridor was dark, yet she could have found her way easily throughout the house, with eyes closed—so much she knew it by heart. She stopped at Donny's door and listened. Very quietly she opened the door, yet Bacon, ever watchful, emitted a low growl. He was laying on the rug by her son's bed.

"Shh," she whispered, and the somnolent dog, recognizing the sound of her voice, wagged his tail a couple of times and, with a sigh, laid his head down and closed his eyes.

The window was open and the moonlight was strong enough to illuminate her son's face. She pulled a curl from his forehead, kissed him and left.

Treading on tiptoe, she went down the stairs and winced when the boards creaked; she did not want to wake up anyone at that time of night. She reached the kitchen without turning the lights on and, without tripping over anything in her way, went out. She loved these nights of full moon, when the world was bathed in a glassy, magic light that made everything stand out, and seemed like they came out of a dream.

Putting on the slippers, she started walking, passing the walled kitchen garden—looking immense under the interplay of light and shadow, a chiaroscuro the moonlight bestowed on the stones that formed it—and continued until she reached a rustic wooden bench that stood under an ancient pergola. Throughout the years the allamanda had taken over the frail construction that now was mostly hidden, showing mainly green leaves and bright-yellow flowers.

Dew-moistened plants and soil, shedding the day's warmth, exuded a pungent scent she inhaled greedily. Cristina just sat there, her eyes caressing the landscape, softly humming Ray Noble's song 'Love Is the Sweetest Thing.' She shrugged off the little mules, down to the grass, and snuggled on the seat. She closed her eyes and listened to the sounds of the night. Suddenly a rustle of leaves behind her made her sit up.

"Who's there?" she asked, and for a brief second, the myth surrounding Lobo occurred to her and a cold shiver ran down her spine.

She was reassured as the tall figure of Rafael Souza, standing a few feet away, came to view. He was wearing the housecoat and slippers Robert had lent him. His hair was tousled, most likely the result of the bath he took before going to bed.

"Sorry. Didn't mean to disturb you. But now that I'm found, may I join you in your nightly meditations? I promise to meditate too." The humorous twinkle stirring behind his eyes went unseen, but she heard it in his voice.

"But of course, sure," she brought her feet down and tried to find her slippers, which, she did not realize, had fallen a little too far for her to reach.

"Allow me," Rafael said and retrieving the footwear, handed them to her. He overcame the temptation of placing them on her delicate feet. He would not trust his hands not to shake.

"Thank you. I think I had too much coffee tonight," she told him, trying to make it sound that it was perfectly normal to speak to a man, in the middle of the night, both in their pajamas. "Kept tossing and turning," and for some reason the word 'bed' seemed inappropriate to her at that moment.

"I normally go to bed late." His voice was very soft.

Standing opposite to her, his face was in the shadows, but she could imagine his eyes fixed on her. He turned his head and walked a few steps forward, away from her. The hill where the house and its gardens stood took a steep tumble down there, where a white wood railing stood to prevent accidents.

"This is a beautiful country." He looked back at her. "Are you happy here, Mrs. Laughton?" When in her presence, he always addressed her formally.

"Yes, I love it here," she answered his odd question. "Don't you like it?"

He slowly assented with his head and went back to contemplating the view in silence. Ahead the ground smoothly descended then rose again into continuously rolling hills. They were covered with grass that, absorbing the moonlight, became an argentine sea. The clumps of trees—mostly on the top of some of these hills—were akin to buildings, so immovable, the soft nightly breeze not having strength to set the leaves in motion. The horizon extended ahead, almost starless; a vault of hazy, infinite deep cobalt blue, so immense it gave one a pang, a longing to embrace it and become it.

He heard her get up and walk to where he was and she stood beside him. He could feel her scent and inhaled it greedily. It was all he could do to control himself and not take her into his arms, kiss those lips he longed for, and tell her how hopelessly, desperately he loved her. He remembered the creamy-skinned face when he had last seen her during winter; now her skin had become the color of golden caramel, from living so much outside. And that was very becoming, and gave her beauty a piquant twist. His brain told him he should not come to Bagé anymore, but his heart reminded him of the impossibility of living without seeing her, even if sporadically. He wondered if she knew how he felt. Something in her way, her inability to hold his eyes for too long, the reserve he had noticed lately, told him she was privy to his secret.

The conversation lagged.

"How are your mother and Mr. Laughton? I haven't seen them for a long time," he asked, referring to Cristina's real mother—who she had met but eight years ago—and Robert's father—who had married that lady.

"They are in Buenos Aires," she smiled, and Rafael felt more than he saw it. "My mother developed a tremendous love for tango and he, well, he'll do anything for her."

"That's how it is when a man is in love," he said, so quietly it was a little more than a whisper.

"Speaking of love," she added quickly, "have you seen Denise— Nurse Krause— lately?"

"Not for quite a while."

"I like her very much." She turned to see his profile, gazing steadily ahead. "You should consider, perhaps…" She broke as he turned to face her. "You're free, and she's a lovely lady. Well, I just think you should seriously consider," she ended, annoyed at his glance that, even in the darkness, told her all she did not want to know, the feelings he had for her.

"I will certainly consider your advice," he answered after a short pause, with a mock-serious expression in his voice.

"Will you? Really?" She held his gaze.

Rafael bent his head in assent. "If it pleases you."

"It would. Very much."

After that they exchanged a few platitudes, then she yawned and he was grateful to her for breaking the spell that had held him.

"Well, I think it's time I go back to… I mean, I'll turn in." From the corner of her eyes, she could see that he was smiling. "Good night."

"Good night," he answered and kept watching until her silhouette disappeared, melting with the shadows in the distance. And when she was far enough, he whispered, "My love." Every time he was in her presence, he felt as if a little bit of her stayed with him. And as long as she existed, no matter where on this Earth, he was happy.

CHAPTER EIGHTEEN

The wise man is safe, and no injury or insult can touch him.
—Seneca.

R obert stood there, a sad expression on his face, looking at the garden beds. It was early in the morning when he first got to the front yard, and the heat was already considerable. He sat back on his heels and, removing the straw hat, used it to fan himself. He had found the old, dilapidated relic hanging on a peg in the work shed when he went there to get tools, and thought it would help him cope with the sun. The area on which he had been working was still shaded, but he was sweating abundantly. Pulling a large handkerchief from the front pocket of his pants, he mopped his damp forehead, then replaced the hat on his head, and went back to work.

Robert and Cristina had planned a party to introduce Max and Desiree to their neighbors, farmers who lived in the area, since that was their first visit to Bagé. Before that, they had always travelled to Rio de Janeiro with their children to meet Max and Desiree. Robert had promised Cristina he would rid the front yard of weeds before the party. The addition of before the party was his downfall; had he not added that, he could have wriggled his way out of the promise. As the day of the event was approaching, Cristina reminded him of his promise and, despite his shoulder still giving him a little bit of trouble, he felt compelled to keep his word. The enormity of his mistake was made more apparent as soon as he had knelt down to work and started sweating. The heat and specially the humidity made his job hard. He got up and removed his shirt. The light breeze on his sweaty body was but a temporary relief. Yet, delaying would do no good, so he went back to work with gusto—and method. A weeder tool firmly grasped in his right hand, he dug under the offending vegetation, gave it a shove, and, grabbing the weed with the left, flung it with a quick jerk of that hand into a battered wheelbarrow standing a stone's throw from him.

A half hour passed in that tedious labor when the loud putt-putt of a car broke the monotony of his silent task. He turned to see a roadster quickly approaching the house. It stopped in front of the gate opening with a screech of the breaks, a beautiful Peugeot 301 convertible coupe with the top down. A smartly dressed young man climbed out of it, but not before carefully arranging his thinning straw-colored hair the wind had disheveled, stretching it back on his scalp with both hands. With that move he revealed the presence of a woman in the passenger seat.

She was a beauty who could have come out of the pages of the One Thousand and One Nights. Her abundant raven black hair was parted in the middle and fell in luxurious waves, framing a beautiful face. It had been tucked in a bun on the nape of a slender neck. Her black eyes, large and fringed with long lashes, examined Robert admiringly.

She was Fátima Kalil, young daughter of the Lebanese Salim Kalil. Salim was the owner of the Salim Kalil store in downtown Bagé, that sold fabrics, clothing and footwear. Fafá, as her family and friends called her, was a statuesque beauty whose curves had been hidden by the prior decade's fashion of low waists and flat-chested boyish bodies. From its inception, the thirties had restored femininity: waists were back to their proper places and women no longer compressed their bosoms. Taking advantage of the new fashion dictates, Fafá made sure her femininity was definitely in evidence. A wide smile from well delineated lips, that exposed two dimples, greeted Robert, who bowed his head in acknowledgment.

Robert did not know Fafá, but he recognized the young man as Sérgio, son of one of his neighbors, Colonel Marcelino Paranhos, owner of Cavalo de Ouro, one of the largest horse farms in the area. He would have been handsome had it not been for his expression; he presented a bored expression to the world, and that detracted from the regularity of his features. During a ball Robert had attended with Cristina, the young man's doting mamma, Dona Maricota Paranhos, had tried to introduce her offspring to the americano but was unable to get a hold of him. They never met, and the difference in age—Robert was ten years Sérgio Paranhos' senior—meant that they did not frequent the same circles, making their acquaintance unlikely. But Robert would never forget Sérgio's receding thatch of hair tightly pulled back, plastered to his cranium with a thick coat of Brilliantine. Sights of that lustrous helmet, shining on the dance floor like a beacon, kept Robert entertained during most of the boring evening.

Sérgio extricated a small wooden crate full of oranges from the roadster trunk and walked up to Robert's crouching form. Seeing the oranges, Robert got up. He knew they were sent by Mrs. Paranhos for his wife. They were going to be turned into a delicacy the older lady had taught his wife—her special orange marmalade.

Robert's clothes and the task he was performing, lead to a misunderstanding. He was wearing old, shabby dungarees—a souvenir of his time spent on a tramp ship[21] a few years ago—and worn-out alpargatas. His naked tanned torso was reluctant with perspiration. Grimy fingers had brushed and smeared his handsome face that was partially concealed under the hat's wide brim. Before he could utter a word of greeting, he found himself scrutinized by the young man's cold stare, which left no doubt of his estimation of Robert's social position. So, the châtelain of Fazenda Minuano was treated with much condescension, which spoke poorly of Sergio's character.

"C'mon man, I don't have the whole day! Get a hold of this," and the crate was shoved at Robert, who was able grab it and save it from crashing to the ground. "Take it immediately inside. Those are oranges, from my mother—Mrs. Maricota, wife of Colonel Paranhos," he intoned, stressing the importance of his papa's rank in the Brazilian Army. "It's for your mistress. Is she in?" Young Sérgio, a seducer and Latin lover in his own mind, was one of the many admirers Cristina had unwittingly acquired since moving to Bagé.

Robert shook his head at the question.

"And your master, is he in?" Receiving another headshake for answer, he asked, irritated: "Why don't you speak up? Are you dumb?"

At this, Robert nodded vigorously and exposed his regular, very white teeth in a successfully mastered clownish smile. Disconcerted, Sérgio

---

[21] Finding Cristina: A New Life

hummed uncomfortably, removed an imaginary speck from his jacket and, before getting back to his car, reminded Robert to take the oranges in—tout de suite! he intoned in bad French, but more gently now, and mouthing the words carefully as people do to make sure a dumb person understands.

As soon as the car took off, Robert rushed inside and, leaving the oranges in the kitchen, went in search of his wife. When he found her, he narrated his latest escapade with colorful details, laughing out loud.

"And to make it more realistic, I watched his lips when he spoke, you know, as if I were reading them. I even silently mouthed the words as he spoke! You should have seen his face," he told her, elated.

"Robert... You didn't!"

After he stopped guffawing, he added for the enlightenment of his distressed wife, "You betcha!"

"He's coming to our party with his parents, hon! It'll be embarrassing if he recognizes you. Have you thought of that?" she asked, dismayed.

"I have not, but now that you mention it, I intend to make sure he does," he answered with a contented smile.

"Oh, you're such a child sometimes!" she chided.

"Come here and I'll show you the child," he tried to get a hold her, but she escaped.

"Get away from me! You're sweaty and stinky, yuk! Go take a bath!" she giggled, running upstairs, trying to avoid him.

"I intend to—as soon as I catch you," and he rushed after her.

CHAPTER NINETEEN

Palestine was on the verge of a new rebellion. The nomads of Arabia were being aroused by foreign propaganda to lift arms against the British and the Jews in the Holy Land.
—Escape from Baghdad, Carl Raswan. 1936.

C ristina heard a car stop at the back of the house; then she heard Maria's voice outside. She was speaking in English, and a male voice, too far for Cristina to recognize, answered. Despite the distance, she could detect a foreign accent. She stepped outside and seeing the man facing Maria stopped short, rooted to the ground.

"You!"

They both exclaimed at the same time, but with quite differing inflections—Cristina with disbelief, and the man, who touched trembling fingers to his large mustache, with alarm.

"Who?" Maria asked Cristina in Portuguese.

At that moment they saw Robert leisurely approaching them, coming from the opposite side of the house.

"Good morn—" He cut his greeting short. Even from afar he recognized the man who Cristina and Maria were facing. "The Polack!" he muttered, while picking up the pace.

Max, who had come out from the kitchen, also exclaimed in disbelief: "The Polack!"

"Who?" asked his wife, who had followed him and was peeking from behind his shoulder at the man who seemed to be the center of attention.

"The Polack?" asked Bunky who, seeing a car approach the house, and hearing his wife trying to communicate with them in English, had decided to see who it was.

"But who is this Polack?" Maria, now out of patience, addressed her husband in Portuguese.

Maria had never been told the story of Cristina's attempted abduction by this very man,[22] who Robert's French friend, Spigot, had dubbed 'The Polack'. Several years ago, while visiting Brazil on business, Bogdan Zietarski—manager of Prince Roman Wladyslaw Sanguszko's stud farm—had spent a few days in Rio de Janeiro. He saw Cristina at a dinner party when she and a friend provided the musical entertainment. Besotted with the young beauty, the man lost his head and attempted to abduct her. That had been thwarted by Robert, who, with some friends, had arrived on the spot in time to save her. Before her rescuers' arrival, the young woman desperately fought off her kidnapper's advances. And she left him with a painful memory of the event, having ripped off part of his bushy mustache in the struggle.

"Will explain later," Bunky answered in his wife's mother tongue, a hard expression on his blue eyes that turned them to the color of steel.

To which she replied with her favorite interjection: "Humph! Why do I feel like the betrayed husband? Always the last to know!"

As Bunky took a step toward the stranger, the man retreated one step, troubled. That action revealed the second man who had stepped out of the car. He had been somewhat hidden from Robert by the angle at which he was coming from.

He was not very tall, but fit and simply, but elegantly dressed. As his companion, at the sight of Maria he had uncovered his head, revealing short cropped blond hair. But unlike the other, his mustache was small and his chin was covered by a discreet goatee. His tanned face was closely shaved, and the observant, deep brown eyes seemed to take on the situation with much calm.

"Carl Raswan[23]?" was Robert's amazed question as he got nearer. And at the stranger's assent, he insisted: "The Carl Raswan?"

---

[22] Finding Cristina.
[23] Carl Reinhard Schmidt, 03/07/1893 (Dresden, Germany) – 10/14/1966 (Santa Barbara, CA). Author, polyglot, Arabian horse expert.

"I am he," was the answer.

CHAPTER TWENTY

Paris was always worth it and you received return for whatever you brought to it.
But this is how Paris was in the early days when we were very poor and very happy.
—A Movable Feast, Ernest Hemingway. 1964.

In the dawn of the Twentieth Century, the descendants of Ubaldo and Héloïse Freitas, founders of Fazenda Minuano, introduced horses to the farm. Their daughter—and the Freitas' last descendant—Vitória, had been in school in Switzerland for several years. After graduating, she chose to live in Paris, seduced by its bohemian life, where she lived in a minuscule studio in the Saint-Germain-des-Prés quarter. She became a constant presence at some of the places frequented by artists and writers: Café des Deux Magots, Café de Flore, and Sylvia Beach's bookshop, Shakespeare and Company. There one could rub elbows with Pablo Picasso, André Breton, Scott Fitzgerald, and Marc Chagal.

In 1927 Vitória's parents—Bernardo and Teresa—went to visit a distant French relative who lived in Montreal—Mlle. Francine Jacquet, who was the last representative of that French family. That year a typhoid fever epidemic hit that city and the three perished.

Vitória was an excellent amazon, but after living so many years away from her birthplace, she had completely lost the taste for farm life, and had no inclination to deal with horse raising. And with her relatives gone, the young woman's first act upon attaining majority was to sell all the horses, keeping just a few for riding and daily chores, while she dealt with the sale of the estate. The second, was to marry an Italian count, Vittorino Albizzi, whom she had met while on the ship returning to

Brazil. Before moving to Italy with her noble consort, the newly-styled Contessa Albizzi sold the farm to the Laughtons.

Unaware of these changes, Bogdan Zietarski included that farm in his and Carl Raswan's visiting route. Zietarski knew Raswan from having travelled with him and Prince Sanguszko to the Middle East in search of Arabian horses for His Grace's farm.

Robert, who was considering rebuilding the horse farm, had avidly read Raswan's articles in the American magazine 'Western Horseman'. After being momentarily distracted by the horse connoisseur, Robert's attention returned to his foe: Bogdan Zietarski.

Intent on preventing a fight, Cristina joined her husband and, holding his arm, pleaded, "Let him talk, Robert."

"I'm not going to knock your teeth out because you came here with this gentleman, whom I admire." Robert's voice was controlled, but the clenched fists held slightly apart from his body spoke of the tremendous effort it cost him.

Zietarski cleared his throat and, in halting words, begged Cristina's forgiveness. "I must have been out of my mind, Madame. I know what I did is unforgivable, but I drop to my knee," and he followed word with action, "and beg your forgiveness."

"Please, get up," embarrassed, Cristina asked him.

"What are you doing here?" was Robert's cutting question, while the other awkwardly got up and brushed the dust from his pants.

"I've been here years ago, looking for studs for my farm, I mean, Prince Roman's farm," he explained.

"Well, the farm was sold to us and there are no more horses here, so get going," Robert remarked, curtly. He was divided between the ardent desire to pick Raswan's brain and a very natural inclination to thrash his wife's offender.

Aware of her husband's dream to restore the horse farm to its former glory, Cristina decided to swallow the distaste she felt for her quasi-abductor, and voiced her forgiveness. That way she hoped to somehow help Robert to be able to meet with Carl Raswan. In the end it was Annie who eased the situation.

Coming home from one of her exploits with her cousin and Bacon, she heard Raswan's name and remembered Donny talking about him.

"Mr. Raswan, tell us some stories about the Bedouins, please, please," she begged him, after introducing herself and shaking his hand.

Carl Raswan felt it would be difficult to resist the charming girl's pleading. He looked at his travelling companion for help, but the man was still in shock from meeting Cristina, his eyes fixed on the ground, in hope of avoiding any confrontation; the scenes of his past encounter with Robert and his friends came vividly to his memory, so he remained silent, decided to draw no unnecessary attention to himself.

"Mr. Raswan could perhaps stay with us tonight. You could drive him back to Bagé tomorrow," Cristina told her husband, coming to Carl's rescue. Then turning to Carl, "You are staying in town?

"Yes, Madame, at the hotel, er… Forgive me if I don't pronounce it properly: Komecio?"

"Hotel do Comércio, on the street with the same name. Downtown Bagé," Cristina helped him. "Can I convince you to stay with us tonight? The adults would also love to hear your stories, if you'd agree."

"Madame, how could I not accept such a kind invitation?" and he gave her a slight bow.

So, it was decided that Carl Raswan would spend the night at Fazenda Minuano. And without the need of a hint, Zietarski discretely said his adieus to his friend, nodded to the rest of the company, and jumped into his car, leaving in such a hurry that it seemed he would have liked to have wings.

CHAPTER TWENTY-ONE

You may be assured I will look after Jadan with more care than if he belonged to me.
—Rudolph Valentino telegram to W.K. Kellogg, 1926.

The forty-year-old Carl Raswan had led an interesting life. He fought with the Turks at Gallipoli during the Great War[24]—the only part of his exploits that bothered Robert. He was fluent in English, French, Spanish, German and Arabic. An accomplished horseman, he had also been the stunt-rider for Rudolph Valentino in the 1926 movie Son of the Sheik. The horse he rode, Jadaan, was owned by W.K. Kellogg—the cereal tycoon. Valentino actually sent a telegram to Kellogg asking for that specific horse, because 'I consider him the embodiment of the finest Arab from every standpoint.' Later on, after Carl Raswan had gone back to his hotel, when told that he had been there, Alcina would curse her luck: she had been staying with her mother who was not feeling well. She had so many questions to ask Raswan about Valentino!

The day was warm, Robert guided Rawan through the walled garden, followed by Cristina, Max, and the children. They sat under the large

---

[24] World War I. Gallipoli Campaign: February 19, 1915 to January 19th 1916. The Germans fought alongside the Turks against the Entente Powers (Britain, France, and Russia).

pergola that stood opposite to the little white gazebo. The clusters of blue flowers and dense foliage from the old wisteria creeper and the tall ferns kept the arbor in the shade and pleasantly cool even on hot days.

With a special dinner planned in her mind, Maria had gone to the kitchen, from whence returned her husband holding a large tray with iced tea, beer and Cristina's beloved Malzbier[25]. Desiree, as soon as she heard Raswan's German accent, quietly went back inside the house. Max empathized with her suffering, yet there was nothing he could do, but be patient and let her have her time alone with her ghosts. He knew she would not join them at dinner and planned to excuse himself and sup with his wife, whom he adored.

After they had refreshed themselves, Raswan started relating how at nineteen years of age he had become blood brother of eight-year-old Bedouin Prince Amir Fuaz, and a member of the Ruala, a Bedouin tribe. He lived, hunted and even participated on their raids on enemy tribes.

"In 1912 I was in the Arabian desert, guest in the camp of Nauaf, eldest son of Sheik Amir Nuri Sha'lan." His deep voice, with the typical rolling rs of German speaking peoples, was soothing. His eyes had that longing, distant look of one who relives a precious memory. And as it was always the case with this soft-spoken man, he held his audience spellbound since the first word.

"His son, the Prince Amir Fuaz, was eight. About your age, I believe, young master," he said, turning to Donny, who listened with parted lips. "He was a good rider—as are all Bedouins—and also a very good shot. One fateful afternoon he and his little companions were practicing shooting with slingshots. They were throwing little pebbles at the wooden pegs that held the tents' cordage. Coming from behind the tent, I unwittingly walked into their shooting range and the stone Fuaz had just loosed, rebounded and hit me right here," he pointed to a small scar on his forehead, between his eyes, lowering his head so the two children could see it. "Foolishly, I thought it was a bullet, and, touching the wound, noticed blood. Still holding the sling, Fuaz ran to me, his face pale with concern. So, I realized it was an accident and scooping him inro my embrace, laughed to ease his concern."

---

[25] Malzbier from Brahma first appeared in the Brazilian market in 1918. A Schwarzbier, but, unlike Porter or Stout, light-bodied, and sweet.

"Lucky it didn't hit one of your eyes," Cristina commented.

"Indeed, it was, Madame." He continued, "But my merriment offended the proud little prince. I can still see him wriggling from my arms and tearing off his veil and headcloth. In so doing, he freed his very long tresses." At his audience's expressions of surprise, he explained, "It is not unusual for a Mussulman man to braid his hair and the Bedouin are not strangers to this ancient custom. I saw tears in the young boy's defiant eyes, but it was with a firm voice that he told me to name the price of my blood." Carl Raswan looked around, as if waiting for a reaction that did not come. "You see, the safety of a guest is sacred to the Bedouin, and Fuaz hoped to give me satisfaction before the news spread—and his father would hear of it."

"What did you do? Did he have to pay something?" asked the enthralled Annie.

"No, I could not create trouble for a few drops of blood. I called the men and children who had gathered around as witnesses and I invoked an ancient Bedouin custom. I told Amir Fuaz what happened was the will of God and my price was his friendship."

"How clever," Cristina exclaimed. "Well done! I bet the little boy didn't expect such a turn of events."

"You are correct. Never did he expect that a non-believer would know his tribe's custom. Moved, he embraced me and, touching the blood on my head he dabbed it between his eyebrows. And so, we became blood brothers," he finished, beaming at his audience.

But the audience was not satisfied, and he had to relate a few more of his exciting experiences among the Ruala. Until Robert, who kept wriggling on his seat, ended the meeting.

"OK, everybody! Now that Mr. Raswan so kindly shared his stories with us, he and I are going to talk horses."

At that Donny and Annie protested vehemently—while Carl Raswan's eyes shone at the mention of his favorite subject. Robert was adamant and soon the children were shepherded away by Cristina, and he and Carl were left alone and embarked in a long talk. The darkening sky found them still in animated conversation.

FINDING CRISTINA: TREASURES ON EARTH

In the background, the monotonous tooting notes from an old Caburé owl[26], named Mr. Brown for his coloration, silenced the two men. Every evening, he showed up for a whistling recital in the walled garden. For several minutes they listened to the little bird's singing before the night's arrival. Then they got up and went through the wooden gate that closed the walled garden and started to leisurely walk to the kitchen, and as they approached, the air was redolent with the scent of the garlic and onions that were being fried. They entered that room to find a lot of activity: Cristina washing vegetables and handing them to Maria, who was chopping them. Robert's cousin, Desiree, stood by the range watching a steaming pot with a bemused expression; to her, a kitchen was terra incognita.

Discretely observing Cristina, Carl Raswan deemed her one of the loveliest women he had ever met. Her beautiful face was enlivened by a pair of extremely dark eyes, edged with long lashes, and surmounted by well-arched eyebrows. She was delicate like a porcelain doll, except for the golden skin, tanned by the tropical sun. At thirty she kept the elasticity and youthful looks of a much younger woman. Despite her short stature, she had the grace of a nymph and the posture of a queen. Her laugh was like the chime of crystal bells.

He refrained from revealing these thoughts to her husband, though. Back to Bagé the next day, having lunch with Bogdan Zietarski, he would still keep them to himself. How would Robert Laughton react if he had told him that Mrs. Laughton's beauty was such that, although he did not condone it, he understood his companion's mad behavior? Perhaps the time he spent with the Bedouin had somewhat warped his judgment? No matter, he decided that it would be better not to share his musings with anyone, nor even his travelling companion. He compared Cristina's beauty to that of the young Austrian actress Käthe Brandt[27], who he had seen the prior year in the comedy No Money Needed. Mrs. Laughton could have been the sensation of movie goers, a star, yet chose to settle on a farm to raise her children. And she seemed extremely happy with such an obscure life. Who can understand happiness, he pondered? Each

---

[26] Ferruginous Pygmy Owl (*Glaucidium brasilianum*)

[27] Hedy Lamarr, who became famous as the lead actress (as Hedy Kiesler) in the controversial German film *Ecstasy*.

person finds it in things that would appear strange to others. As for himself, he felt happier when he was among his Bedouin, riding their wonderful horses with the wind unraveling their manes, watching the setting sun painting the desert sands in mutating tones. How he missed the Ruala. . .

CHAPTER TWENTY-TWO

Like all male creatures Wimsey was a simple soul at bottom.
—Have His Carcase, Dorothy L. Sayers, 1932.

E arly that day Robert had dropped Raswan at the hotel where was staying with Bogdan Zietarski. Robert and Cristina were in their bedroom. The heat of the prior days had subsided in the late afternoon and a nice breeze entered the room through the open windows, brushing past the voile curtains. It was a cozy room, with white walls. A couple of old armchairs covered in floral chintz stood in front of the little iron stove. Between them sat a delicate mahogany Chippendale Pie Crust table where a pile of newspapers and magazines neatly arranged shared the small space with an empty ashtray.

Robert stood facing a picture on the wall—the only one in the bedroom. It was a portrait of Cristina. It was done when they visited Florence, four or five years ago. They came out of the Duomo, and as they stepped on to the Piazza were approached by a young man who had been drawing the church. With much gesturing and a little English mixed to his native Italian, he begged Robert to allow him to draw the signora. He had large, dark eyes and a brooding mouth that intensified his serious expression. It was a chilly morning and he wore a black beret and fingerless gloves. He did not say much, but they learned the nineteen-year-old was originally from Milan and was a student at the Academy of Fine Arts in Florence. The medium used was pastel and in a few strokes the artist had captured Cristina's beauty and freshness. It was signed

87

Pietro Annigoni[28]. Robert wondered if he was still drawing unknown people on the streets of Florence.

On Cristina's bedside table were displayed all her René Lalique treasures: a 'Dahlias' lamp, with its counterpart on Robert's side; a matching, plump little vase, crammed with white gardenias that filled the air with their sweet perfume; a picture of her three children ensconced in a small Lalique glass frame. The small round, opalescent box, Primevères, dotted with primroses, kept Robert's billets doux, mementos from balls and theater tickets. Beside it stood a much-handled old volume of Machado de Assis Histórias da Meia Noite. (For Cristina, the older the book, the more she treasured it. It made her wonder how many hands had perused, caressed the book's brittle pages before her eager ones.) Sitting atop the book was the proverbial clock, a delicate little nothing made of silver, that sang a soft tick-tock, lulling the minutes to pass.

Facing the twin beds, a dressing table held a motley assortment of perfume bottles. An old wooden box held Cristina's jewelry. Beside it sat a large crystal bowl holding a few makeup items—lipsticks, face powder and a fluffy puff, and rouge. Standing against the mirror were two photographs and Robert reached for them.

"Kaishi[29] is what—seventeen?" Robert asked his wife. "She was such a skinny little oaf when I first met them on the tramp." He remembered the day when he woke up lying on a bed on a tramp ship, with no memory of who he was, to see two young faces hovering over his. "And we all thought she was a boy. The two had everyone fooled," he smiled at the memories of the children who were now adults.

It showed the half profile of a beautiful Oriental girl dressed for prom night. Her melancholy almond eyes were highlighted by the delicate arches of thin eyebrows; the black and white hues of the picture did not show the incongruent dark blue eyes, a trait she inherited from her American father. Her short hair was parted on the side and waved down in small curls. The slightly parted lips had been painted with red lipstick and showed almost black. She wore a long dress buttoned down, with

---

[28] Italian painter (June/7/1910-October/28/1988), painted Queen Elizabeth, Princess Margaret, Presidents Kennedy and Johnson, Pope John XIII, as well as the controversial fresco "Deposition and Resurrection" at San Marco, Florence.

[29] Finding Cristina: A New Life.

cap sleeves and Peter Pan collar. The fitted bodice was accentuated with horizontal pleats, repeated near the hem of the flared skirt that was gathered at the waist by a ribbon where a couple of large roses hung.

"Yes, she's just seventeen," Cristina answered, while opening a large cardboard box. "Did you read her letter? It's inside the first drawer, to your right."

"I did. I wonder if she is really serious about going back to Japan after finishing nursing school."

"I think it's a passing fad. Her family is in the States. Her friends, her life, everything is there. I hope she changes her mind. If not, she will be even further away from us," Cristina lamented. The girl and her brother lived with their American family in New York, which was already far; if she moved to Japan, that distance would make travelling more difficult.

"My concern is the political situation in Japan. Things have been heating up since the end of the Great War. There was a coup attempted in '31. And last year some Navy officers assassinated their Prime Minister. That helped Emperor Hirohito, who's backed by the military."

Robert turned to the picture of Kaishi's brother, Ichiro, now twenty-two years old. On him none of his American father's traits were present. He was wearing black tie, sitting with legs crossed, one hand resting on the knee, holding a cigar, the other held a pair of white gloves. His handsome face turned slightly to the left, he gazed downwards with a pensive expression. Both pictures were inscribed on the back to "Uncle Robert and Aunt Cristina."

"How time passes," Robert pondered, replacing the pictures against the mirror.

"I need to get a couple of picture frames for these."

Hands in pockets, Robert turned to his wife. He watched her while she sorted through the books Desiree had brought her—the latest detective novels printed in the United States. She had finally found time to open the large box that contained the volumes, and had little remarks for each title.

"Oh, how wonderful: The Thirteen Problems, by Agatha Christie— I love her!" Then removing the next book: "Another Margery Allingham: Police at the Funeral. I love Campion and Lug."

"Who are these guys? Don't tease me, babe!"

Ignoring her husband's joke, she continued, "Have His Carcase. That's the author Desiree told me about, Dorothy Sayers. She says her books are really good." Then extracting another book from the box, "The Duke of York's Steps, by Henry Wade—yes, I've been trying to get this one since it was published years ago! The Mask of Fu Manchu—Sax Rohmer..."

As she read the titles, Cristina stacked the books on the floor beside her. Meanwhile, Robert approached the window. Parting the curtain and looking down, he saw his heir walking in the distance. Donny was not too far so that he was able to see that the boy was carrying his Hamilton 22-caliber rifle. Then turning his gaze to his left, he saw Annie perched on the swing near the walled garden.

"Mmm... Wonder why Hanz and Fritz[30] aren't together."

"Who?"

"I saw your son marching away with his rifle, but his partner in crime was left behind. Makes me wonder what's going on."

"What?" asked his wife, whose universe, at that moment, revolved around that magical box full of books.

"Never mind," he bent and kissed her head. "Keep playing with your toys, my child. I'll go check what's up with these two."

He was about to leave the bedroom when a shriek from his wife startled him into a stop. He turned to see her face where an enraptured smile parted rosy lips.

"Oh, hon, the latest Freeman!" and she turned the book cover to him. "Another Thorndyke mystery: Dr. Thorndyke's Discovery!" she read and hugged the book.

"You'll give me a heart attack one of these days, woman!"

Outside Robert joined Annie. Bacon was nowhere to be seen; that could only mean that he was in the kitchen, eating, or waiting to be fed.

"You look bored." No reaction. "I see your friend went hunting but didn't take you." The girl's silence aroused Robert's attention. "Do you know where he went?" he asked, feigning unconcern.

"Meet the donkey guy down there." She motioned her head, indicated the direction of the farm's main gate.

---

[30] The rascally twins from The Katzenjammer Kids, a comic strip created in 1897.

"Donkey guy? What donkey guy? What for?" he asked, starting to feel concerned.

"The one that beats his donkey. Donny told him next time he'd be sorry and the man laughed at him, and he got really mad, and promised he'd be the one who'd be sorry."

As soon as the words came out of Annie's mouth, they heard a shot fired in the distance.

Muttering a curse—to the girl's immense delight—Robert took off to where the sound originated, closely followed by Annie, who had jumped down from the swing.

As they approached the gate, they could see Donny standing in the middle of the road ahead, holding his rifle pointed down. In front of him was a donkey cart that had swerved to one side, motionless now, partially blocking the road. Meanwhile, a scruffy little donkey with watery eyes— Robert correctly guessed, his son's latest protégé—chewed at some weeds that grew by the side of the road, his tail flicking listlessly to drive away the flies. Suddenly from one corner of the cart, a head timidly appeared—the driver.

He was a sordid looking type, scruffier than his hoofed counterpart. The man was clearly shaken. Seeing Robert approach, he composed himself enough to threaten him with the law: "This boy tried to kill me! I'll go to the perlice!"

"I shot in the air! I wanted to stop him from beating—"

Robert cut his son short and turned his attention to the man. "It's just a kid's rifle, but I grant you what my boy did was wrong," Robert argued in his best Portuguese, "and he'll be punished. But you shouldn't mistreat this poor animal."

Robert's heavy accent and conciliatory tone had emboldened the man, and he countered Robert's mild rebuke, truculent, "What's 'im to yer? D'ya belong to his family to show so much concern?"

"No, but it bothers me to see brother mistreating brother!"

"I treats 'im the way I wants!" the man riposted, completely missing Robert's meaning.

Robert sighed and shook his head, then turned to his son, "Stay right here, don't you budge." He looked back at the man, now with a thunderous expression.

The man had moved from his hideout and was standing in the middle of the road, hands on hips, in a defiant attitude.

"I ain't afeared!" he challenged his opponent.

But as Robert approached him, he took a step back, his confidence gone.

"Listen here, pal, if the boy had aimed at you, believe me, we wouldn't be talking, 'cause you'd be a corpse." He pointed at the donkey, "But next time I hear you mistreated this animal you'll have to deal with an adult."

He had such a glint in his eyes the man visibly shrank.

"Goramighty, Mistah! No needs to get nasty, no harm done," and he quickly started to straighten the cart. Only this time he gently nudged the donkey. He eyed the whip, but under Robert's hard gaze left it in the middle of the road where it had fallen.

Turning to his son, Robert saw the air of triumph on the boy's face, that quickly vanished under his father's glare.

"No good lowering your eyes! You're in big trouble, young man. Big trouble! Wait till I tell Bunky what you did."

Luckily, with the noise the moving donkey cart made, Robert did not hear his son's muffled chuckle. He bent down, took the whip and broke it in two, deliberately holding it up so it would be visible to the retreating cartman.

"Let's go. And you, young lady, you're in trouble too," he told a startled Annie. "Wait till I tell your dad you sat by while your cousin stirred up trouble."

"What was I to do, Uncle Robbie? He won't listen to reason!"

The intense distress she felt gave her face such a comic look that it was all Robert could do to keeping from laughing.

"That's not true! You thought it was a good idea to teach that guy a lesson so he'd stop beating poor Natalino!" Donny protested.

"Nat... What?"

"Natalino—the donkey." And as his father still did not understand, he explained, "It's from Natal: Christmas. 'Cause he was born on Christmas day."

"I'm surprised he wasn't given the Lord's name! C'mon, let's go, you two ruffians."

"Wohoo! A new word: ruffians," Annie cheered. "I've gotta note this one in my diary. How d'you spell it? And that other word you said when we heard the shot, remember? Can you spell it?"

But Robert did not dignify the girl's questions with an answer. He explicitly slapped the whip against his tight, looking steadily at the slowly retreating cart, then turning to the kids pointed it to the farm gate, "In you go." And the three left.

Robert's stern gaze had operated a momentary change on the muleteer. He gathered the reins and, jumping back on the cart, shook them. The animal slowly moved forward and instinctively his hand went for the whip. But seeing it being held by Robert, broken, that worked even better than the young donkey's avenger would have expected.

He turned to look back and saw no one on the road. Now that he was by himself, his courage returned.

"For'ner, that one is," he thought. "And a meddling for'ner!"

The donkey's slow pace irritated him, but Robert's last words were fresh in his memory, and he did not dare touch the beast. His wrath had to be directed somewhere else. Muttering curses under his breath, he started to dream of ways he would take revenge on the first human or animal that crossed his path. So long as either was of a size he could handle.

CHAPTER TWENTY-THREE

I love thee with a love I seemed to lose
With my lost saints. I love thee with the breath,
Smiles, tears, of all my life; and, if God choose,
I shall but love thee better after death.
—How Do I Love Thee?, in Sonnets from the Portuguese,
Elizabeth Barrett Browing. 1850.

It was an early Friday morning; Maria, Desiree and Max drove to Bagé. Aided by Maria's knowledge of the town, and language skills, they would do some shopping, and have lunch afterwards. Bunky had stayed behind, enticed by the opportunity of taking a peaceful nap on a hammock with a glass of iced tea nearby, while Cristina and her husband took the children to the creek for a swim.

Not long after the family moved to the farm, Robert and Bunky widened one of the creek's rocky turns near the house, and turned it into a large basin. They built a deck, equipped with a bathroom large enough to also serve as dressing room. It was adjacent to the storage room that kept floats, chairs, fishing rods and tackle, and the children's water wings. Not far from the deck was a shed with a door at the landward end, and a double door giving directly upon the creek. Both doors were padlocked. Inside the shed was moored a little canoe, brightly painted in shades of red, white and blue, named The Delaware. The creek as well as the canoe were forbidden territory for the children, unless they were accompanied by an adult. Donny and Annie were allowed to fish there, so long as they stayed on the deck and did not venture into the water.

During their visits to the creek, Cristina liked to lay in one of the lounge chairs sunning herself, after slathering her skin with Jean Patou's Huile de Chaldée tanning oil—that Robert called 'Frog slime.' Meanwhile her husband and the children splashed through the crystalline creek water. Then after so much exercise and a light lunch, the little ones invariably succumbed to a nap.

Cristina, Robert and the twins were in the walled garden, sitting under the large wisteria-covered pergola, taking advantage of the mild temperature the abundant shade offered on these hot days of summer. The twins, Alex and Loulou, were in their little sandpit in the shade, enjoying their favorite game: hitting each other on the head with various toys. Bacon, who did not seem up to brave the afternoon heat and humidity, had demurred when urged to join Donny and Annie on that day's adventure; he lay sprawled on the cool bricks that paved the garden paths, softly snoring. His legs twitching at intervals spoke of wild dreams. Robert was reading—or more accurately, slowly deciphering—the Correio do Sul, the local newspaper. Cristina, the stockings she had been darning forgotten on her lap, was daydreaming, simply taking in the peace and beauty around her.

Two swallows cut the sky above them, performing some daring acrobatics. A hummingbird darted by, a tiny speck of light and color, and landed on a slight branch of the wisteria to immediately take off. Among the white carpet of daisies beyond, roses bled intense red, hanging from verdant bushes, while giant, multicolored pansies opened mysterious pupils, watching their surroundings in amazement. The scent of the mingled flowers and herbs reminded Cristina of her house in Rio de Janeiro.

Blissful. That would be her choice of word if asked for one to describe her life. Not perfect—whose life was perfect?—but the love she and her husband shared, had never wavered but became stronger. She promised herself to take the time to read the gag gift Robert gave her the year before she was thirty: Honoré de Balzac's La Femme de Trente Ans. She was now, as in Balzac's story, a woman of thirty, a balzaquiana in Portuguese. But, as far as she knew of the plot, her age was the only trait she shared with the novel's troubled heroine, Julie de Chastillon. Unlike Julie she did not suffer from uncertainties and vacillations; she was perfectly content with life.

Cristina looked at her husband, sitting across from her. She could analyze his face, completely absorbed on the paper he was reading. The ever-escaping curl of hair lightly touched his forehead, giving him a boyish air. With knitted eyebrows, a concentrated expression she found comical, at times he mouthed the words as he read them, in the effort of understanding that 'darn language,' as he called Portuguese. She thought of the gag gifts he so enjoyed giving. One Christmas, still in New York, with earnest gravity he handed her a beautifully wrapped package that, upon opening, revealed a dozen electric bulbs. To her disappointed expression, he asked, "What's the matter, babe? Don't you need lightbulbs?" Of course, the real present—a pearl and diamond chocker—followed the prank.

At thirty-six, he still had the same youthful air he had when she met him at twenty-six. His mood was constant and reassuring, unlike her volatile temperament, something she appreciated immensely. The years had somehow matured and perfected his beauty. Like wine. And that thought made her chuckle.

"What's amusing?" asked her spouse, peeking from behind the pages of the newspaper.

"You're like wine."

"Inebriating?"

"No, silly," she gurgled with that laughter he loved.

"I know: I make you dizzy, right?"

She made a face at him and turned her attention back to the abandoned darning.

"C'mon, ma'am, spill it or I'll have to tickle you to death!"

"You won't, because I'm armed and dangerous," she warded his attack by pointing a needle his way. "I meant that you're like wine: better with age."

"You ain't seen nothing yet, my beauty. Wait till I turn ninety!"

"We have a good life, don't you think? We've been blessed with lovely children…"

"Lovely—yes, for sure," he said, with a solemn expression.

"Oh, but surely, look at these little angels," she pointed at the twins. Don't you just love them to pieces?"

"Especially when they're asleep."

"I should give you a good spanking for that!"

"Would you really?" and his eyes sparkled mischievously.

"Oh, go back to your paper and leave me to my darning."

"I do as I am commanded."

A few minutes later he burst out laughing, startling Cristina. The twins imitated their papa.

"Oh, this is too good!"

"What?

"'Special session for gentlemen only.' Mmm..." He continued, "'March aw sowlil'—"

"Marche au Soleil," Cristina corrected, pronouncing the words in perfect French. "A French movie? But for men only? That's odd."

Robert lowered the newspaper and gave his wife an impious look. He then straightening the pages back, completely covering his face, and quoted from the paper, "'What is nudism in Europe? Two sessions: eight thirty p.m. and ten p.m.'" He folded the paper and slapped it on the table. "I think I'll go to the ten o'clock session, whatcha think?"

"Humph," was his wife's dismissive response, unconsciously emulating Maria's favorite interjection.

"Oh, well, since you won't let me go, I'll just read the rest of the paper." And he started reading out loud the social news and advertising. "Now, here's a pearl: a poem by Ogustow doos Anjews: Oo lamntow das cosas.'"

"Augusto dos Anjos, O Lamento das Coisas," she corrected him. "Please, don't commit a crime against his poor afflicted soul by reading his poem, I beg you. He suffered enough when he was alive."

"Now, that will interest our tots: 'Circo Sul-Americano.'" And at these words the twins stood still and stared at their father. "What did I tell ya?" Robert asked his wife, indicating the children with a head motion. "Too bad Donny and Annie have gone in one of their camping trips today. Uncle Bunky will take you, babies," he told the children, who clapped their hands and smiled broadly in anticipation.

"Shame on you for committing Bunky without his knowledge," Cristina chided her husband and got a chuckle for an answer.

She turned her attention back to darning, Robert resumed reading, now in silence, and the children went back to playing in the sand. After a few minutes of working in silence, she smiled, again remembering her husband's peculiar sense of humor. When they first came to live on the farm, they were told the area was plagued with poachers. Robert immediately painted signs in Portuguese that read 'Poachers, welcome to our property'. These he and Bunky nailed to the fence, in different areas of their farm. The text was startling, but somehow it worked: they never encountered anyone sneaking in, nor any unaccountable shots were ever heard. Bunky, another practical joker, explained to Cristina that the very peculiarity of the signs would look suspicious, therefore stopping in their tracks anyone coming to poach.

A sound made Cristina raise her head from her darning.

"I think I hear the car."

Robert was too absorbed reading, so without disturbing him she walked out of the garden and went to the garage, where she met Maria and Desiree. Max was getting several packages out of the car's back seat and piling them on the floor, in preparation of carrying them to the house.

"For you," and Maria handed an envelope to Cristina.

On the cover was written Departamento dos Correios e Telégrafos.

"A telegram," Cristina said a bit surprised.

She started to turn when Maria stopped her: "What is it? Is everything fine?"

"Will tell you as soon as I read," she told Maria and went back to the garden.

As Cristina read the telegram, her face took an expression of concern: 'Sonya sick come telephone company strike.'

It was signed Anatoly, which was unusual. Why did Sonya's doctor, Dr. Anatoly Orlov, send the telegram, instead Irena, Sonya's companion?

CHAPTER TWENTY-FOUR

*Great eddies of air were swinging me to and fro. I was navigating somewhere in
the belly of a cumulus whose thickness I could not guess. I rose to seventy-five
hundred feet and was still in it.*
—Wind, Sand, and Stars, Antoine de Saint Exupéry. 1939.

Seeing his wife's serious expression, Robert put the newspaper
down. "What is it, princess of mine? What's wrong?"

"Not sure." She hesitated, then related the contents of the
telegram to her husband, explaining at the end, "Dr. Orlov signed it. You
remember him. Which means that he sent it. But why didn't Irena send
it?"

"Maybe she was just too busy taking care of Sonya and the doc
wanted to help," Robert suggested, then wondered, "Yet, we spoke with
Sonya just a few days ago—last Saturday—and she was fine."

Every other Saturday Cristina and Robert went to the Telephone
Company in Bagé, to call Sonya.

"She's not a kid anymore," Cristina wondered, concerned.

"Yet Helena is about the same age as her and is healthy as a horse."

"Well, yes, she's not much older than mother, but she never really
recovered after my father—I mean, Vasili—after Vasili died. I must go
to Rio," Cristina turned to her husband and before he started protesting,
continued, "We can't both go, you must see that. Someone has to keep
an eye on the children."

"Bunky can do it."

"And there's the party. You know how it is—noblesse oblige, kiddo."
She smiled at her husband and took hold of his hand with both hers.

"Noblesse oblige my—"

"Husband!" she admonished him, and motioned her head to indicate the twins. "Language!" Then she continued, now serious, "There's an airplane from VARIG leaving for Porto Alegre[31] at eleven on Saturdays—I saw it in the paper the other day. I'm sure I can find an airplane to Rio de Janeiro when I get to Porto Alegre. Or even a ship if the planes are all booked." And seeing his brow furrow, "Please, don't be difficult. It's the best solution." He did not look convinced, so she added, "I'll be fine."

And that, her husband knew, was final.

Cristina's decision was irrevocable, and Robert was forced to accept it. Reminding her of the occasional political turmoil the country had been experiencing for the last several years was of no effect. So, early on Saturday morning she prepared a small suitcase, with only the basic things she would need for a short stay. She went downstairs dressed in a smart linen suit, a one-button jacket with a straight skirt. Her hair, that she had grown longer again, was gathered on a small chignon on the nape of her slender neck. A coquettish little hat perched on her head, leaned towards her right ear. Her gloves matched the clutch, belt, and the comfortable low heel oxfords she had chosen. To avoid a scene, Bunky had been instructed to take the twins to the river for a little canoe trip. But Cristina knew it would unavoidably happen later. Donny had said his goodbyes the night before, together with Annie. And even before anyone was up, both children had stuffed food in their haversacks and left for another excursion, so Cristina did not see either of them.

Despondent, Robert drove his wife in her two-seater to Bagé, secretly hoping the plane was booked to capacity.

"I'll be back and you won't have time to miss me, you'll see," she assured him. "You'll be so busy with the party too," she added, trying to console him, unsuccessfully. "Oh, hon, you know I don't want to go."

"So, don't! Let me go instead. There's still time."

---

[31] Capital of the state of Rio Grande do Sul.

"Sure, you must see that I have to be the one going, Robert." She tried once more to convince him.

"No, I don't!"

"I won't budge, you must accept my decision," she told him, now with a sharp note to her voice.

Their arrival at the airfield prevented this exchange from evolving into an argument. It was a little after ten in the morning. At the counter Cristina was told that there were four passengers and her disappointed husband watched her purchase the fifth and last available place on the airplane. She was told she could take her seat if she wanted, so, accompanied by a very unhappy Robert she walked to the airplane.

The Junkers F-13 had just parked on the landing field. Robert handed Cristina's luggage to a mechanic who put it with the mail bag which had been on the plane since nine o'clock that morning. He then helped his wife reach the stirrup on the side of the plane. She climbed the two little steps on the wing and got in. He followed her, squeezed through the narrow opening into the small craft, and sat beside Cristina, looking miserable.

"What a sardine can," he sulked, looking around the cabin.

There was a two-seat chair with its tall, padded back against the plane's fuselage. Right in front of it, leaving not a lot of leg space, were two separate chairs, facing a little glass window that gave to the open cockpit.

"Were the airplanes you flew bigger?"

"No, but at least I had the cockpit all to myself," he told her, referring to the period he flew in France, during the Great War. Turning pleading eyes to her, he tried to dissuade her to go to Rio. "There's still time, I can still go in your place." And before she could argue he added, "I can buy everything I need when I get there."

"Stop making puppy eyes at me. It won't work, you know."

"It used to," he grumbled.

Cristina laughed and tousled his hair. "You look like a kid whose toy was taken away!"

"But my toy is being taken away from me!" He crossed his arms and frowned—which make him look so much like his son—and sat back, the knees of his long legs jammed against the back of the chair on the front row.

Cristina gurgled with laughter. Stretching up on her seat to reach his face, she gave him a kiss on his cheek.

"Consolation prize, kiddo."

"I'll show you how it's done, Mrs. Laughton."

But as he started to embrace her, the pilot poked his head through the door and smiled at the scene that met his eyes.

"Hello folks—sorry about the interruption. The two of you going to Porto Alegre?"

"No, just my wife," Robert answered.

"OK. Will let you know when we're ready."

"How easy it is to get a flight to Rio de Janeiro from Porto Alegre?" Robert asked before the man left, hoping against hope to discourage his wife.

"There are the hydroplanes from Condor and Air France that fly do Rio; they leave from Voluntarios da Pátria Avenue, from a pier at the Guaíba river, instead of the airdrome. We'll get to Porto Alegre in one hour thirty minutes, depending on the wind and at the Aeródromo São João your wife can get the information."

"What about ships bound to Rio?" Cristina asked, hopeful.

The man rubbed his chin thoughtfully. "Now, that I really don't know, ma'am. Sorry." And with that he jumped down to meet another man coming their way—the mechanic. They conferred for a few minutes, then the pilot escalated one of the wings and, from there, jumped into the cockpit.

Time passed too quickly. The pilot turned back in his seat and, opening the little window that communicated with the interior of the plane, addressed Robert: "You'll have to leave, sir. We're about to take off."

This time Robert was able to steal a kiss from his wife unobserved. He then held Cristina's left hand and removed her glove.

"What are you doing?"

"Making sure you have your wedding ring."

"Oh, really, hon!" She snatched her hand from his and put on the glove again.

"I love when you call me hon. I feel like melting," he winked and gave her an impudent look.

"We're getting ready. You have to leave, sir," the pilot insisted and slammed the window shut.

Robert gave his wife a last, quick peck and scrambled out of the aircraft.

"Not going to wait for the other passengers," they heard the pilot tell the mechanic. "I'd be late and you know how the boss takes pride on our punctuality."

At that moment they saw a car fast approaching, honking, an arm frantically waving from one of the windows. It came to a sudden stop right beside the plane. They saw Carl Raswan come out of it. The next one to come out did not surprise Cristina nor Robert.

"Oh, no," Cristina grunted.

"I'll be...," her husband hissed under his breath, then out loud, turning to her with a somber expression, "The Polack!"

CHAPTER TWENTY-FIVE

Certainly, it is valuable to a trained writer to crash in an aircraft which burns. He learns several important things very quickly. Whether they will be of use to him is conditioned by survival.
—Ernest Hemingway, Paris Review, interview by George Plimpton. Issue 18, Spring 1958.

Dismay was plainly inscribed on Bogdan Zietarski's face. It was quickly replaced by an expression of fear; the last thing he wanted was a physical confrontation with the American. He turned to Carl Raswan for support and, together they approached the airplane. Robert stood by, arms crossed, legs astride.

"Hon, don't cause a scene, please. The man can hardly try anything, with Mr. Raswan on the plane," Cristina whispered.

"Mr. Laughton, are you joining us in this trip?" Raswan smiled at Robert, then removing his hat, turned to Cristina, who was perching out of the door, "Mrs. Laughton. How nice to see you both," he addressed both of them with his calm demeanor. "Are we to have the pleasure of both your company?"

Robert responded the greeting with a cordial hand shake, while ignoring Zietarski.

"My husband is staying, Mr. Raswan," Cristina answered, and added quickly, to prevent Robert from making any comment, "The pilot was just going to start the engine. It seems they are very punctual. So, why don't you hand your luggage to the mechanic and take your seats?"

As unhappy as he was, Robert was nevertheless forced to step aside so the two passengers could climb the little steps that led to the door.

Zietarski removed his hat and gave Cristina a nervous side look. His stays creaked as he bent and squeezed inside the cabin, making his way to one of the front seats. His presence evoked stressful memories on Cristina and she remembered the first time she saw him. She and her friend Solange were the entertainment at a private party in Rio de Janeiro. They had been playing—respectively, the piano and the harp—when a man with huge mustache made his entrance. The two girls thought of a walrus, and could not help laughing. The mustachioed man was Zietarski. That was nine years ago, but it felt like a century had passed since that day.

"I'll telegraph from Porto Alegre," she told her husband who was standing by the wing. "Then if the strike is still on when I arrive in Rio, I'll send you a telegram. But I'm sure things are now completely under control," she added, referring to the last revolution—one of many—that had broken in the state of São Paulo the prior year, 1932. The revolutionaries had surrendered in October of that year. "And remember to keep Bacon away from Mrs. Valentim at the party," she urged him, right before the airplane door was shut.

The dog had an inherent distaste for that lady. A few times he tried to relieve himself on Mrs. Valentim's legs, causing a terrible brouhaha. Cristina saw her husband's gloomy expression slowly ease into a wide smile after she made her request. It was a clear sign that he was planning to do just the opposite.

"Oh, God," she whispered to herself, briefly closing her eyes. She knew there was nothing she could do, so she sat back, resigned.

The pilot opened the main fuel tank valve, turned the nob of the auxiliary tank valve, and was turning the fuel selector when he saw another car approaching at break-neck speed. It came to a screeching halt. From it came a couple of young people, both very blond. He was tall and slim with horn-rimmed glasses, a small bag in each hand. Wearing pants and with very short blond hair, at first sight the girl looked like a teenage boy; she was petite and had a pretty, piquant face. Despite the heat, as she came out of the car, she put on a battered leather flight jacket, which she proceeded to button up.

The young man handed the bags to the mechanic, scrambled up the wing and entered the airplane cabin, sitting beside Cristina. The girl sprang to the wing like a gymnast, closed the door of the airplane as she passed by, and, placing her left foot into the kick step on the side of the craft, hopped in and landed on the seat beside the pilot. He seemed to know her. She quickly put on a flight helmet, then adjusted a pair of goggles over it and put on a pair of leather gloves. She exchanged a few quick words with the pilot while he checked the fuel quantity floor gauge to make sure it was full. Turning her head to see the passenger area, she grinned and gave thumbs up to the young man sitting beside Cristina; he returned her gestures in kind.

The pilot went through the whole starting process until the motor started and the airplane slowly moved ahead. Cristina leaned toward the little window and waved at her husband, blowing him a kiss. Jogging alongside the aircraft, Robert was able to keep up with it for a short while, until it gained speed. Soon it lifted off the ground. Cristina kept watching until her husband was a mere dot, then sat back with a sigh. The first time she traveled on an airplane, she enjoyed the speed of the trip. But the rattling din of the motor and the turbulence were such inconvenience she decided only dire circumstances would force her to fly again. She still felt the same way.

"I am Heinrich Jürgen Kramer, but you can call me Harry," the young man beside her addressed her in an English tainted with heavy German accent. "I heard you and the gentleman speaking the language—I mean, English."

"Pleased to meet you, Harry. I am Cristina Laughton," she said, shaking his hand, "and the gentleman you saw is my husband, Robert." She then turned to the front seats, addressing the two men. "Mr. Carl Raswan, and," she hesitated, "Mr. Bogdan Zietarski, this is Harry Kramer." She had to almost scream to be heard.

Both men managed to turn in their seats to shake the young man's proffered hand.

"Raswan?" Harry asked. "Du bist derjenige, der mit den Beduinen lebte!"

"Yes, I'm the guy who lived among the Bedouin," Raswan answered in the same irreverent style the young man used. But he expressed himself in English for the benefit of Cristina, who he knew did not speak German. Carl was a bit taken aback by Harry's use of 'du,' instead of the formal 'Sie' that Germans employ when addressing older people, or someone not intimate.

"Who is the young lady?" Zietarski asked Harry, also in English.

"And why does she prefer to sit with the pilot?" Cristina added, voicing the question that was on everyone's mind.

"She's my cousin Karola Teresa Kramer. Terri is a pilot. Her airplane is in a hangar near this airdrome, being fixed. She recently bought a 1927 Stearman C3 in America and flew it here," he explained. "She also has a degree in veterinary from the University of Leipzig." And at the surprise expressed on everyone's faces that a woman had been to college, he explained that their grandfather had been a great benefactor of that institution; when Terri decided to join, they felt obliged to accept her. "Besides, Terri always gets what she wants," he finished and turned with a beaming expression to where the young lady sat with the pilot.

A half hour later, in the cockpit, the pilot was pointing out a large extent of clouds to his companion. Their airplane was headed straight to it. The towering of puffy cumulus clouds would be above them and she knew what it meant: turbulence—the plague of aviation. It would be a bumpy ride until they passed it.

"Thank the gods it's not a cumulonimbus," she told the pilot above the noise of the motor, to which he heartily agreed.

Encountering that monstruous cloud formation known as cumulonimbus, a pilot would have been forced to either turn back, fly lower, or avoid it by completely changing the course of the airplane.

He indicated to her that he was going to warn the passengers to keep their seatbelts fastened. He proceeded to disengage his own and, turning backwards, he opened the little window and yelled a warning to the passengers: there would be some turbulence ahead. He then told them to make sure their seatbelts were fastened. As he closed the little window shut, the plane, having reached the cloud formation, stalled and violently dropped in altitude, rattling ominously. The passengers were saved from being pitched forward as, having been engaged in conversation with young Harry, they had not thought of unfastening their seatbelts since the plane took off from Bagé. Caught unprepared, the pilot's head slammed into the overhead. He fell limply onto his seat, and the weight of his body having landed on the yolk, it pushed it forward, forcing the airplane into a nosedive.

In the passengers' area the occupants were also pitched forward, but were held from tumbling down by their seatbelts and by grasping the seats' arms or whatever they could reach. In the chaos Raswan and Zietarski exchanged a quick glance, panic in their eyes.

Cristina smothered a scream; her hand convulsively grabbed the back of the chair in front of her, until the knuckles shone white through her tanned skin. A horrible death seemed unavoidable, and, in her despair, her thoughts went to her husband and children, and she tried to say a quick prayer. But when she turned to look at young Harry, he appeared to be strangely unperturbed.

CHAPTER TWENTY-SIX

If you are looking for perfect safety, you will do well to sit on a fence and watch the birds; but if you really wish to learn, you must mount a machine and become acquainted with its tricks by actual trial.
—Wilbur Wright address to the Western Society of Engineers. September 18, 1901. Published in the Journal of the Western Society of Engineers, December 1901.

While the airplane went into a nosedive it shook the passengers like beads inside a maraca during Rita Montaner's interpretation of El Manicero[32]. Meanwhile, the girl in the cockpit desperately tried to pull the pilot back onto his seat. Through the window, Raswan saw her frantic, unsuccessful efforts. Unleashing his seatbelt, he fell forward, crashing against the partition that separated the cockpit from the interior of the plane. Taking hold of the hand Zietarski held to him, he balanced and straightened himself, and reached for the window. With a tremendous effort to keep from being pitched against the partition, he managed to open the windowpane, then tried to squeeze his chest through it, to get access to the cockpit. Impossible: it was too small. Besides, the space in the cockpit was minimal, barely enough for two. He decided to stretched his free arm and, with a little effort, was able to reach the collar of the pilot's jacket. With his firm grasp and Terri's help he managed to pull the pilot against the back of his seat, while Terri laboriously lashed the man's

---

[32] The Peanut Vendor was a Cuban song. Rita Montaner made it an international hit in 1928.

seatbelt. The girl then quickly pulled his yolk back to the correct position. Grabbing the yolk in front of her, she took command of the aircraft. After several anxious moments, when it seemed they were doomed, the airplane was brought up to a safe altitude.

Raswan fell back into his seat with a loud sigh of relief, sweat pouring down his face. After mopping his also wet forehead with a large handkerchief, Zietarski patted his friend on the shoulder. He could not yet vocalize his thanks and hoped the gesture conveyed that. Cristina, her eyes shut, sat with her head against the seat's back. She took a couple of deep breaths and only then was able to open her eyes. Upon which she encountered Harry's admiring ones.

"You have the most, wunderbar—how do you say that in English?— oh, yes: marvelous! You have the most marvelous face, Frau Cristina! And such eyes! I could sit here and look at you for hours," he added, dreamily.

"How come you remained calm thought this?" Still recovering from the near-death experience, Cristina did not really grasp the meaning of the young man's words, but could only think of his calm expression during that desperate moment.

"Ach du lieber Gott! But if Terri was in the co-pilot's seat!" he told her, as if that should explain his calm reaction throughout the scary moments. "I knew she'd bring us out unscathed."

"Your faith in your cousin is—how do you say in German? Wunderbar," she said and both laughed.

It amazed her that, in such dire situation, that young man had concentrated not on the prospect of being smashed to the ground, but on the beauty of her eyes!

It was just past one in the afternoon when the airplane reached the Aeródromo São João, the airdrome that served the city of Porto Alegre. The pilot, a big bruise on his forehead, and after thanking Terri wholeheartedly for her sang froid, said his goodbyes to the passengers. He was grateful for Terri's promise that she was sure to convince the passengers not to report the accident; had they done otherwise he would certainly lose his job.

FINDING CRISTINA: TREASURES ON EARTH

All the passengers were travelling to Rio de Janeiro—although Raswan and Zietarski planned to stay in town for a week. Zietarski specially felt he needed some rest, but not because of their long trip that had lasted a month; the tension of being confronted with Cristina and her family had drained him almost completely.

There was no flight available to Rio until the next day, and they had to find accommodations in Porto Alegre. Terri and Harry, who reserved rooms at the Grande Hotel in advance, suggested they all stay there. Cristina, stayed there with her husband when they were in the process of buying the farm in Bagé, and already planned to try that hotel, so she accepted their suggestion. Her only concern was having Zietarski so near, but she trusted Raswan would keep him in hand.

The hotel was located at the corner of Andradas and Caldas Junior streets, in the heart of downtown Porto Alegre, with one side facing the large Praça da Alfândega—the Customs Square. When the Laughtons stayed there it had just been expanded and renovated. As the five travelers arrived at the hotel, they discovered that it was full. Summer was a time when families from small towns went to Porto Alegre to enjoy the beaches; Vila Assunção, Tristeza, and Pedra Redonda, among others, all properly illuminated with electric light and of easy access by tram, where areas that attracted these wealthy families during the hot months. Besides, February was attractive due to the Carnaval balls private clubs organized in the capital. Wealthy Gaúchos shied away from street festivities—frequented by what they described as the riffraff—working men and women, blacks, and, the worst offenders, groups of men dressed as women, all people with whom they refused to mingle. Nevertheless, street Carnaval was very popular, and was actively promoted and encouraged by the local newspapers, who wrote lengthy articles with photographs of the events.

Upon learning of the lack of rooms, Harry turned to his cousin, and they conferred in German for a couple of minutes. Then, turning to Cristina and the two men, he explained, "I'll share my room with you gentlemen. My cousin will share hers with Cristina."

Cristina's eyebrow went up a fraction; she was surprised that in only a few hours that young man had felt such familiarity as to dispense with formalities, calling her by her Christian name. Harry's cousin noticed Cristina's reaction, but made no comment. The plan was agreed upon

111

and the cousins collected the keys, then guided the three guests through the elegant lobby. Its high ceilings were held by two large columns covered in marble, at the end of which was the staircase and the elevators. The cousins had adjoining rooms on the top floor; each of their luxurious rooms had private bathrooms, with no need to share such facilities, something common in hotels.

"Oh, I'm dying for something to eat." Terri threw her coat on a chair and stretched herself on one of the beds, then lit a cigarette. "What say you if we went out for a bite?" she asked, Cristina while making smoke rings and watching them disappear, then added, "Confeitaria Colombo is just a couple of minutes from here, at the corner of Andradas and General streets"

"Excellent idea."

Cristina removed her heavy clothes and dressed a soft pink cotton frock. She exchanged the heavier stockings she wore for the trip for some fine gauge silk ones, and stepped into a pair of low-heeled soft calfskin pumps, in the same shade as the dress. She opened the French door to let air in and walked onto the balcony. Looking down she saw a multitude of cars, honking, stopping here and there to avoid the throngs of people crossing to-and-fro. The emerald top of the trees of the nearby Alfândega Square reached up to their floor. She turned her head back, to the room, to be heard by Terri, "Why don't you change into something lighter? It's quite hot outside."

"Righto!" was the girl's answer.

Getting up, Terri removed her pants and shirt, and threw them on the bed. She rummaged through her bag and pulled out a pair of light cotton, wide leg pants which she then put on, following with a skimpy sleeveless sweater. She put on a pair of open-toe Spanish espadrilles she had embroidered herself. Perching a little beret on her head, she went to the balcony to join Cristina.

"I'm ready! Should we go?"

If Terri thought she would shock her room companion, she missed the mark. Stifling a sigh, Cristina turned to the door, thinking that the young woman was just craving attention.

CHAPTER TWENTY-SEVEN

Mrs. Nísia Floresta Brasileira Augusta has the honor of participating to the public that on the 15th of February next she will open, at Direita Street, n° 163, an educational school for girls, in which, in addition to reading, writing, counting, sewing, embroidery, and everything else that concerns a girl's domestic education, the grammar of the national language will be taught using an easy method.
—Jornal do Comércio, Rio de Janeiro, 1838.

As Cristina expected, the sight of a young lady wearing trousers, smoking, and, to make matters worse, exposing painted toenails in a scanty pair of sandals[33], caused a big sensation since their exit from the hotel, until their arrival at Colombo. There Terri insisted on getting a table in the first floor. That was area where the gentlemen sat, the mezzanine being reserved for ladies and families. Unlike the one in Rio de Janeiro—that had no business ties with this one, and where Cristina and Robert first met—the Colombo in Porto Alegre was quite conservative, reflecting the population of that city.

"You will be much more comfortable in the mezzanine, ladies," the anxious waiter pleaded.

"Why? Are the chairs there more comfortable?" Terri asked and looked up, scrutinizing the mezzanine. "They look the same to me," she concluded and stared at the waiter.

---

[33] In the early 1930s ladies rarely wore open-toe sandals; they rarely wore trousers, or painted their toe nails.

So, the poor, harassed man had to allow the two ladies to remain in the men's sanctum sanctorum. Several of them openly stared at the young woman. When she stared back at them, they dropped their eyes and went back to conversing amongst themselves. From the mezzanine the shocked ladies looked down at Terri; she became the center of their attention, and object of whispered conversations. Cristina pondered if they might not be jealous, not having the courage to break with convention, all so obediently adhering to some predestined role in life.

She and Terri placed their orders and the waiter left.

"I like it here," Terri said, while admiring the beautiful wall paintings and large, sparkling mirrors that decorated the walls. "It's not like Confeitaria Colombo in Rio, but it's nice enough. And the grub is very good." She lit another cigarette.

Cristina watched the girl. At first glance she looked no more than a teenager. At closer inspection she appeared more mature. She ignored that Terri was her own age—thirty.

"Forgive me, but I must ask you something. Why do you like to call attention to yourself?" She was amused at the girl's surprise look. "You've been getting attention since we left the airfield, you can't possibly have missed that," she insisted. "Why?"

"I guess I just don't like conventions," Terri answered after a long silence, nonplussed.

"But you don't need to dress differently to defy conventions. I believe a woman can challenge conventions wearing a pretty frock."

The arrival of the waiter stopped the flow of conversation. Cristina thanked him, and started pouring the tea in two dainty porcelain cups, handing one to Terri. She took a long sip of hers and continued, "In a way, I defied the status quo," a statement that produced a surprised look from the other girl, who started to listen more closely. "Well, I'm not a pioneer and didn't do anything too out of the ordinary, but years ago, when my father died, we were left with all kinds of bills to pay—and no money. So, I went out and carved out a living playing the piano. It may not sound like a big deal to a woman who has a college degree. But in Brazil, where men think a woman's best book is a cookbook, it was a big deal. We're mothers and wives, and supposed to stay at home embroidering dainty handkerchiefs, taking care of children, and cooking.

To my mother the only solution to our situation was my marrying. I didn't."

"So, you are a feminist," Terri interposed.

If she thought Cristina had never heard that word, she was mistaken.

"I think I am too busy to take the time to define myself as feminist. Or anything else for that matter. Having a farm is hard work, young lady."

"I think you are a very conventional country," Terri said, pensively.

"Yet some of us don't conform. Rita Lobato, for example; she was the first Brazilian female doctor. She graduated in 1887. And Edwiges Becker was our first female engineer, who graduated in 1917. And in the early 1800s Nísia Floresta opened a school for girls in Rio de Janeiro—Colégio Augusto. Listen," she continued, "I didn't mean to turn this into a lecture. What I'm trying to say, is that shocking people with your appearance doesn't change their minds; it just makes them suspicious of you and even more entrenched behind their ideas. You are a veterinarian; that is an accomplishment that can change the status quo. Now, go out in the world and don't just try to shock people: make a difference!"

"Boy, you're some straight talker!"

"Well, when I'm with someone whose purpose in life seems to be to shock others, and who didn't bother to ask me if I minded being part of her act, I feel entitled at least to speak my mind" and she took a bite from one of the dainty savories on her plate.

"Touché!" Terri poured some sugar into her cup, swirled it, and took a long sip. "What about your husband? What does he think of your ideas?"

"Robert has an open mind. It's just one of his many qualities that I love. He doesn't expect me to be subservient. I'm his equal—and I make sure he knows that," at which they both laughed.

"You and your husband aren't at all as I expected. Not at all," Terri told Cristina with a thoughtful expression.

"What d'you mean? Have we met before?"

"No."

"So how could you expect us to be one way or another?" Cristina enquired, mystified.

She noticed the girl's troubled expression, but it was gone so quickly she could not be sure it was not her imagination.

"I mean, we never met, but I've seen you and your husband in Bagé a few times. I did not think you were, you know, just regular people. You know, like me and Harry." She laughed, "Well, especially not like me. I mean," she searched for words, trying to convey her feelings, "you're a regular person."

"I sure hope I am," was Cristina's comment.

"You're not a snob, like some rich people I've met. You're quite accessible and likable."

"Now, that's a nice compliment, thank you. And we should drink to that."

Cristina raised her cup to Terri, who touched it with hers.

"To making new friends," Terri smiled and gulped the tea.

"And keeping them!" Then, changing the subject, "You were incredible in the plane," Cristina told Terri. "Not for you taking control and we'd be all dead."

The girl just shrugged her shoulders. "It was nothing. I know how to fly, so, it was just a matter of taking over. With Raswan's help it was easily done."

"No matter! One needs a lot of self-control to remain calm in a situation like that. And I'll drink to that again!"

Both laughed and toasted with their teacups again. At this point Harry joined them. He did not seem to be surprised to find Terri so attired, and sitting in the gentlemen area of Colombo.

"What were you toasting? And with tea!" he exclaimed with a disgusted expression, but continued, not waiting for an answer, "They told me at the hotel the hydroplanes leave early in the morning. Quite a long trip, almost whole day," he said for Cristina's benefit, then tried to steal one of the minuscule sandwiches from his cousin's plate, only to get his hand slapped hard. "Ouch!" he exclaimed and turned a scowling face to her. Then addressing Cristina, "We could have a very early breakfast before we drive to the hydroplanes. Place's not far from the hotel."

"No breakfast for me, thank you very much," said Cristina, thinking of the turbulence they had experienced in their trip from Bagé.

The conversation became generalized. Harry pulled a chair from a neighboring table, and after a long wait was able to get the waiter's attention and placed an order for more tea, cakes and sandwiches.

CHAPTER TWENTY-EIGHT

In midwinter, when real flowers are too expensive, porcelain ones take their place—unless there is a lunch or dinner party.
—Etiquette, Emily Post. 1922.

The day of the party dawned sunny and bright. Not a cloud marred the azure of the limpid sky. Early in the morning Desiree drove a party in the truck to the farm's little old chapel. With her went Donny and Annie, Maria and Alcina, the latter's mother having stayed with her younger son, Claes, who was in bed with—he claimed—a cold. On the open deck of the truck sat some of the farm hands. Father Valentim—Fidêncio Valentim's brother— officiated every other Sunday, and as the mass was in Latin, Desiree could follow with no trouble.

Upon returning to the house, each went about their activities: food preparation, cleaning, decorating, and all the many little details that seem insignificant, but are so necessary for a successful party. Before the ball there would be a dinner, sitting a total of fourteen people, with the guests coming from the surrounding farms. The kitchen was bubbling with activity; it was populated by Maria, Alcina, and a couple of old ladies, Candinha and Benta, famous for their culinary skills. One of their most requested delicacies was Galinha ao Molho Pardo. That Portuguese specialty was prepared by blending fresh chicken blood with vinegar. The mixture was then added to the chicken when that was almost ready, and cooked until thickened. To the more finicky of palate, the outspoken Candinha would advise "Don't dismiss it till you tried!"

A chicken, a turkey and a suckling pig had been dealt with—before Donny and Annie were aware and could plea on behalf of the victims. The pig was being slow-roasted on an open fire outside, under the expert supervision of João Silvano. Roasting the chicken and the turkey was a task exclusive for the kitchen. There, the ladies were using the gas stove. That modern contraption, while easier to deal than the wooden stove, unfortunately did not prevent that place from becoming excessively hot. So, two fans were placed on opposite sides of the room, running constantly. The door, left ajar, helped dispel the heat and bring in some outside air. Near the door the twins stood in the playpen. Alex, with a concentrated expression, played with some building blocks, his Humpty Dumpty forgotten. Meanwhile Bacon patiently suffered Loulou tying ribbons on him; he had been imprisoned with the twins to keep them quiet, so the ladies could work in peace.

Had Cristina been at home that day, she would have been barred entrance into the cooks' shrine, since she was never lured by culinary arts. Instead, she would have been charged with setting the table and decorating the rooms. When she decided to travel to Rio de Janeiro, she deputized the duty to Desiree. That lady, also absolutely helpless in a kitchen, was an expert when it came to room decoration. Foreseeing that Maria would stay in the kitchen throughout the dinner—she and Bunky always found an excuse to avoid attendance—and with her own absence from the table, Cristina also had to decide on the fourteenth diner; she picked Alcina. She did not see the girl before she left for the airfield, and asked Maria to inform her. But overwhelmed with the dinner preparations, Maria forgot her task. When at last she remembered, she removed the young woman's apron, told her to get dressed, that she would be among the diners, and started to motion Alcina out of the kitchen.

"Me? But I could never—"

"Oh, stop whining, girl," Maria cut her. "Can't you see we're busy? I don't have time to waste. Go on girl!" and she pushed the astonished Alcina out of the kitchen, shutting the door behind her.

Robert's cousin had been to the garden and, with the help of her husband, returned to the house with armfuls of flowers and greens. Vases had been washed and dried, and were lined up like a small army. She filled them with daisies, roses, gardenias and ferns, and placed them around the house. For the dining table she filled an oblong silver centerpiece with gardenias and ferns, coupled with two massive three-candle silver candelabra. Max and Robert were sent back outside with the task of cutting long, thin branches from the two ipê[34] trees. Desiree then placed these yellow and purple flowers into large milk cans. Filled up with water and the flowering branches, they were placed outside, near the chairs that stood in the shade of trees, around the dancing floor the hands had put together the day before, and in the tea tent.

An awning was stretched to protect the musicians from the sun. Opposite to it, in a large tent, two big tables brought together were covered with a snow-white tablecloth, with chairs awaiting the diners. A few heavy stones were placed on the table's ends, serving as weights to keep the cloth in place. Tableware, glasses and dishes were neatly arranged on a tall sideboard, everything covered with large napkins to protect them from flies, waiting to be receive food and drinks. A couple of milk jugs laden with flowers sat on each side of the tent opening.

Close to the start of the party, Desiree was entrusted with preparing her favorite dish: Oscar Tschirky's Waldorf Salad—which, together with scrambled eggs with smoked salmon, was the only food she knew how to prepare. She kept it as simple as the recipe in the cook book Oscar published in 1896: peeled apples cut into half inch pieces, and celery cut the same way, everything carefully mixed with the Hellman's mayonnaise she had brought all the way from the States.

To Max had fallen the choosing of the wine, which he did after studying the menu. That consisted of a satiny piece of paper, containing the dinner fare, written in purple ink in his wife's beautiful round hand script. She spent two hours the prior evening laboriously cutting the paper to size, and writing everything down, leaving space at the end for the beverages.

"I see that we'll have Oscar's salad. I remember seeing a 1921 Riesling in the cave and I think will go very nice with the salad," Max said after

---

[34] Respectively, *Tabebuia alba* and *Tabebuia avellanedae*.

thinking for a few seconds. "Roasted chicken, turkey and suckling pig," he continued to read the sheet of paper where his wife had listed that evening's fare. "No oysters? 'Course they don't have access to oysters here," he corrected himself, then continued, "And… Borsch?"

"It's Maria's special recipe. Nothing to do with the original thing; it's her version of Borsch. She passes the cooked beets through a mill, and adds cream. And it's served cold."

"What a strange version: passed through a mill and cold, eh, what?" he wondered.

"I think it's going to be delicious. And with this heat would you like the poor souls to have hot soup?"

"'Course you're right, old girl. Well," he continued, addressing the listed dishes, "the vegetables will be served with the meat. So Demi-Sec Champagne throughout the meal. I'm guessing this is supposed to be dessert?" he asked, pointing at the word Sobremesa.

"Yes, but don't ask me how to pronounce it! Maria is making Baked Alaska. With ice cream she made herself. Must be scrumptious," she said, excited. Baked Alaska was one of Desiree's favorite desserts.

"You know I don't care for dessert, but Baked Alaska with homemade ice cream! Sounds too good not to try. Let's pair it with that excellent 1850 Port. Oh, and we must have ice water," he told his wife, as an afterthought. Then he continued enthusiastically, talking about wine, "Robert took me to their cave the day after we arrived. Well-stocked. I saw some 1926 Bordeaux and Burgundy and a few old Bollinger champagne. Can't wait to try 'em," and he rubbed his hands anticipating some future degustation.

"Well, I'll leave you with your bacchic dreams, and I'll go back to my room to finish my job. I still have to write the place cards."

"Don't forget the list," he waved the sheet of paper in which he had noted the beverages.

"I think I can remember: Demi-Sec Champagne, Riesling, Tawny Port and ice water," she counted on her fingers. "And I'm sure there'll be coffee—served in those thimble-sized cups Brazilians love! Strange people…"

And with that comment she left the room.

"Brandy and cigars after dinner," Max told himself, considering the bottles of cognac he had seen in the cave, which he would sequester with views to the after dinner, when the men would remain in the dining room, while the ladies would retreat to another room to sip some Chartreuse or Cointreau, and gossip.

Coming out of the kitchen still stunned by the invitation to join the diners, Alcina met Robert. She told him about his wife's request, that had just been imparted to her by Maria. If she expected him to disagree with Cristina, she missed the mark.

"Yes, my wife told me before she left. You'll be fine," he assured her, reading the anxiety in her eyes. "Desiree," he turned to his cousin, who was just coming down the stairs with the bundle of menus and place cards she had finished, and addressed her in English, "Can you help Alcina get dressed? You know Maria never abandons her kitchen and Alcina is to join us at dinner tonight."

"With pleasure—right after I place the cards. I'll meet her in my room. Please, explain that to her, will ya? I'm sure we'll be able to communicate fine—with sign language," she joked.

"And, please, remember not to dress excessively smart. These are simple people, not that bunch of snobs who you frequent back in New York." His cousin made a face in response. "They might be simple, but I like them—well, most of them," Robert said, thinking of Sérgio's mother. "They are the salt of the earth."

In the kitchen Maria found time to help Annie prepare a dessert specially for the children. The recipe was from a leaflet of Baker's Dot Chocolate, and had travelled with Annie from New York for that purpose. The kids would have a separate table laid out for them, and would have their dinner served earlier. Their table would have white, starched tablecloth and napkins, and menus and place cards, just like the adults'.

"Chocolate Coconut Glossies," Maria read.

Annie stood by, looking very competent in an apron, too large for her small frame. She felt very important, coming to the kitchen to help prepare the desert that would be served at the kids' dinner.

"I set all the equipment and ingredients there," Maria indicated the large kitchen table, where a space had been kept and displayed an array of items. "Can you read the recipe for us, Annie?"

"Eight squares—one package—of Baker's Dot Chocolate," she read.

"We'll use Nestlé. There's no Baker's in Brazil, but Nestlé is very good quality," Maria explained, opening the package. With the girl's help she started chopping the chocolate into small pieces, which they dropped in a bain-marie pan that had been simmering over low heat.

"Two thirds cup of sweetened condensed milk," the girl continued, giving Maria time to measure the ingredients. "A pinch of salt, one cup of shredded coconut, and one teaspoon of vanilla."

"Which we'll skip, because—and I hope you agree with me—I think we already have flavors enough, with chocolate and coconut," a statement that received the girl's approval.

"Heat the chocolate over boiling water," Annie read on, "until partly melted. Remove from boiling water and stir rapidly until entirely melted. Add condensed milk, salt, and coconut; blend. Drop from teaspoons on waxed paper. Chill in refrigerator or let stand at room temperature several hours, or until firm. Makes about three dozen."

Under Maria's close supervision, the girl slowly stirred the pan with the chocolate, then proceeded as the recipe directed.

"Very well done, Annie. You're a natural! You can join us in the kitchen anytime you want, and learn more about cooking."

"I'd like that very much," Annie answered, excited.

"Now, there's no space in the refrigerator, so I'll put your Glossies in the larder, since the kitchen is too hot."

"Can I serve them when it's time for dessert?"

"Sure. When you kids approach the end of the meal, come to the kitchen. I'll have 'em on a tray, ready for you."

Annie was hot, her little brow sprinkled with tiny beads of sweat, and there were a couple of smears of chocolate on her cheek, but she felt very proud of herself: her first incursion in a kitchen had been a success. She thanked Maria then rushed to her bedroom to wash and get dressed for the party.

CHAPTER TWENTY-NINE

If you neither understand nor care for dogs or children, and both insist on climbing all over you, you must seemingly like it; just as you must be amiable and polite to your fellow guests, even though they be of all the people on earth the most detestable to you.
—Etiquette, Emily Post, 1922.

The children, dressed in their finery and on their best behavior, were having a private dinner. Bunky, his face displaying a lugubrious expression—that did not scare anyone—stood by, ever vigilant, ready to nip any trouble in the bud. Beside him Bacon sat patiently, waiting for bits of food that he seemed to expect would drop to the floor.

Meanwhile, almost all the guests had arrived and congregated in the large living room, where small cordial glasses of apéritif were being distributed by Rafael Souza: Campari, Sherry and sweet Vermouth.

Robert was crossing the room to join the police chief he had noticed standing near the French window in a group, when Mrs. Valentim cut his progress right as he was about to get to his friend. Unable to avoid her, he was forced to stop. In her own mind a queen among hostess, the matriarch of the Valentim clan expressed concern that, due to Cristina's unexpected trip, the table would be composed by an odd number of guests. She had a way of talking down her nose, in a shrill tone, that never failed to irritate Robert.

"Don't worry, we'll be an even number. My wife thinks of everything," Robert informed her in his laborious, heavy accented Portuguese.

As he tried to move pass her, thinking he had put her mind at rest, she held him. "Someone else was invited? Who?"

"Alcina will make the even number," he answered, holding back a sigh of frustration.

"Isn't that the young lady who works in the kitchen?" she asked, alarmed.

"Yes. Lovely lady, ain't she?" Realizing her discomfiture, he decided to add to. "And very talented. She studied at the Cordon Bleu—you know, that famous culinary school in Paris. André Terrail tried to get her to La Tour d'Argent, but she couldn't stay in France." He saw the lady's eyes widen at the mention of one of the most exclusive restaurants in Europe. "When her father died in an accident—you might recall—they were left almost destitute due to some bad investments he made," he continued, "and so she had to return to Brazil."

At that time Alcino was also affected by the tragedy and had to interrupt the Veterinary course at the Federal University in Porto Alegre. Both he and Alcina came back to Bagé and got jobs at Fazenda Minuano.

"You're right across from Alcina at table, Mrs. Valentim, so you'll be able to ask her all about her life in Paris. Now, if you excuse me, I have to see a man about a dog," he winked at her and walked away, happy at having annoyed her. And it was with a mischievous smile that he joined the group congregated around the police chief.

"What were you up to?" his friend asked him, receiving a broader smile for response.

Hearing the word 'dog," Mrs. Valentim started, thinking Robert was referring to her arch-enemy, her nemesis, and Donny's beloved pooch, Bacon. With that danger in mind, she slowly moved forward, looking around anxiously, expecting to see the odious dog at each step. And thus, she almost collided with her husband.

"What's it, Quininha?" Fidêncio Valentim, her long-suffering spouse asked her.

"That infernal dog," she hissed, getting hold of his arm with an iron grip, making him wince. "I think he's in this room!

"Nonsense."

"I should have brought some poison to give him," she said, her voice rising in her fear.

"Shhh, don't talk so loud!" he admonished her, as heads turned their way inquiringly.

"And guess what I just learned? That their kitchen maid is going to sit at the table with us, to make up an even number. What the world is coming to, I don't know…"

Kitchen maid, her husband wondered, not daring to voice a question. Having been married to the woman for over twenty-five years, he knew he would be unable to get a coherent explanation while she was in her present mood. He resigned himself to merely wait until she calmed down, or, as it was so often the case, for the next embarrassing episode, when he would have to extricate her, then hear about how mistaken he was for interfering with things that did not concern him.

And nearby, one of the heads that turned, was that of Mrs. Maricota Paranhos. That lady disliked Quininha Valentim and pitied her husband and son. To her both would go straight to Heaven after death, just for having coexisted with that woman.

"Her majesty fears the appearance of that dear little dog—what's his name again? Presunto?"[35] asked Maricota Paranhos.

She stood beside the police chief, Aparício França, her arm threaded through his, her bejeweled hand holding a tiny cordial glass with her second Vermouth. Maria Augusta de Sá Paranhos, known to all as Maricota, was petite, of a delicate frame, which made this fifty-something year-old lady look like a girl at first glance. Her hair dyed platinum-blonde was cut short with spiral curls plastered to the forehead and cheeks.

The police chief, was slim and tall, in his early forties. He was a quiet man, with a luscious moustache that was his only display of vanity. Today, having been coaxed with a thin coat of perfumed pomade, it remained obediently in place.

"Her majesty?"

At Aparício França enquiry, Mrs. Paranhos explained, sotto voce, wrinkling her nose, "You know: Joaquina Perpétua da Silva Gama Valentim. Her majesty, if you please!" She made a mock courtesy, bobbing her head, and that made her look like a puppet out of Punch and Judy.

---

[35] Presunto: Portuguese for Ham.

Her husband grunted, but the police chief found her joke quite amusing.

"Right animal, but wrong type of meat," he told her. Her puzzled look encouraged him to provide an explanation, "The disliked canine in question is called Bacon. It was Donny, Laughton's son who gave him the appellation."

"Oh, I so love that dear little boy, God bless'm! How creative. And bless the li'l dog too for hating that witch." She confided to the police chief, then looked around, her sparkling black eyes searching every corner of the room.

"Can I help you find something, dear lady?" Aparício asked her, solicitous.

"I was only wondering where she parked her broom. Must have left it outside."

"Don't bite your tongue, my dear. It might prove fatal," was her husband's advice, to which she laughed wholeheartedly.

"Mr. Lawton, Mr. Lawton!" that lady called Robert, slaughtering his last name as was her wont. "Yoo-hoo," she waved her free hand at Robert.

"Why not call me just Robert? Aren't we friends?" Robert told her when he joined them and stood beside the lady.

"Oh, but I like to show my knowledge of English," she winked at him. "Make people think I can speak the language, eh?" Mrs. Paranhos giggled and took possession of Robert's arm. "I know just a tiny little bit of English. En passant, as the French say, you know."

Robert concealed a smile and her husband sighed, refraining from correcting his wife's misuse of the French expression.

"Madame," said Robert and made a deep courtesy, to which Mrs. Paranhos responded in kind.

Suddenly she waved the little cordial glass in the direction of a young man who had just entered the room and stood looking around with a bored expression.

"Sérgio, my pet," she called out loud and stood at the tip of her toes, "come here!"

Robert and Aparício eyed each other; the police chief knew how little his friend wanted to meet young Sérgio. He empathized, since he had never taken to the young man. He liked his parents and his married sister,

Onélia da Silva, who lived in the capital and had brought her children to spend summer on the farm. But he avoided the snob Sérgio as much as possible.

As the starched young man stood in front of his mother, she began the introduction she had longed to make. "Mr. Lawton," and as he raised a warning eyebrow at her, "oh, well, Robert," she simpered, then continued, "I'd like to introduce my son, Sérgio Paranhos." Turning to her son, "This is Mr. Robert Lawton."

"Very pleased to meet you, at last." the young man said in a haughty matter. "My mother talks heaps about you. And thank you for the invitation."

"But we met before. Don't you remember?" Sérgio looked confused and Robert explained, "A few days ago you came to the farm and we spoke." The young man still did not seem to remember, so he elaborated, "I was clearing the front yard from weeds. You came to deliver the oranges your mother sent to my wife."

Realizing his blunder, Sérgio grew pale.

"You see," Robert turned to the people gathered around him, "I was sweaty, dirty, wearing a pair of disreputable trousers and an old hat. Sérgio here," and he patted the other's shoulder, "thought I was a farmhand. He even told me to hurry in with the oranges," Robert ended, shooting Mrs. Paranhos a mischievous side glance.

The whole group laughed at the funny misunderstanding, but Sérgio's mother laughed the harder. So hard that the cordial glass she held leaned in a perilous angle and was retrieved in time by her attentive husband. The only one who did not enjoy the joke was Sérgio. He turned from pale to crimson, then pale again, and after a few minutes stammered his excuses and walked away.

Later on, Aparício França approached Robert with a warning. "You might like to steer clear of young Paranhos, Robert." His friend appeared surprised at the advice, so he added, "He's a terribly conceited idiot, with a huge ego and even bigger self-esteem. I saw the look he gave you after you were introduced."

"If eyes could kill and all that?"

"Well, you catch my drift. Just watch yourself, my friend. He has a group of other spoiled, rich brats, who are actually old enough to know better, but don't."

"I'm shaking in my boots," Robert laughed and took the warning lightly, but Aparício remained serious.

CHAPTER THIRTY

It may be due to the war period, which accustomed everyone to going with very little meat and to marked reduction in all food, or it may be, of course, merely vanity that is causing even grandparents to aspire to svelte figures, but whatever the cause, people are putting much less food on their tables than formerly.
—Etiquette, Emily Post. 1922.

Suddenly there was a lull in the conversation: Desiree and Alcina stood at the door threshold, looking like starlets from Motion Picture magazine. Both were blond, but there ended the resemblance. Desiree, tall and statuesque, and of a classic profile that would have inspired Botticelli. Alcina, petite and delicate, the exquisite result of mixing the blood of a southern Brazilian Native and a Norseman. Desiree dressed a simple pink lace and chiffon gown, with ruffles for sleeves, and a wide black grosgrain ribbon tied around her waist, ending on a large bow on her back. Her flaxen hair was parted on one side, with simple waves; it was a little longer on the back, which turned upward in a double roll. For the young woman, Desiree had found the perfect dress in Cristina's closet: an empire waist, with square neck opening and short puff sleeves in deep blue silk—which deepened the azure of Alcina's eyes. Her hair was collected on the nape of her neck in small ringlets, and a white silk cabbage rose was pinned on it.

"Oh, such beauties!" exclaimed Maricota Paranhos, admiringly.

"The kitchen maid," raged Quininha Valentim and would have gnashed her teeth at the sight had they not been artificial.

Max was the first to recover. He quickly made his way through the crowd, and, offering an arm to each lady, brought the two beauties into the room. Jô Valentim, under the iron grip of his mother, who had quickly reached him, was unable to join Alcina. When he was finally able to break free, the lady of his dreams was engrossed in conversation with Rafael Souza, whose eyes left no doubt of his admiration. Naturally shy, Jô decided to wait until he could have a moment alone with Alcina, ideally without his mama's knowledge.

Sometime before dinner was served, the children came into the room. Donny and Annie eloquently protested the unfairness of not being allowed to at least watch the dance that would be held later. Mr. Valentim, who was fond of children, suggested to Robert that they should also be allowed to enjoy themselves. Robert relented and the children ran outside to see the set that had been readied for the event. The accordionist and guitar player were already in place and indulged the children with some pieces of Gaúcho music they would play later on. Dionisio Bello, who excited at the prospect of a ball, had been idly walking up and down in his best finery, stepped on to the wooden platform and offered to teach Annie how to dance—which she quickly accepted.

Bunky walked into the room with a very butler-like demeanor—which, in Robert's appreciation, was the reason people were confused about his station in life, since it was not uncommon to see Robert and his factotum en a tête-à-tête at the Sorocabana, enjoying a coffee. Standing straight as a rod, he said, in his booming voice, in order to be heard above the din of conversation and the gramophone: "Dinner is served, lady Walston-Armstrong."

Robert cringed. Desiree jumped, then giggled. The guests were startled. After his words were translated and everyone regained their composure, they started to slowly move towards the dining room. Desiree—the aforementioned Lady Walston-Armstrong—holding Robert's arm, saw that Quininha Valentim had rushed ahead of everyone and was already in the dining room. So, throwing Robert's arm and etiquette to the wind, she got to the room in time to stop Jô's mother from interfering with the table sitting arrangements. Mrs. Valentim had quickly run through the place cards, and was annoyed to see Alcina's at her son's left. She was about to take the girl's card to replace it with another guest's when she felt her elbow grasped by Desiree.

"Here, let's find your place, shall we?" Lady Walston-Armstrong dimpled smile did not belie the steely glint in her eyes.

The startled Mrs. Valentim dared not resist and was firmly carried to the other side of the table and securely seated on her chair, while Desiree pointed at her name on the card. She had not understood Desiree's words, for she spoke no English, but her actions had been quite clear.

There was a bit of shuffling of people, while all the guests entered the room. Having more gentlemen than ladies, Desiree did what she could to distribute the diners. She pointed out the places, mispronouncing their names, causing hilarity. When the correct placements were finally found, the gentlemen chivalrously pulled the ladies' chairs.

To Desiree right sat Mr. Valentim—the more senior of the gentlemen—then followed Alcina, Jô, Sérgio—seething at not being allowed to sit beside Alcina—Max, and Divina—Aparício's sister, Diva Maria França. To Robert's right sat Maricota Paranhos—the older among the ladies—Rafael, Onélia, the police chief, Mrs. Valentim—livid at seeing her son in such mongrel company—and Colonel Paranhos. Aparício had caught up with Onélia when they were still in the living room. Together they reached the dining room and were delighted to find themselves sitting side by side.

"You look beautiful tonight, if I'm allowed to say so."

"Yes, please, do," she smiled at him, her light brown doe eyes shining softly, a delicate blush suffusing her cheeks. "Men should make a habit of repeating these little compliments to women—even if they don't feel it, or if the object of their comment is not really worth," she teased him. "There's nothing a girl likes more, you know. Well, except, of course, flowers," and her hand stole to the beautiful gardenia she wore on her bosom, then her eyes met his adoring gaze. She had received the flower that morning, with a tiny card that read 'Wear it tonight,' but had no signature. In the language of flowers, Gardenias sent to a lady meant secret love; but Aparício's love was no secret to her.

Onélia could not be called beautiful. Her lips were a bit too full and the face was angular-shaped. The softness in her eyes, their serene expression, were carried to the face, smoothing its angles. And her shiny wavy brown hair made a beautiful frame, coupled with a clear complexion. To her gallant admirer there was no woman in the world who could compare to her. You see, he loved her since they were children. And love is not blind, as the saying goes, but sees the beauty no one else does.

Aparício's feelings were forced to become latent, as one day a dashing young man captured Onélia's heart; they married and had two children—a girl aged nine, Antonia, and Virgílio, a seven-year-old little rascal, who became Donny's pal from the moment they met. The boy was the police chief's godson; but there was an even deeper trait to unite godson and godfather: Virgílio was the name the police chief had taken at his Confirmation.

Meanwhile, across from them, Jô tried to force his hand to stop shaking. He was barely able to eat at the proximity of his beloved. Mr. Valentim, all smiles, was engaged in deep conversation with Alcina, ignoring his wife's outraged looks across the table. That young lady noticing Jô's silence, tried to engage him, but only caused him to choke on a mouthful of food he had just swallowed. Sérgio Paranhos, happy to find a way to release some of his anger, viciously slammed his neighbor's back under the guise of help, causing Jô to tumble a glass and spill water all over his plate. The plate was quickly removed and a new one brought in.

"I'm so sorry," Jô kept trying to say, while still coughing.

"Have you heard what that despicable li'l man, Arnold Hitler has done?" Maricota Paranhos asked to no one in particular.

"Adolf," growled her son from the opposite side of the table.

"Who's this Adolf?" that lady asked, wondering if he might be Arnold Hitler's relative.

"It's Adolf, not Arnold, mother. Adolf Hitler," he stressed. 'Please, don't embarrass us' was the message conveyed to her in the angry look her son gave her.

"As a matter of fact," Robert interposed, coming to the lady's rescue, "I always get his name confused. Arnold, Alfred, Adolf, at the end it's the same despicable little man, as you say, Mrs. Paranhos."

And at that gallant recovery, she gave her host a grateful look. Robert raised his glass to her and they both drank to each other's health.

CHAPTER THIRTY-ONE

If you leave a kiss within the glass, I'll not ask for wine.
—Toasts and After-Dinner Speeches, in The Complete Buffet
Guide, V.B. Lewis. 1903.

D esiree looked at Robert, who, understanding his cousin's meaning, addressed the company in Portuguese, "My cousin asked me to convey to the ladies that they will be more comfortable taking their digestif in the drawing room."

Robert got up and the other men followed his example, helping the ladies with their chairs. Desiree bowed, acknowledging her cousin's help and left, followed by the ladies, leaving the gentlemen to enjoy their cigar and brandy.

In the drawing room Desiree and Alcina served the digestif in tiny crystal cordial glasses. After one taste, Maricota Paranhos rushed and hooked her arm through Alcina's. She directed the young lady to a couple of comfortable armchairs that stood near one of the windows.

"My dear, this cinnamon cordial is absolutely delicious! Where do you buy it?"

At that question all eyes turned to the young woman.

"I actually make it," she answered, shyly, embarrassed at being the center of attention.

Hearing that, Quininha Valentim ostentatiously sat her untouched glass on the little table beside her chair, crossing her arms, an unmistakable expression of distaste on her face.

"I should have suspected," said Sérgio's mother. "And may I enquire at the recipe—or is this some secret brew you learned in France?" Unlike

Mrs. Valentim, and due to her son's marked interest in the girl, Maricota Paranhos was aware of Alcina's having lived in Paris while attending the cooking school.

"It's very simple, really. It's not a French recipe, and no secret by any means," Alcina told her. "It's from a precious little book I found in the Marché aux Puces," she said, referring to the Parisian flea market located in Saint-Ouen.

"So, can you share the recipe with me?"

"Sure! Let's see," Alcina thought for a few moments, then continued, "You need four ounces of cinnamon—and I use Ceylon cinnamon. Pound it, just enough to break it into pieces, then put that in one quart of brandy, and let it macerate for ten days. After that time, strain the brandy, then add one drop of essence of orange peel and a few cardamoms. The book suggests adding some caramel to intensify the color, but I just leave it as you see now," and she motioned to the little glass she held, raising it to the window, letting the light reveal the liquid's beautiful amber color.

"Oh, but you need to write this down for me, my dear. I know I'll forget the instructions by the time I get home."

"I'd also like a copy," said Onélia and Divina França.

"I'll do that with pleasure," and that said Alcina pulled the drawer from the little table that stood between their chairs and took a block of paper and a pencil.

"And, since you're writing it down… That pickled okra—you know, the one with the appetizers. It was simply marvelous. Could I also have that recipe?" Maricota asked, blinking her eyelashes at Alcina.

"Sure. I have it by heart." Alcina answered, giggling, and quickly wrote down both recipes, handing the paper to Maricota. She then made a couple of copies, and handed those to Onélia and Divina, ignoring Quininha Valentim's disapproving looks.

Meanwhile, Desiree, who did not speak Portuguese, but had picked a few words she knew, understood the conversation centered on recipes. Not her forte, she just observed the ladies and, especially, the haughty Mrs. Valentim, whose forbidding expression assumed a comic tinge to her.

"You have such beautiful handwriting," said Maricota Paranhos gazing at the paper on her hand—a comment that prompted similar reactions from the two ladies holding their pieces of paper. "My handwriting, my son says, is like a bunch of drunken spiders running next to each other, trying to figure out where everyone is going."

They laughed at her sally, while Onélia translated the meaning to Desiree, then they continued chatting about different subjects until the gentlemen joined them.

Outside, the party had not yet started. But the chimarrão was making its way around, while meat, skewered in long spits, was slowly roasting under the expert eye of João Silvano. He constantly mopped his sweaty brow with an enormous red scarf; like all self-respecting Gaúchos, he always carried the versatile scarf as protection against cold and dust, to wipe the sweat from his face, or, on festive days, to decorate his neck. Near him, under a tree, a long table displayed bottles of wine and spirits of different sizes and shapes.

The farm workers were all there, wearing their best pilcha, a little awkward in their formal attire. The men had starched shirts with scarves tied loosely around the collars and hair slick with pomade under hats that had been brushed until they almost looked new. They all wore dark, short jackets or vests. Some bombachas were decorated with smocking along the side seam or just below the waistband, and others still were plain, but all looked like they had been carefully laundered and ironed. Their boots shone like mirrors and their moustaches were perfumed and combed; while the younger men displayed smoothly shaved faces. Their ladies—wives, sweethearts, mothers, sisters—wore their best Sunday dresses that had been kept in cedar trunks, wrapped in tissue paper; from some emanated the delicate scent of cloves and rosemary sachets; others of lavender. The dresses were decorated with precious laces; delicate cameos adorned collars. Some ladies had braided little flowers or silk ribbons through their hair; others wore a rose tucked above the left ear—the side of the heart—or one or two richly decorated combs firmly holding long tresses in place. Colorful shawls wrapped around their shoulders, mary-jane shoes discreetly picking from under long skirts, they smiled and accepted, delighted, tiny pieces of meat stolen at great risk from the ferocious João Silvano; or a cup of tea smuggled out of the tent that held the large samovar; others shared a sip of chimarrão with their inamoratos.

João Silvano gave the sign that the food was ready and people poured forward like a disjointed, noisy wave, in a rush to see who could get to the plates first. The musicians, who had been portentously adjusting and testing their instruments and sat nearby, advanced ahead of everyone and it took the old man and other cooler heads to stop an ensuing fight among the entertainers and the farmworkers. Tempers were suited. They lined up sedately, plates in hand, and were given juicy slabs of meat Silvano and his helpers distributed. They sat around the large tables, and all feasted on the various dishes they were offered. Then, the parties satisfied, the men just dallied lazily chatting with their neighbors. But the ladies were intent on getting the Laughtons' anticipated dessert and the gentlemen were forced to invade the tea tent to discharge their commissions.

As the group were finishing dessert, Robert stepped outside with his guests, and found places to sit. The musicians, taking that as a cue, rushed to their instruments and started playing. The company waited for Robert and Desiree—who was filling in for Cristina—to open the dance floor. For a few minutes their graceful figures, both blond and tall, kept the audience spellbound. They looked like brother and sister, so alike they were. But the spell was broken when Annie dragged Donny to the floor and, taking firm grasp of his hand, tried to force him to dance. The onlookers laughed and applauded, and, furious, Donny broke free and fled in the direction of the house. Pairs started forming. Seeing that the farmhands felt shy of joining his guests, Robert invited Mrs. Christensen, who, nervous, tripped when stepping on to the platform.

"Would you do me the honor?" Alcino asked his sister, beating Joca and Sérgio, who were both making a beeline to Alcina, their eyes shining in the anticipation of holding her on the dance floor. She bowed graciously to her brother and, led by his hand, they joined the other waltzing couples. Soon the sound of shoes scraping the wood floor mixed with laughs and the musical instruments.

Onélia took her children, Antonia and Virgílio, to the house, following Donny's theatrical exit. She hoped they would be asleep at the time she and her family were ready to drive back to their farm. Meanwhile, Annie, always rebellious and defiant of rules, stayed with the adults. Frustrated in her attempt to join the grown-ups, she sat dejectedly, watching the dancers. It seemed that everyone was dancing, save what the uncharitable child called the methuselahs. And, to her chagrin, she eyed one of these antediluvian specimens approach her.

"May I join you?"

Turning to look, she identified Mr. Valentim, and in view of his earlier pleading their case—to let the children stay up longer to watch some of the festivities—she decided to be nice.

"Please, do so."

After a short spell watching the evolutions on the dance floor, he directed his attention to the girl sitting silently beside him. "Young lady, you seem bored. Can I do something to alleviate your predicament?"

She did not say anything for a few seconds, scrutinizing him with a serious expression. "Actually, I wonder… Do you know anything about Templars?" And by the puzzled look on his face the girl realized he had never even heard of those brave warriors of Christ.

So much, she thought, for being nice to that ancient baggage!

CHAPTER THIRTY-TWO

A semicircle of mountains, which appear spectral, as weightless as blue aluminum, are crested delicately with a green lining…further down, domes of blue porcelain, red dice, white cubes: Rio de Janeiro!
—From Roberto Arlt's column "Aguafuertes." El Mundo newspaper. Buenos Aires, Argentina. April 1930.

That same Sunday, having taken a hydroplane from Porto Alegre, Cristina, Terri and Harry landed in downtown Rio de Janeiro, at the pier at Ponta do Cajú. At that beach in the XIX Century, Antonio Tavares Guerra, a rich coffee merchant, built a large house. In 1810 then prince regent João—who in 1807, with his royal mother, the Portuguese court and the royal library, fled Portugal from Napoleon's invasion—developed a wound on his leg. It was caused by a tick and the wound became infected. The future king of Portugal was advised by his doctor to bathe in the Cajú beach. For that purpose, he started using Mr. Guerra's house. Since his kingship that house became known as Casa de Banhos de Dom João VI—Dom João VI Bathhouse. More than one hundred years later, Brazilian columnist Charles Julius Dunlop wrote about Cajú that it was 'a beautiful area, with beaches with white sand and crystal-clear water, where one could see the bottom of the Bay of Guanabara, and its inhabitants, shrimp, seahorses, sardines.'

Cristina had not realized how much she missed the ocean until she could see the beach from the hydroplane's window. The Guaíba River in Porto Alegre was nothing to compare to the glorious beaches of Rio de Janeiro. They had left Porto Alegre at noon and, after the stopover at

São Paulo, it was late afternoon when the hydroplane landed, and the sun was getting ready to dive behind the mountains.

After their goodbyes, Cristina got a taxi cab to take her to Copacabana. When the cab got to Atlântica Avenue, the sea was a glassy teal blue, the white ribbon of sand slowly turning into a deeper, creamy hue, as the light on the sky faded.

On the tallest peak to her right, far away, she could see the statue of Christ the Redeemer, its white stone delineated against the fiery sky, blessing the city of Rio de Janeiro. Soon, at night's descent, it would be illuminated by a battery of floodlights, making it a focal point. At the statue's inauguration, on October 12 of 1931, Guglielmo Marconi switched these lights remotely, by shortwave, from the living room of his house in Rome. Then, Pope Pio XI defined that feat as 'a new marvel of science showing the illuminated Christ like a celestial vision of splendid light among the shadows of the night.' And so it was: the majestic statue of Christ, His open arms forever blessing the Cariocas[36].

It was as if she had never left. Rio de Janeiro. What a marvelous city, Cristina thought. She could not know then, but in one year that term would become a very popular music performed by Aurora Miranda, Carmen Miranda's sister—Cidade Maravilhosa, the marvelous city. Yet, at the same time that this city attracted her, Cristina realized that her life on the farm was also a vivid presence, so dear to her. Where her loved ones were, was where she wanted to be.

The flight had been smooth, without incidents. But coupled with a relatively long trip by car to Copacabana from the airdrome in Ponta do Cajú, near Downtown, she was ready for a bath, a light meal, and then jump into bed. She got out of the taxi, paid the fare and, carrying her light suitcase, walked the short walkway to the front door. Quickly climbing the steps, she opened the door with her latchkey.

The house was in darkness. Not a sound greeted her as she entered the hall. Silence. Not that depressing silence that seems to inhabit a dwelling empty for, say, a month. But the silence of recent occupation, that leaves behind scents and memories lurking in the shadows.

---

[36] Carioca: (from Tupi *kari'oka*, "house of the White man") From, or belonging to or relating to the city of Rio de Janeiro. Natural or inhabitant of the city of Rio de Janeiro. Novo Dicionário Aurélio da Língua Portuguesa. 1995.

Cristina turned the switch—she knew by instinct where everything was in that house—and the place was flooded with light, the memories in her mind becoming reality in a mere instant. She called several times and no one answered. She went halfway up the stairs to the second floor, calling Sonya and her companion, Irina. She listened for a few seconds, but the silence remained. Back to the entrance hall she noticed that the two large ferns that flanked the door had been recently watered.

She raised the telephone's handset to her ear and listened. No dial tone. That meant the telephone company was still on strike. On the telephone table was a folded sheet with a message from Dr. Anatoly Orlov. As if his spidery scribble wasn't already difficult to decipher, Cristina also had to figure what the doctor passed for a message in Portuguese, a language he never really mastered. After a few minutes trying she was able to gather that he had admitted Sonya to his Clinic. She fumed at the aggravating man for omitting any detail of the patient, or the reason for the absence of Irina. But that was typically Orlov's habit. Another was to just hang up the telephone as soon as he had said his piece.

Cristina sighed. There would be no bath and no light meal. And specially no bed. She looked at her watch: the promised telegram to Robert would have to wait. Taking hold of her purse, she locked the house and went back out, now in search of a taxi to take her Downtown, to Senador Dantas Street, where Anatoly Orlov now ministered his art, having purchased the clinic from Dr. Edivaldo Bittencourt[37]. As the taxi cab stopped in front of the building, she saw that the sign now read 'Clínica Anatoly Orlov.' The door was opened by nurse Denise Krause. She had not changed much since the last time Cristina saw her. The same peaches and cream complexion, and serene demeanor. Partially hidden by a white cap, her blond hair was tied in a bun on the nape of her slender neck. Her blue eyes were as bright as ever. The two had met almost five years ago, when Robert was abducted and secretly brought to the clinic. Cristina had wanted to meet the nurse who tried to help them find and return him to his family.

At that time Cristina thought Denise and Rafael, who saw the nurse for information when investigating Robert's disappearance, had become

---

[37] Finding Cristina: A New Life

romantically involved. She hoped he had found someone to love and help him forget his infatuation with her. Unfortunately, it was not so. Although he never declared himself and always treated her like he did everyone else, his love was written in his eyes when he looked at her, and that made her uncomfortable. Cristina liked him, but aware of his feelings, she would always be reticent when in his presence.

As Miss Krause did for Dr. Edivaldo, she was still, under Dr. Orlov, the clinic's head nurse. She took Cristina to the same room that, years ago, Maria and Bunky had sat and waited to speak to her. It had lost it's gloomy, Victorian looks. Now as her private office, it was a reflection of its owner: light, and fresh.

"I just arrived in Rio. I read—I mean, I deciphered Dr. Orlov's message," at which comment Denise smiled, "and rushed here. How is she?" was Cristina's anxious question about Sonya.

"You must be in need of something to eat," Denise said that while pushing a little bell on the wall that connected with the kitchen. Before Cristina could protest, she added, "Mrs. Abramov is sleeping and I think she needs that rest. Seeing you might be a little overwhelming to her. Dr. Anatoly is out visiting patients and I want him to make that decision." And as the other seemed to accept the logic in the nurse's reasoning, she continued, "There's no need to fret, Cristina. Mrs. Abramov is well. The blow to her head did not cause any damage. But she fell on her face and the poor dear has a big bruise under the right eye."

"Blow on her head?" asked Cristina, shocked. "What happened, who hit her?"

But at that moment a little maid in a perky white apron and white starched cap came in and, making a little curtesy, asked if Miss Denise had called. Cristina had to wait patiently, in silence, until the maid left.

"Please, bring some tea, and ask Mrs. Tavares to prepare a light meal and send up as soon as she can. It's for Mrs. Abramov's daughter. Thank you."

The girl stole a look at the lady sitting in the chair by the window, and, bobbing a little courtesy again, left to discharge her mission.

"Apparently," Denise started explaining, "Irina got involved with a crook. A neighbor actually saw him going into the house several times, but didn't think much of it. Sonya was unaware of these visits, since Irina did it secretly. That day the man landed a blow to Mrs. Abramov's head that rendered her unconscious. It is fine, my dear," she assured Cristina. "Luckily that night the doctor was driving by and, seeing the house in darkness, decided to check that all was well. He found Sonya unconscious on the kitchen floor and Irina gone."

Cristina closed her eyes and took a deep breath. When she opened them again, they were black as coal. "Why did Irina get this man in the house? I don't understand…"

"He certainly ingratiated himself to her. Dr. Anatoly went to the police station nearby and reported the incident. He gave them a description of Irina and her documents; the foolish woman left them behind in her haste, I suppose. The doctor went to the house with the police. After a thorough search they noticed that jewelry and money were gone."

Dr. Anatoly, not only their doctor, but a friend of the Abramovs for years, knew Sonya's habit of keeping cash in the house instead of the bank. He was also aware that her jewelry was in an unlocked drawer in her bedroom's chest of drawers. Many a time he had admonished her for her careless habits.

"What an ingrate!" Cristina fumed. "She is the daughter of a widow friend of Sonya, deceased already, and we took her not only for the company for Sonya, but to give her employment and a place to live."

"Well, it seems that no good deed goes unpunished. But here is your tea and you can learn more details when you see the doctor and Mrs. Abramov. Now, how was your flight?"

"Oh, you can't begin to imagine what happened during the flight from Bagé to Porto Alegre," Cristina said after taking a long sip from the hot tea that preceded the arrival of a more substantial meal. She went on to narrate the accident and how they were saved.

Supper arrived and since it was not meant for an invalid, Mrs. Tavares turned the light meal into a lavish dinner: half a chicken breast, its skin golden and crispy, yucca sautéed in plenty of butter, a big chunk of carrot soufflé and a glass of milk. To tie it all up, a small bowl where stood a large, trembling slice of Manjar Branco[38] encircled by a crown of prunes swimming in the blondest of syrups. Sonya had endeared herself to Mrs.

---

[38] A pudding made with coconut milk, sugar and cornstarch. In our house it was served with prunes in syrup. See Appendix for recipe.

Tavares by always sending praises with the empty dishes returned to the kitchen. So, upon hearing Cristina's relationship with that lady, the cook had outdone herself. At the first forkful Cristina realized how ravenous she was—and the food was simply delicious. Denise doubted that such petite, svelte lady could possibly eat all that food. She was proven wrong.

"I am so sorry," Cristina asked Denise, while putting the white, starched napkin on the left side of her plate. "I did not eat anything before getting on the plane—for fear of turbulence, you know."

"I like to see someone with an appetite. Most of our invalids are very picky and generally not very hungry. Now, tell me again the name of the young lady who landed the airplane."

"Terri."

"No, I mean, her last name," the nurse explained.

"Kramer. Why?"

"I seem to recall this name. Something to do with your husband's abduction, I think," she hesitated.

Cristina sat up. Kramer! Suddenly, she remembered why the girl's name had seemed vaguely familiar. As it is not uncommon with people who go through a lot of stress, Cristina had locked that knowledge in a dark recess of her mind and thrown the key away, blocking a lot of memories related to Robert's abduction. At the airfield in Rio, they said their goodbyes before they went their separate ways—Terri Kramer and her cousin Harry were bound to the ferry to Niterói where she wanted to see an airplane that was for sale. The girl had held Cristina's hand in both hers and told her most effusively how happy she was that she had finally met Cristina; that Cristina and Robert were not as she had always thought them.

Always? That meant. . . Cristina turned to Denise, realization showing in her eyes.

"I thought so," said the nurse, easily reading Cristina's expression. "I never learned all the details, but Mr. Souza mentioned the captain's name. Karl Kramer, I'm quite sure. I never forgot his name."

"Yes, Karl Kramer and his wife, Terri Kramer."

Cristina went on to tell Denise the details of Robert's abduction the nurse did not know. "And now I am willing to bet that their trip to Bagé was linked to Robert."

"That seems quite probable," Denise said without hesitation. "I suggest you be careful while you are in Rio. Who knows what this young lady might do."

"But before we parted—when we arrived in Rio—she told me Robert and I weren't like she imagined us. Which puzzled me then, but takes on a very different perspective now that I think of all these details."

CHAPTER THIRTY-THREE

A little morphine in all the air. It would be wonderfully refreshing for everyone.
—Lady Chatterley's Lover, D.H. Lawrence, 1928.

When Bunky was fifteen years old he ran away from Huron, his hometown in Ohio, to escape a forced marriage. A distant cousin—Terri Griffith—had accused him of putting her in the family way. In the city's harbor Bunky found a ship bound to New York and stowed away. For two years he lived among the dregs of society in New York until one day, in a most unusual way, he saved three-year-old Robert from being run over by a car. Tired of constantly hiring new nannies for the boy, his father, John Laughton, hired Bunky on the spot and he became Robert's guardian, practically raising him. More than twenty years later, in Rio de Janeiro, Bunky met Terri Griffith, then Terri Kramer. Her husband, Captain Karl Kramer, was in business with a certain Francisco Ferreira, who was in reality Daniel Cabral[39]. Unrequited love for Cristina had led Daniel to plan and execute Robert's abduction as a means of revenge. The finding of Robert, who had lost his memory during abduction, and some details related to his return, Denise knew.

"I never learned what happened to Daniel," Denise told Cristina. "Rafael never told me. Is he in jail?"

"They found him dead of an overdose of morphine in the hotel he was staying. Didn't you read?"

---

[39] Finding Cristina: A New Life

Denise shook her head. "At the time I was in bed, sick, with terrible flue coupled with headaches and reading was the last thing in my mind.

"They said it was suicide." Cristina shuddered at the thought of the moment when, almost five years ago, Daniel, under the guise of Francisco Ferreira, revealed himself to her. She explained that to the nurse. "And to complete his revenge, he married Solange, who was a close friend of mine. Very calmly he told both of us he married her to upset me. He wanted to hurt my friend, because he knew we were very close, and that way he'd hurt me too."

"What a terrible man," Denise said, shaking her head in disapproval. "He must have been a very unhappy person."

Cristina poured some tea and sipped it meditatively. She recalled her parting from the young Germans when the hydroplane arrived in Rio. After Harry made his goodbyes, the girl held her hand and, with a frank smile, looked straight into her eyes and told her how glad she was they had finally met.

"You won't understand," Terri had told Cristina, "but I now believe you and your husband are very good people. Whatever happened was no one's fault." And she bolted to a taxi her cousin had hailed, not giving time for Cristina to ask the meaning of that enigmatic comment.

The night before in the hotel, the French windows open to let the cool night air in and the lights in the room off, she and Terri had chatted until both fell asleep. The girl had told Cristina that her mother was American and the father German; he had died a few years ago, and was in the transport business—ships, she had said... Terri's father was none other than Captain Karl Kramer; and Cristina now understood that the young woman meant the death of Kramer—that happened in the ship, when he tried to kill Robert—was no one's fault.

At that point Dr. Anatoly Orlov stormed into the room, interrupting her musings.

"Ah, you are here finally, girl! Very good. Come, let's go see mama, Cristina." He said that and left, giving Cristina no time to greet him.

"You can't stay in Sonya's house alone," Dr. Orlov told Cristina. "You will stay here!" He delivered this speech—more of a command—

with a prodigious amount of head shaking and brow knitting. "You agree, nurse?" he turned to Denise and added, without waiting for her answer, "Tell the girl, tell the girl!" and pointed at Cristina with his big hairy paw.

"Don't worry, Dr. Orlov. During the house renovation a few years ago, Robert made a hidden compartment in our bedroom. We keep a pistol there. I'll sleep with it under my pillow."

"And you know how to shoot with pistol, girl?" he asked, sullenly.

"Of course, I do. Don't worry about me, doctor. And thank you for taking such good care of Sonya," she got up to leave and, before he could stop her, she kissed him on the forehead.

"I'll drive you home. No arguing! While you are in Rio, I drive you!" And, indeed, there was no arguing with him.

CHAPTER THIRTY-FOUR

"You bet we have more clues!" exclaimed Frank eagerly. "And real clues this time."
—The Hardy Boys: The Tower Treasure, Franklin W. Dixon. 1927.

That Sunday night, after everyone was asleep, Donny sneaked into his cousin's bedroom. They talked in whispered tones. With the help of a little flashlight Donny read out loud from Dr. Costa's book about the Templars.

"'That same day my assistant Pedro Rocha, a native of the area, found this tablet-like stone with the following inscription in Portuguese, which our guide translated: 'Full it gave life./ Empty it became dangerous./ Deep inside, within the darkness,/ Lies the treasure of the Templars.' We were digging near a little hill skirted by a creek; on top of the hill there was a derelict building covered with ivy. The tablet laid between a large rock and the creek's shore. The rock was forty-five centimeters in height, and had an unusual, somewhat conic shape that reminded me of the old-fashioned sugarloaf cones[40], similar to the Sugarloaf Mountain in Rio de Janeiro.'"

He and his cousin read that riddle so many times they knew it by heart, yet they were no near to understanding its meaning. He snapped the book closed and extinguished the light. In the darkness the sounds from the world outside were magnified, a perfect background for their silent brooding—wind tousling the leaves of the nearest trees; frogs

---

[40] Sugarloaf: sugar molded into a cone. Sugarloaf in Rio de Janeiro takes its name from it—Pão de Açúcar in Portuguese.

croaking a plaintive, repetitive melody in the distance; the stridulating crickets nearby; the flapping wings of Mr. Brown, the owl.

Further in Dr. Costa's book, she thoroughly described the area where the tablet was found—the hill, the conical rock, and the creek that came so near it almost touched the hill's base. She also planned to return the following season to continue her research. But while hiking on the Himalayas she had an accident and not long afterwards died as a result of her injuries. Headless, her crew dispersed and the site was forgotten. It was due to the diligence of her assistant that her manuscript was even published by the Livraria do Globo in Porto Alegre. With his meager savings Pedro Rocha was able to get fifty copies printed. But to Pedro's chagrin Dr. Costa's work was not well received by the archaeological community. The copy Donny and Annie found in the farm's library had been sent to Bernardo Freitas by Pedro, since the Freitas family had been great supporters of Dr. Costa's research. Inside the book the children found a note scribbled in pencil on a piece of paper, which also had a sketchy map. But unfortunately, the graphite had been almost completely rubbed off, for, just as with the book, it had seen much handling.

"I'm getting tired of this treasure hunting business," Donny said, despondent. "I feel like dumping this book in the trash can!"

In his frustration, he threw the book away and it hit the wall across the room, making a loud thumping noise.

"Don't do that. You're gonna wake everybody up," Annie hissed, and her cousin shrugged his shoulders in response. She got up and picked up the book. "Look at what you've done!"

With the shock the book cover had become detached. Annie started to replace it around the pages that were still held together, planning to fix it later, when she noticed the tip of a piece of paper sticking out from the head of the spine. It was tucked between the spine and the lining. Intrigued, Annie pulled it out. It was a long piece of paper, folded a few times in order to fit inside the narrow confines of the book's spine.

"What's that?"

"A piece of paper. When I picked up the cover, there was a little corner of a paper sticking out of it. I pulled it and this came out," Annie motioned to the folded sheet she held. She unfolded it, then spread it on the floor, smoothing its creases. "Shine the light here."

It contained some notes and a sketchy map. It was written with fountainpen, in a beautiful, clear hand. Unlike the other note they found in the book, this was in pristine condition, having been protected inside the tight space in which it was concealed, and the fact that ink was used, instead of pencil. The cousins analyzed the map. It was a schematic representation of a hill, a river and a little building with a cross on its top. They were all numbered, and a list below detailed each corresponding name with a few notes. It was written in Portuguese and Annie had a little bit of difficulty understanding everything.

"Listen to this. Looks like the last owner of this farm did some digging and found a cookie tin. A cookie tin?" Donny looked at his cousin, mystified. "Anyway, they found this tin not far from where the archeologist found the inscribed stone. And there was a note inside the tin," Donny continued. He quickly went through the text, then translated to English, reading it out loud: "'Inside the sacred image lies the key to a treasure. At the third quadrant plus one find the shadow of the cross.'" He looked up at her and shook his head discouraged. "I hate riddles!"

"Sacred image... Makes no sense, Donny." Annie said and both relapsed into silence.

"Wait a minute," the boy suddenly sat up. "Imagem in Portuguese also means statue. That makes more sense, doesn't it? I mean, a statue could have something inside it. A hollow statue, that can be opened? Unless you're supposed to break it."

"Nah. Don't think so, otherwise there'd be some kind of clue indicating that. Still, what statue and where's it?" Annie asked, mystified.

"I think if it's a statue and there's a cross involved, it must be a church."

"Yeah, I think you're right. But the second sentence, I can't make head or tail of it."

"I think it refers to time." Despite Annie's skeptical look, Donny continued, "Now, listen! One day has twenty-four hours. If you think in quadrants, that gives us six. If I'm right, then the third quadrant is noon. And if you add one, we have one hour in the afternoon."

"I see," the girl looked at him approvingly and added, "You know, you aren't as dumb as you look!"

"Who could be that dumb?" he teased her back.

The two giggled, then sat in the dark, in silence, thinking, their little brows creased in concentration. Bacon jumped on the bed and rested his front paws on the windowsill, looking outside. Annie held the flashlight her cousin had put down on the floor and absentmindedly turned it on, directing the beam to the dog. The light projected his silhouette against the white wall. Looking up, Annie saw it and froze.

"Donny, look at the wall behind you."

"Why?"

"Just look," she commanded.

The boy saw the dog's projection on the wall and turned to her, "The shadow," he whispered, excited.

"I think you are right about the second sentence having to do with time. So, at one in the afternoon the sun will project the shadow of a cross on something. Perhaps on the statue?"

"Could be! But... Which statue? And where's this statue?"

Again, they sat in quiet contemplation, not sharing their thoughts. Not many minutes passed when Annie's voice, in the silence of the room, startled her cousin: "You're right it must be a church!"

"Or a chapel!" both said at the same time.

The farm's little chapel! They looked at each other, barely able to see in the dark, elated at being able to lift part of the veil hiding the mystery of the Templar treasure hidden in that area. They quickly made plans to wake up early the next day and walk to the farm chapel. They would sleep in their clothes and Donny would set his alarm clock to six in the morning. They would take water and food—after all, it was a dangerous treasure hunting expedition and they needed to be prepared for all eventualities! They looked at Bacon. The dog was curled up in bed, already asleep, softly snoring, in dereliction of duty. They decided they would leave the unreliable animal behind.

Monday morning dawned. The blue sky was marred by a few pregnant clouds, their immaculate white tinged with gray, foretelling heavy summer showers to come. The air was humid and the temperature was slowly rising. Annie and Donny had sneaked out of the house a little after six in the morning, and after a little over forty minutes of leisurely walking arrived at their destination.

The little chapel was squat, rough, constructed with stones and wood beams. A short tower, like a bump sticking out of it, housed a bell. On its top a cross, the signs of time imprinted on the rugged wood. The building stood on the crest of the highest hill of all. A well-trodden stone path led to it. Inside a couple of glass windows shed light, but still kept the chapel in semi-obscurity, so welcoming to silent prayers. On the left window, in delicate tones, Christ preached to his disciples. The right window had more dramatic, darker tones: it showed Christ at the cross. Two niches, below each window, housed beautiful wooden statues; on the left side was the Virgin Mary, and on the right, Saint Joseph, both examples of Brazilian Baroque. The altar was a small, tall table, but beautifully hand-carved, of a Rococo style, although more subdued, that sat on a slender stone slab. On the wall behind it, a large wooden cross with the image of Christ in lighter wood, probably carved by the same hand who did the statues.

The altar was covered with an embroidered white linen cloth, heavily starched. A beautiful crystal vase held flowers that had already served their purpose and needed changing. It was flanked by two heavy silver candlesticks. A beautifully French carved oak armoire standing against the back wall on the right, held the accessories the officiating priest would need: the golden chalice and ciborium, crystal cruets for wine and water, as well as lavabo and pitcher, and ecclesiastical vestments. These costly adornments were bestowed upon this rustic edifice by the farm's first mistress, the French Héloïse Jacquet. But instead of clashing with the little building's rusticity, these lavish items actually enhanced its simple beauty. All these precious gifts were hidden during the more violent periods of civil unrest, after an elaborate golden chalice disappeared during the Guerra dos Farrapos—the Ragamuffin War— that broke in 1835, when the Gaúchos fought to secede from the Brazilian empire.

After Héloïse's death, the place was abandoned and the decorations taken to the farmhouse and stored. With the passing of years, Nature recalled the little chapel, embracing the building with ivy, in an attempt to protect its sacred identity; yet, these vivid green bejeweled filigrees reflecting the sun would not have looked more beautiful if done with real emeralds. Upon her family moving to the area, Cristina, entranced with the little edifice's charm, restored it to its original state, returning its liturgical objects and decorations. She also arranged for messes to be regularly said there on Sundays.

Sweaty and tired, the children sat down with their backs against the chapel's cool stone wall. Hunger decided them to have breakfast—hard boiled eggs, canned sardines and water. They killed time planning what they would do with the treasure they were sure they would find. Then as the day went on, the heat overtook them and they dozed in the shade for a couple of hours. They woke with the rain pelting on their heads, got up and ran to find protection at the chapel's threshold. They remained there, watching while a mini deluge ran down the hill, until it was over and the sun showed its implacable face again.

"This wait's killing me!" Annie complained after they had stood there for a long time. "I'm bored to tears."

Their attention was diverted by the creek not too far down. It was reached by a meandering rough track carved on the side of the little hill. Someone was fishing, his golden hair shining under the bright sun.

"Claes," Donny said. As if feeling the children's stare, the boy looked up. Donny waved, but Claes turned his head back to the creek, ignoring the friendly gesture.

"I don't like him. He has snake eyes."

Donny burst out laughing. "You're in love with him," and he laughed harder as the outraged girl punched him repeatedly on the shoulder.

"Am not!"

"Are too," he insisted and moved away from her to avoid her fists. "Who taught you to punch like that?"

"You, dummy! You don't remember? Never mind." She turned to look at her watch—her pride, a brand-new Ingersoll Mickey Mouse with stainless steel charm bracelet she got last Christmas. "Ten minutes to one. Let's go inside," she pleaded.

"What, you aren't going down there to say hi to your beloved?" Donny teased her and was barely able to avoid being slapped by his irritated cousin.

"That's not funny!" She made a face at him.

They pushed the heavy door open and entered the chapel, letting some of the day light in. Inside the small building was cool and very quiet. They dipped their fingers in the rustic stone fount filled with holy water, touched one knee to the ground, and made the sign of the cross. Their eyes wondered around the room, trying to predict what would be revealed to them by the afternoon sun. Despite having been there for mass, they had never analyzed their surroundings, but there was not a lot to occupy them in that little space, and the minutes passed excruciatingly slow. Impatiently, they watched the path the sun travelled on the stone floor, from the right-side window.

"One o'clock." Annie's voice was whispered, as if she were saying a prayer.

With bated breath the children saw the sun project the image of the cross from the stained-glass window upon the statue of the Virgin Mary. They reached the statue at the same time. Annie reverently removed it from the niche, exculpating herself with the Mother of Christ. After a little bit of handling and searching, she found a well-disguised opening on the back of the image. She had to wriggle it until she was able to pull the cover out. Inside there was a little piece of paper. With some difficulty—it seemed to be stuck—she removed the brittle parchment, not noticing that half of it remained concealed inside, affixed to the statue's hollow interior by the action of time. Annie carefully unfolded it and Donny read it out loud: "Sob o local de culto/ O tesouro foi oculto."

The two raised their eyes together from the paper, and gazed for a long moment at one another in speechless dismay. Donny was the first to voice their thoughts.

"Another riddle..." he said, discouraged.

CHAPTER THIRTY-FIVE

Not to us, Lord, not to us, but to Your name be the glory.
—Psalm 115:1, motto inscribed in the Beauceant[41] banner of the Knights Templar. In A New Encyclopaedia of Freemasonry. 1970.

A nnie closed the opening on the statue's back and carefully replaced it on its niche, making the sign of the cross. Taking the manuscript from her cousin, she read it out loud, "If my Portuguese is right, I think it says something like beneath the place of worship, a treasure was hidden?"

"Yup. And this is a place of worship. That means the treasure is under the chapel. Which also means we must dig. Great, that's all we need," he told his cousin in a despondent tone.

"No, I don't think so. But I think you're right: the treasure must be in here. But where?" Annie asked and started looking around the place. "I don't think there's anything to do with digging, otherwise there would be some clue in that piece of paper," she said while standing near the altar.

Suddenly she gave a little cry, startling Donny. "I think I've got it," she turned to him, triumphantly. "It's the altar!" And as he looked at her, uncomprehending, she explained, "The altar is the place of worship! Isn't that so?" Annie asked her cousin, barely containing her excitement.

---

[41] Noum: the black-and-white banner of the Knights Templars; interjection: used as a battle cry by the Knights Templars. Merriam-Webster Dictionary. For more information: Dictionnaire de l'Ancien et Moyen Français, Frédéric Godefroy. 1881.

"Yes, I think you're right," he agreed, but, still, doubt lingered in his speech.

He joined her beside the altar and they walked around it, analyzing the stone that formed its base. Crouching down the boy noticed a depression on the front right angle of the stone; it went all the way through to the other side. He passed his hand on the angle, feeling the surface with his fingers.

"I think this was carved on the stone," he turned to his cousin, who had kneeled beside him.

He analyzed it closely, then tried to insert his fingers through the hole. "I think this hole was drilled so they could pass a rope through it. That's probably how they brought the stone here—dragging it up the hill with a rope. And I'm pretty sure if we pass a rope through this hole, we can move the stone."

"How? The slab's thin, but it looks very heavy," the girl told him, discouraged. "We're not strong enough to move it, Donny."

"Let's get the rope and I'll show you!"

The children ran to their haversacks and each brought out a coil of rope.

When they first entered the chapel Donny had noticed the narrow stone column that helped hold the tiled roof; it sat in the center of the building, several paces from the altar, before it.

"We'll use that as leverage," he pointed at the rough column. "Join the ropes with a knot, while I'll work this end through the stone."

Donny easily passed one end of the rope through the hole in the stone and tied a knot. Then, holding the other end, he went around the column. Stretching the rope, he instructed Annie, "Stand behind me and get a hold of the rope. We'll pull it together."

The effort was tremendous and they had to stop several times to rest. But inch by inch the stone, with the rattling altar atop, was moved, until there was a gap large enough for one of them to sneak in. Two sweaty faces looked down into a dark void revealed by a round opening not much wider than three feet. With the flashlight they were able to see inside. It looked like a well, but it was dry and it looked like there had been no water in it for many years. It was a deep tunnel with walls covered with stones, maybe fifteen feet long, that widened slightly as it went down. The irregularities on its length projected dark dimpled shadows upon the walls. Pieces of rotten wood still attached to the structure spoke of a long-gone crude ladder. At the bottom they could see something that looked like an opening on one side.

"I'm going down and—" Donny started and was cut short by his cousin.

"No way! I'm first!"

"Don't be daft. I'll go first and make sure it's safe."

"Because you're a boy and I'm a girl?" she made a face. "Now, listen," she stopped him, "I have an idea! Let's decide who goes first with a new game called 'Paper, Stone, and Scissors' my mom taught me that she read in a book[42]." And as Donny looked at her suspiciously, she explained, "It's a good way to decide this, you'll like it. First, we put one hand behind our backs. On the count of three we bring our hands forward. Clenched fist means stone, fingers extended means paper, and the two first fingers extended, scissors. The paper wraps the stone, stone blunts scissors, and scissors cut paper. Understand?"

Upon his agreement, they tried the game. Donny brought forward an open palm, while Annie's hand showed the index and middle fingers extended and separated: scissors.

"I win!" she screamed, elated.

"Fine. Go ahead. Just don't mind the spiders—or the rats—you'll find down there," he told her nonchalantly.

"What? I'll wait here," the girl relented, eyeing the dark opening on the floor with an anxious expression. She had not considered the possibility of these detested little creature setting their homes with the treasure.

Women, thought Donny. Afraid of spiders and rats. Shaking his head, he undid the knot that gathered the two ropes, but kept the one he had tied to the stone base of the altar. He then threw down the rope he was holding into the well. That done, he laid flat on the ground, directed the light of his flashlight to the opening, and started feeling the walls with one hand as far as he was able.

"Watcha doing?"

"Checking the walls. There are all kinds of pieces of wood and stones sticking out that I think I can use to help me get down there. Keep the

---

[42] Scissors Cut Paper, Gerard Fairlie.

flashlight directed down so I can see where I'm going. Like so," he showed her the best angle to direct the light beam, then pulled the rope tight and slowly eased himself down.

The descent was not too difficult. As he hoped, the protruding chunks of stones and wood served almost as steps. But suddenly Donny put his weight on a piece of rotten timber that gave way. He slipped and, unable to keep a hold on the rope, fell down with a crash that, combined with Annie's scream, echoed mightily inside the quiet building.

"Donny," she called down. No answer. "Are you all right?" No answer again. She projected the beam of flashlight down and saw her cousin's body twisted in a way that sent a shiver down her spy. Cold sweat started to form on her forehead. "He's dead! What should I do?" she asked herself, and after a brief hesitation, jumped into action.

She secured her haversack to her back and, holding the flashlight on her tight lips, grasped the rope and, very carefully, went down the well. It was a little damp and smelled of musty soil, the result of being sealed shut for so many years. When she reached her cousin, she was relieved to see that he was alive. Pouring water from her canteen on her neckerchief with trembling fingers, she pressed it upon Donny's brow. Then, as he did not react, she poured the rest of the water on his face. The boy came to with a start and the sharp pain on one shoulder.

"Stop that!" he complained. "I think I dislocated my shoulder," he said and sat up with difficulty. "I'll be fine once my dad puts it back." And at his cousin's confused look he explained, "Once he was attacked by some thugs and he dislocated his shoulder in the fight[43]. It didn't heal properly so it happens again sometimes and he had to learn how to fix it." He looked around and saw the opening they had noticed when looking down into the well from the chapel's floor. "Point the flashlight to that opening," he asked Annie. "Let's see what's inside before we get out of here."

"I think I should go to the farm and bring someone to help fish you out of here."

"No, I'll get out by myself."

"You can't possibly—"

---

[43] Finding Cristina

"Sure, I can," he cut her, annoyed. He was a man, and as such he would escalate the wall and get out of that hole, even with a dislocated shoulder. "But first we must explore down here."

Annie gave a sigh and shrugged her shoulders. "Men," she muttered and directed the light as requested.

It revealed a small room, not much more than a large cupboard, barely five feet high and three deep, roughly excavated and reinforced with mismatched stones, a few of which had collapsed. Inside it, against the wall, stood a large trunk. The girl squeezed past Donny and entered the room.

"This thing is rotten, falling apart," she said after examining the wood and corroded metal that held it precariously together. She opened it and looked inside. "It's filled with stones—looks like those polished stones we get on the river, you know. And some yucky rolls of fabric and pieces of wood. There's no treasure," she turned to her cousin, disappointed, then, frowning, asked, "But why leave all these clues if there's not really a treasure?"

"I don't know. Maybe someone had nothing better to do than trick other people into thinking there was a treasure under the church? Or maybe someone else was here before us, took the treasure and left these things in the trunk. I just don't understand why they would. Ouch!" When Donny leaned one hand on the ground to try to straighten himself, it was pricked by some sharp object. "Rats!"

"Rats!" Annie screamed, frightened. "Where?" she asked and anxiously looked around.

"Not real rats, silly." He picked a little object from the ground, and putting it on the palm of his hand, showed it to her. It was a ring. "Really big; probably from a man."

The girl picked it up and held it close to the flashlight. Indeed, it was a large signet ring, and from its size, for the hand of an adult. It had an octagonal face with an engraving, and was made of iron, corroded by time. "There's an inscription." The girl rubbed it with her handkerchief. "Looks like Greek."

"And how would you know?" Donny sniggered.

"I was studying Greek in school before…" she hesitated, not wanting to talk about the reason for her leaving the school in Switzerland. "Well, I think it's Greek! I'm good with languages, if you must know," and she stuck her tongue out at him. Then she turned the ring so he could read the inscription on the flat, octagonal face:

Ἰάκωβος

And at that moment, having looked pass her cousin's head, Annie gave a loud gasp.

"What?"

"The rope," she pointed and Donny turned to look. "It was right behind you. It's gone," she finished in a whisper.

While they had been distracted exploring the bottom of the well, and talking about the ring, someone removed the rope.

CHAPTER THIRTY-SIX

Sometimes we meet a fool with wit, never one with discretion.
—Maximes, François de La Rochefoucauld. 1665.

E arly that Monday morning Robert and Bunky drove to Bagé. Bunky was left at the Sorocabana where he would meet his crony and owner, Osman Sadik. The Turco, as his sobriquet implied, was born in Turkey. He was a large man in his fifties, with wavy graying hair tamed in place with very strong, perfumed pomade, and an eternal unlit cigarette dangling from flashy lips. The two would sit at one of the small tables on the sidewalk, watching the traffic and the people walking by, while drinking coffee and chatting. Turco had learned English while a stevedore and working as deckhand on an American tramp ship for many years before moving to Bagé and opening the Sorocabana. Of Portuguese he learned only the essential, picking words here and there, misusing expressions he could barely understand, but always with a smile that endeared him to the bar's habitués.

Robert drove to General Osório Street, where stood the building of the Correios e Telégrafos, the Post Office and Telegraph. Having found no telegram from Cristina, he jumped back in the car and, turning left, then left again onto Gomes Carneiro Street, parked in front of the Telephone Company building, where another disappointment met him: he was told the workers of the telephone company in Rio de Janeiro were still on strike.

He was frustrated, upset, but aware that there was nothing he could do but wait. Since he was in Bagé he might as well do some shopping. He needed a new belt—his wife having condemned his favorite one—

handkerchiefs and a new Panama hat. He also wanted to buy a few things for Cristina—those little baubles he knew she rarely indulged in and he wanted to spoil her. Cristina was gone two days and he already desperately missed her. With shopping in mind, he drove to the Loja Salim Kalil at the corner of General Netto with Marechal Floriano streets. He parked the car and proceeded to the store.

At one of the store windows, waves of blue satin fabric cascaded down from the ceiling, creating a water-like backdrop for the diving ladies' lingerie—a collection of white, dainty little nothings in silk and lace. Another window displayed mannequin busts, their glamorous faces half hidden by little veils, wearing 'the latest fashion from Hollywood' in women's hats; in the background, on a raised platform, a few hatpins and a poster proclaimed them a thing of the past: 'An elastic band placed under the hair will secure your hat!' Inside the store, headless mannequins stood tightly swathed in soft silk and gossamer chiffon, while more ordinary fabrics—printed cotton and voile—artistically emulated airy summer dresses. On both sides of the store, behind counters, floor to ceiling shelves displayed an extensive array of goods stored in boxes or inside drawers. A couple of glass counters in the middle of the store revealed lined-up open boxes with neatly folded gloves, handkerchiefs and silk stockings. The back wall of the store displayed the gentlemen session, and to that Robert directed his steps. There, male mannequins displayed the latest fashion in dress shirts and silk ties, with matching kerchiefs tucked in their pockets, while Panama hats balanced on the heads of expressionless faces.

The place was busy, that Monday being Kalil's big annual sale. Still, Fafá Kalil, who was standing behind a counter helping a customer, spotted him. Unceremoniously she passed her customer to a harassed clerk, who was already helping two other people. She then hurried to the gentlemen session. A shawl thrown on her shoulders, in the manner of Flamenco dancers, she wore a red dress with large white dots and ruffles on the sleeves and hem. Robert though she only needed a Spanish comb and a flower in her hair to compete for the title role of Bizet's Carmen. He was greeted with a wide smile from generous red lips, two dimples making a charming appearance.

Sérgio and two of his friends had been lingering there, killing time until noon, when he planned to take Fafá to lunch. He saw Robert walk to the end of the store and his girlfriend's maneuver to reach the American as he got to the counter. Signaling to his friends, he leisurely walked to were Robert stood conversing with Fafá, and leaned on the counter beside him.

"And how's the beauteous Cristina?"

"Mrs. Laughton's fine, thanks for asking." Robert answered, barely turning to look at Sérgio. "These kerchiefs and the black belt, yes. Can I try this Panama, Miss?" and he followed word with action. The hat fit perfectly and he consigned it to Fafá, with the other items he had decided to purchase.

The young woman watched him with adoring eyes. In her mind she liked him to the statue of David she had seen in the Galleria dell'Accademia when staying in Florence the prior year. So much beauty should also be on a pedestal!

"I heard she left. Took a plane . . ." and despite the factual character of the comment, Sérgio's tone insinuated Cristina had left her husband.

"You heard right," Robert answered, this time without looking at the young man.

"Don't bother Mr. Laughton, Sérgio. And what are you mugs doing here anyway if you aren't buying? Get lost!"

"Don't worry. I'm used to dealing with children. I have three at home." Robert smiled at Fafá. "Now, can you show me some ladies' handkerchiefs?"

"Pleased to, Sir," the girl showed all her beautiful teeth, delighted to be of service to Robert. "This way, please," she indicated the counters on her right.

Sérgio and his friends followed them, and were again ignored.

"Two men in the plane accompanying her, I was told," Sérgio said to his friends, loud enough to be heard by Robert, a smirk on his face. The two young men sneered and observed Robert.

"Sérgio, stop this! Scram," and Fafá pointed at the door.

"Leave my wife alone, boy." The muscles on Robert's face tightened, and his voice acquired a different tone, that, unfortunately for him, young Sérgio did not recognize.

"If she only left me alone," the young man laughed, and deliberately turned his back to Robert. His friends sniggered at that.

"I was told, and didn't believe, but you are Brazilian trash."

The smile died on Sérgio's friends' lips. The young man spun around to face Robert, seething. "I'll show you what trash is, Gringo!" he snarled and took a wild punch at Robert's face.

Robert pivoted to the right, avoiding the other's fist, and Sérgio then took another swing, now with his left fist. Robert simply dodged it again. But at this second attack, his instinct to counterpunch overpowered common sense, and his right fist landed a harsh blow square on his opponent's nose. The impact was such that it sent Sérgio reeling backwards and he collapsed on the floor. Robert gripped the young man's lapels and, finding no opposition, pulled him back onto his feet, then pushed him to a vacating chair a startled customer had quickly vacated. The young man sat there, dizzy, crumpled like a bundle of dirty clothes.

For a few seconds there was absolute silence. Then it was pandemonium. A few ladies celebrated the event in the usual manner—emitting piercing shrieks, and, having fainting fits, comfortably collapsing on chairs nearby. Customers poured out of the store, like milk left to boil over a stove. Cries of 'murder' were heard coming from outside—some unintelligible, that sounded somewhat like 'young lady.' And Sérgio's companions, who a few minutes before were jeering at Robert, unmanned, vanished and where nowhere to be seen.

Sérgio's nose was bleeding profusely and a good amount of it decorated his once crispy linen suit. Robert looked around, searching for something to use to stanch the flow. Seeing Fafá hugging to her breast the handkerchiefs he intended to buy, he grabbed them and, gathering them into a bundle, walked to his opponent, who had remained on the chair, stunned.

He thrust the kerchiefs in the young man's hand and commanded, "Hold this on your face. And tilt your head back, this way," he pushed Sérgio's head backwards, not too gently, until it rested on the chair's back. He then stepped back and watched the young man's face, a frown marring his brow. "Why did you have to do this?" Then turning to the unnerved Fafá, he pointed at the bloody mess Sérgio held against his face and commanded, "Add these to my bill."

Meanwhile, alerted by the uproar and screaming, the Law arrived in the person of Sargent Gumercindo Goudene. He was an imposing figure; two hundred pounds, and so very well distributed through six feet in stature, that not infrequently his sudden appearance overwhelmed, and helped stop crime before it was committed. But Gumercindo, when not fighting villains, was the gentlest of souls, whose hobby was painting. Most of his free time was spent in front of a canvas, depicting some bucolic scene in the countryside. As for the quality of his productions, only experts can opine.

"What's this, what's this?" he said his habitual lines as he entered the now almost deserted store.

There the bemused lawman beheld a triadic tableau vivant: Sérgio, his head thrown backwards, recumbent on a chair holding a bloody mass of handkerchief to his nose; behind him the white-faced Fafá Salim, who had come out from behind the counter, watched the young man; and Robert, standing by, his eyes also beholding the sitting man. The three suddenly came to life, each trying to explain what took place.

"Ahem," Gumercindo trumpeted. He hooked his thumbs in his belt and, with a demeanor that brooked no refusal, ordered, "Very well! The two gentlemen and the young lady: follow me. All to the clubhouse," and he motioned the three to the door, "toodsweet," he added, butchering that beautiful language of Victor Hugo. "'Opefully you'll get a long bit," he said, wishing them a long stay in the city jail.

As they marched to the nearby police station, they formed a strange procession that attracted the passersby's attention. Cars, bicycles and horse carts slowed down, causing a small traffic congestion. Street urchins who prowled the neighboring streets, gathered little pebbles and threw the missiles at the group. That triggered a stern reaction from that stalwart representative of the Law in Bagé: he unerringly aimed his stick at the ones who dared to get too close, and the quickly formed gang disbanded also as quickly. To the relieve of Goudene's captives, their brief excursion ended with no further contretemps.

CHAPTER THIRTY-SEVEN

They gave me a report and I said 'look for the woman.' That made them laugh.
I questioned the injured man. The imbecile was amusing himself watching a grisette
undress in her garret. He missed his step and he fell. Let's look for the woman, Mr.
Salvator, let's look for the woman.
—The Mohicans of Paris: Drama in Five Acts, Alexandre Dumas
Père. 1864.

Aparício França's office at the Police Station building was exactly as he found it when elected to that post. It had belonged to others before him; men who, for lack of time, interest, or perhaps taste, had not added anything to the room's original appointments. During the many years since the building was erected, a feminine hand never touched that chamber with the charm that only women can bestow. Consequently, the room was somber. A positive trait during summer, it turned into a hindrance during the icy winter days, when the Minuano wind penetrated that chamber through the gaps and cracks in the windows and doors. The walls were covered with dark green paper sprinkled with fading golden crowns—vestige of the time when Brazil was an Empire—with dark smudges here and there, now only mementos of the gas lit fixtures that were used throughout the building. A bulky desk of jacarandá wood, it's top full of files and sheets of paper neatly organized, shelves protected by glass doors, a heavy office chair and facing the desk two incongruently light No. 14 Thonet chairs, a bit wobbly from many years of wear.

Aparício França sat back on his chair, pensively. Crossing his left arm over his chest, he rested the right elbow on it and started to smooth his mustache with index and thumb. He looked at the trio facing him, then turned to Gumercindo Goudene, who stood framed by the door, a marshal figure with a grim expression on his face.

"So, am I to understand that Mr. Paranhos here," and the chief of police indicated Sérgio with his head, "having stepped on some, er, how should I say? Unknown substance? Yes? He then proceeded to slipped and fall down, hitting his nose. Is that it?"

Sérgio, still holding the bundle of handkerchiefs to his nose, tried to say something, but only emitted a stifled groan as one of Fafá's delicate feet, clad in sturdy Oxford shoes, came in abrupt and painful contact with the young man's shin.

"Keep the kerchiefs, darling," she told him. "You don't want to bleed all over, do you?" and she gave him a warning look.

"Also," Aparício França continued, turning amused eyes to Robert, "that you, Mr. Laughton, being in the right place at the right time, and being of a most charitable disposition, helped him?"

"That pretty much sums it all up—yup," Robert told his friend with a straight face.

"Excuse me, sir, but these two were fighting over the dame here."

"Why, I'd never!" gasped the dame in question.

"Gumercindo," growled his superior, warningly.

"Sorry, sir, I'm sure. But it's clear as daylight," he continued. "As them Frenchies say, shurshay la fame," parroted Goudene, repeating the chauvinistic French saying, cherchez la femme, and so loading all evils of the world onto the shoulders of one of Eve's sisters.

"All right, thank you, Gumercindo, you may go now. And close the door behind you."

The outraged lawman left, not before emitting a low harrumph, thus making patent his disapproval of his superior's light handling of the situation.

The police chief drummed the table with his fingertips and analyzed the trio facing him. "Get out of here—you and you," he pointed at Fafá and Sérgio. "And if I hear of any more trouble involving you," he addressed the young man, "you won't get out that easily." Then turning to Robert, after the door closed behind the two young people. "Now, spill the beans."

Robert dutifully related the whole story to his friend. Standing outside, near the door, Gumercindo Goudene could hear the two men burst into laughter and shook his head in disapproval.

"And to say that I came to town with the innocent goal of getting news from my wife," Robert exclaimed, sighing and feigning distress. "Which, by the way, I didn't. Then I was minding my business, and, well, you know the rest."

"Yup, you're a model of rectitude and patience. Who knows, you might be immortalized in a bust—or even a statue. They might put you in the central square," França teased Robert.

"Think so?" he joked. Then seriously, "I'm a bit anxious to get news from my missus. If I don't hear from her tomorrow… I can't wait until Saturday to take a plane to Rio. I'll go nuts if I have to wait that long."

"C'mon, man, give her some time to breath."

"It's not that. She promised to telegraph from Porto Alegre, and she didn't." Aparício pooh-pooed his concern, so Robert added, "She told me she'd do it as soon as she got there and that little lady is as good as her word—always. I'm really getting anxious, França."

"Mmm… If push comes to shove, I'll commandeer an airplane," Aparício assured him.

"Can you?" Robert asked, and the police chief answered with an assenting headshake. "Well, then tomorrow I'll come to town, and if no telegram, I'll try to call. Failing that, I'll hold you to your word."

When Robert left the room, he was sternly addressed by that paragon of policemen, Gumercindo Goudene. "I don't know what trick you played to get off clean . . ."

"Oh, put it down to my irresistible charm, officer," Robert interrupted him.

Hands in his pockets and a crooked smile, he left the Police Station.

"Forget about shopping! I need some hooch," he told himself and drove to the Sorocabana to join Bunky and the Turco, with the intent of dipping into the latter's stash of Raki, the Turkish brandy that gentleman kept for very special customers.

CHAPTER THIRTY-EIGHT

I fear to lose the marvel
of your statue-like eyes and the accent
that at night places on my cheek
the delicate rose of your breath.
—Sonnet of the Sweet Complaint, Federico García Lorca.

T he first lights of Tuesday morning found Robert driving to Bagé by himself in Cristina's two-seater. The prior night he informed Bunky that, in the eventuality that he did not get news from Cristina in Bagé, he would find a way to travel to Rio de Janeiro.

"You and Maria are in charge in my absence, as always."

Arriving in town he made a beeline to the Telephone Company and then the Post Office. Both proven unsuccessful, he rushed to the police station.

Aparício França looked up from his littered desk as the door of his office burst open and in came Robert. His friend tried to keep a calm appearance, but the police chief read the signs that betrayed his concern.

"You've got to get me that plane, França," Robert told him.

Following on Robert's footsteps the dispatcher, Ezequiel Goudene, a toothy, lanky youth with a mop of black hair, who had unsuccessfully tried to stop Robert's incursion into the police chief's office—fuming at such a breach of etiquette. Ezequiel, brother of the intrepid

Gumercindo, was his brother's antithesis and had been easily brushed aside by Robert, as would a thin leaf of pampa's grass by a mere breeze.

"Sorry sir," he apologized, his face growing red under his superior's scrutiny. "He wouldn't stop," Ezequiel complained and gave Robert a resentful glance that went unnoticed.

"That's all right, Ezequiel. No harm done," then turning to Robert, as the door closed behind his minion, "Sit down, old man," he pointed the chair in front of the desk. Getting up he went to his private restroom. He was back with a glass containing a little brandy. "Take this—c'mon, drink up! That's better. I assume you're here because you got no news from your wife?"

"You assumed right!"

In a few words Robert related his unsuccessful trips to the Telephone Company and the Post Office. Again, he stressed that she had promised to be in touch when she arrived in Porto Alegre. That was on a Saturday. It was now Tuesday and the lack of a word from her troubled him.

"You see, that blasted Polack was in the plane!"

"Polack?" the police chief asked.

"Oh, it's a long story. But. . . Guess I'll have to tell you! Before we were married this guy tried to abduct my wife—"

"Abduct? Your wife?"

"Rats! Stop repeating what I say and listen," Robert growled, annoyed at the interruptions. "He was in Brazil buying horses. Saw Cristina and got dizzy with her. I happened to be on the spot—with some pals of mine—right when he tried to abduct her. We were all packing heat, broke into the guy's den in the nick o' time." The memory of that incident made him grind his teeth. "Now this goon had the nerve to show up at our farm," a statement received with raised eyebrows by Aparício; he could not understand what the Polish man was doing in Bagé, but dared not ask. "It was all I could do not to blip him. Luckily to him, Carl Raswan was with him." Another name unknown to Aparício. "You don't know Raswan? Never mind. Listen, let's jump in my car and I'll tell you all about the Polack and Raswan while I drive us to the airfield."

"Give me the key. You're in no condition to drive."

While they rushed to the airfield, after giving more details of the kidnapping incident, and of Carl Raswan, Robert told his friend how

Raswan and Zietarski had travelled to Porto Alegre in the same airplane as his wife.

"It doesn't result that the Polish—"

"Polack," Robert corrected his friend.

"OK, Polack! What I mean is that it doesn't necessarily mean the Polack kidnapped her, Robert."

"I wouldn't be so sure!"

There was no way to assuage his friend's fears, so França diverted the subject to the trip.

"I am hoping we find a friend of mine when we get there. Quirino Robaina. He's a retired engineer. Don't think you know him." And as Robert said he was not acquainted with the gentleman, Aparício continued, "He's a very nice guy. Airplane aficionado. Just bought one— well, I should say, another one. I'm sure I can convince him to take you at least to Porto Alegre."

At the airfield the Robert's luck held: Aparício's friend, Quirino Robaina, was lovingly inspecting his new acquisition. He was a sturdy man of middle height in his late fifties, with a military demeanor and a bushy mustache that partially hid his mouth. Wide eyelids gave a dreamy expression to his hazel eyes. Quirino had recently arrived from the United Sates where he purchased a Mohawk M2-C Chieftain and was easily swayed to take a trip to Porto Alegre. Upon learning of Robert's predicament, he offered to take him all the way to Rio de Janeiro. The urgency of the American's errand resolved him to try the trip in one day.

"It'll probably mean two fuel stops. Let's see," and that saying he grabbed a map and, unrolling it, spread it on a desk that stood on a corner of his hangar. With a stubby finger he indicated a couple of areas to Aparício and Robert. "I'll just fill the tank with gas and we can leave," he said, excited at the prospect of the pleasure the many hours of flying would afford him.

The tank full, Robert and Aparício helped him pull the airplane out of the hangar.

"You'll need this," Quirino threw Robert a jacket. "It was on the back seat and I only saw it when I got here. The fellow who owned it must have been about your height and weight. It should fit you. And you'll need these too," he said, handing Robert a pair of goggles and a leather flight helmet. "It gets cold there," he explained, pointing at the sky, "so you'll also need gloves. Let me show you how to adjust the goggles."

"My friend, you're talking to an expert," Aparício slapped Robert on the back. "He piloted a plane in France during the Great War."

"You don't say! Must have been an incredible experience, lots of fun," the man turned a searching gaze to Robert, impressed.

"Not that much fun, I assure you. Seeing a plane go down in flames—even if it wasn't one of your own—isn't a sight I enjoy recalling."

"'Course not," the other said, embarrassed, cursing his own lack of tact.

In a few minutes the two men donned the necessary garments and were ready.

"Well, shall we go?" Quirino rubbed his gloved hands together, pleased, like a child who unexpectedly found some forgotten candy in his pockets. He escalated the wing and, with agility unusual for his girth, squeezed through the window into his seat. Robert said his goodbyes to his friend and followed into the cockpit.

Quirino started the engine and taxied the airplane to the runway—a mere grassy lane from whence the airplanes took off. The Police Chief watched while the little airplane gained speed then was airborne. Going back to the car, he turned it around and drove it to the police station. Things were quiet at the station, so he decided he would drive the car to Fazenda Minuano after he had his lunch. When later on Gumercindo showed up, Aparício França instructed him to stay and hold the fort while he and Ezequiel went to Fazenda Minuano. He then told Ezequiel to drive his own car, while he would drive Robert's.

If Robert's mind were not so absorbed in his concern for Cristina, he would have enjoyed the trip. The necessary stop for refueling, although quickly handled by Quirino Robaina, sent him into paroxysms of desperation. The minutes dragged and every moment he remained in this uncertainty was torture. To make it worse, the memory of the botched kidnapping of some nine years ago—when he, Max and his Italian friend, Andrea Calvetti, broke into Bogdan Zietarski house in Rio de Janeiro—kept him from admiring the beautiful views the flight afforded. If the

Polack so much as touched a single of Cristina's hair… He tried to imagine the ways in which he would punish the man. Then he started blaming himself for allowing her to go alone. Anything that happened to her would be his fault.

Night was falling when they arrived in Rio and it was with trepidation that he stepped on terra firma. He dismissed Quirino's suggestion that they should go to a hotel.

"Not a chance. And you're coming with me; you'll stay with us. C'mon, let's not waste time. I can't wait to make sure my wife is fine. Taxi," and he almost ran in front of a cab that had just dropped a fare and was starting to leave.

"You goofy or sometink!" the driver yelled at him.

"Yup, sometink," he said, and pulling the surprised Quirino after him, jumped inside the car. "Copacabana," he told the chauffer and gave the man the address to Sonya's house.

It was not a very long ride, but Robert was on tenterhooks and to him it seemed to take ages. Upon arriving he was surprised to see the house in darkness. A light pole that stood on the sidewalk right in front of the entrance gate shed some light on the house façade. Robert looked for the hidden key and not finding it, knocked at the door. Silence. He walked to the back and repeated the process at the kitchen door. No answer. He and his companion eyed each other, but neither said a word, for both wondered the same thing: where was Cristina?

CHAPTER THIRTY-NINE

As you think, so you become. Avoid superstitiously investing events with power or meaning they don't have. Keep your head. Our busy minds are forever jumping to conclusions, manufacturing and interpreting signals that aren't there.
—The Art of Living, Epictetus.

Robert sat, dejected, on one of the steps that led to the front door of the house. Not knowing what was happening, Quirino stood by, uncertain what to do or say. Suddenly a car stopped in front of the house and a man got out of it and came around to open the door near the sidewalk. In the dark Robert could only make up a silhouette and a big moustache.

"The Polack?" Robert spat out, baffled at the man's nerve of showing up.

His surprise grew when he saw the man help none other than his wife out of the car. He shot up from the step where he had been sitting, and, without a word, took off like a fury. It all happened so fast it took everyone by surprise. In a moment Robert had the man by his lapels and was shaking him like a ragdoll.

"Stop, Robert! Are you crazy," his wife screamed, trying to pry his fingers from the man's lapels. But she soon realized the reason for her husband's aggression, and added, "It's Dr. Anatoly Orlov! Stop!"

Robert let the man go and looked at his wife, embarrassed. "I thought it was the Polack. It looked like just him in the darkness…"

"Shame on you," she threw at him, her voice trembling with outrage. Then turning to the doctor, "I am so sorry, Dr. Orlov. My husband took you for someone else."

Fuming, the doctor straightened his jacket, frowning at the dejected young man. "Need glasses? Go to optometrist! I can indicate good one to you." Then turning to Cristina, "Call me if husband goes out of his mind again. I'll send him to Hospício Pedro II," referring to the mental hospital located at the nearby Praia Vermelha neighborhood.

A penitent Robert handed him his hat that, in the melee, had fallen on the sidewalk. The doctor grabbed it and stuck it on his head. Giving his aggressor a last venomous look, he turned to Cristina. "Mother will be released in a couple of days. Nurse Denise will call to let you know."

"Thank you. And, again, I apologize for the misunderstanding."

The doctor harumphed mightily and entered the car. "In Russia we used knout to cure crazy people! We should bring good old czarist custom to Brazil!" he told Robert in his thunderous bass voice. Slamming the door, he turned the ignition on and took off.

"What is it with you? And why are you here?" Cristina had turned blazing eyes to her husband, and, arms crossed on her chest, faced him, waiting for an explanation.

Recognizing the early signs of a storm, he tried to pacify her. "I got here and it was all dark, no keys—"

"Didn't it occur to you that I might be at Dr. Orlov's clinic? Sonya's there, remember?"

"Oh, princess—"

"Don't you princess me. Why are you here?" she repeated.

"Did you forget you promised to send news as soon as you got to Porto Alegre?" At that he noticed a sudden softening of her expression and continued, rallying, "Well, that was Saturday," and he let that sink in, watching her with a knowing expression. The situation had reversed and he started to breathe more easily. The clouds were dispersed; he was safe.

"Oh, my God, you're right," she turned penitent eyes to him.

It was amazing how her mood changed so quickly, her husband thought, thankful.

Robert woke up. In the darkness of the bedroom, he could barely distinguish the objects around him, yet he knew there was an intruder in the room.

It was very quiet and the only sound he could hear was that of his wife's soft breathing in the bed beside his. Yet, he was certain that a third person had joined them. At first, he thought of Quirino having come to ask something, to immediately discard the idea: the man would hardly barge into their room in the middle of the night, unannounced. If he needed something, he would have knocked at the door. It was an intruder and he must try to reach the gun in the hidden compartment before it might be too late. Trying to maintain calm, he continued to breathe regularly, to give the impression that he was sleeping. But when he slowly turned to reach the wall behind the nightstand, the springs of his bed made a noise.

And then he heard a sound he remembered from his years in the Great War: that of the safety being released on a pistol. And it came from the foot of his bed. The intruder was right in front of Robert.

"I'm going to reach for the light," he said, calmly, in a voice that was just above a whisper. "Whatever you want, you can have it, no need to shoot."

The light revealed a slim boy wearing a large cap, pushed down, almost covering a face where no trait of beard showed. He was holding a Mouser. For a brief second Robert relived an experience he had during the war, when he did an emergency landing behind enemy lines, in Germany, and found himself facing the same kind of pistol. Fortunately for him his opponent's weapon was empty and his was not.

Cristina woke up and sat up abruptly.

"But... What are you doing here, in my bedroom?" Cristina recovered from her initial surprise and now, outraged, she confronted the intruder with a stormy expression.

Her husband's discomfort increased when, showing no sign of fear, she stood up and turned to the boy with a menacing frown.

"Don't do that, hon! He might shoot you!" and he tried to hold her back.

"Leave me be," the now furious Cristina slapped her husband's hand and addressed the intruder, "Give it me right now and stop making a spectacle of yourself." Cristina's voice was rising, she was clearly getting more worked up. "Did you hear me? Stop this right now! You're acting like a spoiled child."

"He killed my father," the girl—for it was not a boy, but Terri Kramer—motioned the pistol to indicate Robert. "And now I'm going to kill him."

"No, he didn't and you won't, you silly girl." Cristina stretched her arm and commanded, "Take your finger off the trigger and hand me the gun this instant." And as the girl hesitated, she added, "Your father almost killed my husband. His death was an accident. Give me the gun and we'll tell you the true story."

"You lie!" the girl screamed. "My mother told me how it happened."

Sensing the tension mounting, Cristina started to speak softly. "How could she know if she wasn't on the ship?" She saw the girl's hardened expression waver and, taking advantage of that momentary softening, she continued in a gentler tone, "Please, give us a chance to tell our side of the story. Hand me your gun, Terri," she pleaded.

The young woman's resolve was clearly wavering, but at that moment the door, that was left slightly ajar when the girl entered the room, opened and Quirino peeked in. Startled, Terri stepped back, tripped, and inadvertently gripped the trigger and the gun went off. A loud report resounded, made more preponderant in the relatively small room.

Cristina felt a sharp, burning pain. She heard Terri scream—only it seemed to come from far away. And that was strange, since she knew she had been standing quite near the girl. Everything seemed to be happening in slow motion. She looked down at her side where a red blot was forming on her pajama.

"How strange," she said out loud, an expression of amazement as she looked at the red stain, and the feeling of warm chocolate oozing down the side of her waist.

Cristina touched the red spot and looked at her fingers. Red. The color of blood. And suddenly everything sped up, scenes succeeded so fast she could barely understand them. She saw Robert shoot up from his bed. Why was he doing that? She was not falling, just floating in the air, a feather, an airborne speck of dust, so light.

"I'm tired," she whispered. "I think I'm going to sleep."

She reeled and Robert was beside her in an instant, holding her.

"No, no!" Robert screamed desperately. "Cristina! Cristina! Stay with me, princess! Please, please, babe!"

Cristina felt her husband's arms holding her against his chest, as one holds a baby. She smiled at his worried expression. Tears running down his cheeks, Robert choked back a sob. Anxiously, he looked at his wife's limp form in his arms. In horror he saw her eyes flutter and close, while her face slowly grew pale, and her lips became colorless. He turned wild eyes to the girl standing in front of him, a horrified expression on her face.

"You killed her," he uttered in a strangled voice, desperate, his eyes welling with tears. "Damn you!"

CHAPTER FORTY

Thus are things decreed by fate.
—Heraclitus.

Quirino rushed into the room and grabbed the pistol Terri, unnerved, had dropped to the floor. He shoved it in the pocket of the house coat Robert had lent him.

"Did you check her pulse?" he asked Robert, who, shaken, stood there, with the limp body of his wife in his arms. "Take a hold of yourself, man!" Quirino grabbed him by the shoulders and shook him. "Put her down on the bed and check her pulse!"

Blinded by tears, Robert squeezed his eyes shut. Things seemed unreal. It must be a dream, he thought. The light weight in his arms— that must be a nightmare. He looked at Quirino, as if coming out of a dream, and very gently deposited Cristina on his bed. Kneeling beside her he touched her neck with index and middle finger.

"She's alive," he told himself, then, turning to the other man, with a sense of urgency in his voice, "We must take her to a hospital."

"I'll go out and try to find a taxi and—"

He was cut by Terri who had come back from her stupor. "I have a car outside. Come!"

Robert quickly slipped in a housecoat. He wrapped Cristina with the bedcover, donned his slippers and, holding the light burden that was his wife, followed Terri. Quirino, also wearing a housecoat and shod, had already reached the front door, which he opened for them, following on their footsteps.

Outside, there was a car parked right in front of the gate, a four-door Chevrolet with the lights off. Robert was shocked to recognize the person at the wheel: it was Solange[44], a friend Cristina had not seen for several years. She had been married to Daniel Cabral—at the time under the assumed name of Francisco Ferreira. After Daniel's demise, Cristina had tried to locate her friend, but in vain.

Solange believed Robert had something to do with Daniel's death; and Terri's mother—Bunky's cousin Theresa Griffith and Solange's friend—believed Robert killed her husband. And now, there was Solange at the steering wheel of a car, waiting for Terri, he surmised, and no doubt the instigator of that almost tragedy. The two women were the instigators, the reason for the girl showing up in the middle of the night, pointing a gun at him. Despite his anguish, the irony of the situation was not lost on him: both Solange and Terri were going to help save his wife's life. Those thoughts passed through Robert's mind like a lightning bolt.

Terri ran to the car and yanked the back door open.

"What are you doing? What's going on?" asked Solange, stunned to see Robert carrying the unconscious Cristina. And as he entered the car, followed by Quirino, she yelled, "Get out of my car, now!"

Robert ignored her. Terri closed the back door and walking around to the driver's side, shoved the outraged, cursing Solange to the other seat. Grabbing the steering wheel, started the motor. "Shut up," the girl growled at Solange. The car jumped ahead and took off screeching. "Directions," she asked, addressing Robert.

The car fled through the deserted streets of Rio de Janeiro, but to Robert it seemed that they were crawling. Holding the light burden close to his heart he tried to pass his warmth, his life to her. He alternately implored and threatened the Deity, kissing his wife's cold, silent lips, her beautiful eyes that remained closed. He looked at her hands, holding them on his large ones—so small, but deceivingly strong.

Even before the car had completely stopped in front of the clinic, Robert threw open the car door and jumped out, holding his wife tight against his chest. He ran to the door and, his hands busy, he started kicking it. It was open by a sleepy looking, very young and very shocked nurse, who he unceremoniously pushed aside.

---

[44] Finding Cristina.

"Get the doctor immediately," he told the stunned woman in English.

Quirino, who followed Robert into the clinic, translated to Portuguese. "There was an accident," he added.

The nurse saw the blood that oozed on to the cover wrapped around the prostrated figure the tall man was holding, and quickly took them directly to the operating room. She left Robert placing his wife on the table. She explained to Quirino that the doctor was awake, monitoring a patient, and would be down directly, then went in search of Dr. Orlov.

A few anxious minutes passed until the doctor arrived, huffing and puffing. Furrowing his bushy eyebrows, he looked from Cristina's limp body on the table to Robert.

"What's this, what's this? Killed your wife, now! You madman," he continued, not understanding Robert's confused expression.

"Listen here, I did not shoot her, it was an accident," Robert tried to explain, now irritated by the man's mulishness.

Once again, Quirino interpreted the words for the doctor's benefit.

"Out, out! Everyone! Close door, nurse," Dr. Orlov shooed Robert and Quirino out of the room, and, unceremoniously pulling the nurse inside the room, slammed the door closed.

Less than one hour later the door of the operating room opened and the doctor came out to the corridor. Removing the face mask and surgical gloves, and brusquely throwing them to his assistant, he observed the three anxious faces. Robert, Quirino and Terri—who had refused to budge and had sent Solange packing. At the sight of him the three jumped up from their seats.

"Bullet went through, between spleen and stomach. Lucky, very lucky," said the taciturn Dr. Orlov, expressing himself in English, with a very heavy accent, not caring if the other two understood him. He gave Robert a menacing look and wagging an accusatory finger at him, admonished, "No shooting your wife anymore or I'll call police."

"I tried to explain to you that I didn't shoot my wife—I love her, I'd die for her," which elicited an approving head shake from the doctor. "It was an accident."

"Cristina will have difficult sitting up—"

"Difficulty," Robert corrected.

"Yes, as I said! She'll have difficult sitting up, until muscles heal. I gave her a sedative, very mild. She's awake, but don't bother her. I'll go see my other patient and will return in," he checked his watch, "half hour." He then bowed slightly to the three assembled in the corridor and started to walk away.

"God be wi' you: let's meet as little as we can," Robert muttered.

"What?" the doctor asked turning his head back, an eyebrow raised in disapproval, not recognizing the quotation from Shakespeare's play.

"Just thinking out loud," Robert explained, with an impudent smile.

"Very peculiar man!" the doctor told himself. He shook his head in disapproval, turned his back to them once more, and, without a second thought, left to see his patients.

"My cousin—Harry—he'll kill me when he hears what happened," Terri said, then added, for Robert's benefit, "He's head over heels in love with your wife, you know."

"Yeah, I know," he inclined his head in agreement. "She tends to have this effect on most men. Not her fault, though."

CHAPTER FORTY-ONE

You've no conception of the mistakes my mother may be making.
—Lord Peter Wimsey in Whose Body?, Dorothy L. Sayers. 1923.

Cristina moaned and opened her eyes. The first thing she saw was her husband's face close to hers. His eyes looked so bright—brighter than she had ever seen. He smiled and it was like a sun coming into the dark room. She looked around and realized it was not her bedroom.

"Good morning, princess. Are you hungry?"

She tried to sit up and felt a sharp stab on her left side that made her fall back.

"Ouch! What's this?" she asked, pushing the sheets down to look at her body to find a bandage under the gown.

"You don't remember?"

She frowned and looked at her husband, confused. Then all of a sudden, the memory of the prior night's events became clear to her mind—Terri, the pistol, a shot.

"She shot me!" and she looked at Robert, shocked.

"Yup. D'ya want me to kill her, babe?"

"No: I'll do it! That little cow actually shot me!" Another ouch when she tried to sit up again.

"Language, young lady. Dr. Orlov forbids. Don't incur his rath or he will use knout on your derrière," he emulated the doctor's accent.

"Don't make me laugh. It hurts when I laugh."

"My poor little darling. What can I do to make you feel better? What about a kiss?" and he passed from word to action. "Feel better?"

"Get some pillows and help me sit up."

Robert found a couple of extra pillows in the closet. He carefully pulled his wife with one hand to a sitting position, while with the other hand he placed the pillows behind her. She sat back with a little grunt of pain.

"Is that little, er, is Terri here by any chance? I'd like to talk to her," Cristina said with a severe expression.

"I can see you're feeling yourself already—I recognize the militant air. Good news! And yes, the wench's here. I'll fetch her for you this instant, mon général," he saluted and added before he went out to do her bidding, "I am sure you remember that murder is still illegal in Brazil." He shook his head, and shrugged his shoulders. "Strange people, I know, but, well, there you have it: no killing. So, limit yourself to a good verbal thrashing," and with that advice he left.

Terri came in. A penitent expression on her pallid face, eyes cast down, she stood silently beside Cristina's bed, waiting.

"What happened, Terri? Just a few days ago we said our goodbyes on friendly terms. What changed?"

"I'm sorry," the girl mumbled.

"Not good enough," Cristina told her, searching the other's face with earnest gravity. "Something happened that affected you so much that you invaded my house in the middle of the night to kill my husband. I want to know what happened!"

"Someone told me about my father's death[45]; confirmed my mother's story... that I always doubted. That's what happened," she finished, defiantly.

"Who was it? Someone who was on the boat?" Cristina waited a few seconds and as Terri did not answer, she added, "Only two people witnessed what happened. The cook and a friend of your father—a shady character who jumped ship at the first opportunity, and sent your mother a telegram telling a pack of lies. And my husband reported your father's death to the authorities as soon as the ship arrived at the next

---

[45] Finding Cristina: A New Life

harbor." She scrutinized the other's pinched face and insisted, "Who was it, Terri?"

"Solange."

"Of course! I should have known she'd be behind this," Cristina said under her breath.

"She hounded me for two days with her stories. At the end I was so raw I was ready to do anything!" The words came tumbling out of Terri.

"I didn't think you were the kind who could be easily convinced to commit a crime…"

"And she showed me the article in the paper," Terri continued, disregarding Cristina's comment. "There was a big scandal involving her husband and my father. Drugs were found in my father's tramp, but Solange said they were planted."

"Of course she'd say that!" Cristina exclaimed, losing patience. "Solange was not on the ship, Terri! And she holds a grudge against my husband for something he didn't do."

"He killed her husband too," was Terri's aggressive remark. "Even if indirectly," she added giving Cristina a defiant glance. "Francisco Teixeira—her husband—committed suicide and left her, pregnant, alone and without a penny. Mother, of course helped her—opened a music store for her to manage here in Rio. And when the child died at birth Solange almost went crazy with grief and mother took her to Germany for a while. And when she was feeling better, she came back to Rio. But she's not over what happened, never will be. And I do understand her!"

Cristina let the girl talk, spill all her frustration and confusion, until she thought Terri had said all she wanted. She sighed heavily, which caused pain. She was too upset at having to touch that subject after so many years, but there was no way around it if she wanted to clear the mess the young woman had been fed.

"Bring that chair here; I need to tell you a story." She waited until Terri was seated beside the bed to continue. "Several years ago, Daniel—that was Solange's husband's real name: Daniel Cabral. He tried to force me to marry him using blackmail."

She recounted the whole story to Terri. At least the story she knew, since she was never privy to the real identity of the man who gave Daniel the means to blackmail her: Alexandre Rebelo de Oliveira, the father who Cristina and her mother, Helena, still believed died before she was born. What she told Terri was the official version. The facts related to Daniel's frustrated blackmail were only known to Robert, his father, John Laughton, Bunky, and Sonya Abramov.

"Thank God I escaped his clutches," Cristina told Terri. "After that no one heard from him, until he reappeared, wearing a disguise, with a different name, married to Solange. The last time I saw him I was with Solange; he told me—right in front of her—that he had married her to get back at me by making her suffer."

Terri seemed troubled and Cristina knew she would feel worse at the end of this meeting.

"I am sorry, but you need to know: your father and Daniel were trafficking drugs. Daniel shanghaied Robert and took him to your father's ship—with your father's consent." She pitied the suffering she was inflicting on the girl, but someone had to tell her the truth for once and for all.

She told Terri how her father had gotten the ship's owner, Captain Taylor, drunk and, cheating at a game of poker, won the ship; the story had been told Robert by Taylor's son, Kaleb, who was among the ship's crew. How Robert won the ship back by the same means—a poker game, straight this time—and returned it to Captain Taylor. And how afterwards Terri's father, knife in hand, had charged madly at Robert who had been leaning on the ship's rail. Taken by surprise, her husband tripped on some ropes, and fell on the deck, that way avoiding the strike. But Captain Kramer lost his balance and toppled over the rail into the sea.

"All this can be confirmed with the people involved if you're ever interested. Robert has kept in touch with most of them."

Terri got up, turned around and stood there, in silence, facing the lace curtains on the window softly brushed by the outside breeze. The morning sun had been slowly making its appearance. The world kept turning on its axis, evolving around the sun. Life and time did not stop, but pushed ahead and a new day had already started. For a long time, she had suspected her father of illicit commerce. His ships, their routes, could not bring so much money. But she stuck to her studies, turning a blind eye to his possibly shady business. Besides, it troubled her that both her parents were associated with that lunatic, Hitler. Last year she and Harry had practically escaped Germany, to avoid their parents' insistence that they joined the Socialists, Adolf Hitler's party; now that he had been appointed Chancellor, God only knew what that man would do. And then there was Solange—who seemed so disgruntled at times, with her passionate entreaties for vengeance. But after hearing Cristina it was hard to believe Solange's claims. Cristina's explanation no longer seemed absurd. The facts she related seemed quite likely and were all falling neatly into place.

"Was your visit to Bagé connected to all this? Where you and Harry there with some purpose?"

Contrite, Terri turned to Cristina and agreed with a headshake. "I wanted to meet you and your husband. To see how horrible you both were—just like my mother and Solange both kept saying you were." She shook her head, despairingly, "I saw you. I discreetly asked people about you and your family. Then you and I spent some time in Porto Alegre. My beliefs were shaken by then. But when I got here Solange wouldn't let go, constantly droning her story on me, hour after hour, until I thought I'd go mad. Now that I heard you, my thoughts are finally clear. And to tell you the truth, I think Solange's unbalanced." She shook her head, upset. "The worse is that my mother knew all my father's business very well. They were partners with Francisco—I mean, Daniel. I know it's lame, but I felt I must be on her side. You need to understand that it's hard to believe one's parents are, well, crooked. I can't explain better. I can only beg your forgiveness."

"So, no more shooting?" Cristina asked her lightly, trying to dispel the heavy atmosphere.

"I promise," the girl smiled back and shook the hand the other offered.

Robert and Quirino were waiting in the corridor when Terri left Cristina's room. Robert gingerly opened the door of his wife's room and peeked inside. Cristina was laying in the same position he had left her, a satisfied expression on her face.

"What's the score, princess? Brazil one, Germany zero?"

CHAPTER FORTY-TWO

[T]he plays of children are not performed in play, but are to be judged in them
as their most serious actions.
—Essays, Michel de Montaigne.

I t was the afternoon of the day Robert had gone to Bagé to look for news of Cristina and ended up on a plane with Quirino Robaina, on his way to Rio de Janeiro.

On the farm, the late afternoon sky was an angry mix of blazing red, pink and purple, where a few deep mauve clouds seemed to be fighting to hide the dying sun. It had rained copiously, starting late the prior night, ending an hour or so after noon. The air had stayed cool, impregnated with the pungent scent of the soaked earth.

"Where are those brats?" Bunky said. He and Maria scanned the horizon, straining their eyes as if the effort would bring Donny and Annie into view.

He and his wife were standing beyond the wall of the kitchen garden. Beside them stood Bacon. His ears up, little eyes attentively fixed ahead, the dog knew something was amiss; his young master's absence rendered him restless. He turned to Bunky and barked a few times, as if asking for some action.

When Alcina joined them, they were speaking in English, a language she was somewhat conversant, but understood enough to realize what the subject was.

"You know how they are," Maria tried to assure her husband, hiding her concern behind a calm façade. "They don't understand the concept of time as we do; they're children." She turned to Alcina, "We're talking

189

about Donny and Annie," to which Alcina assented understanding. "They didn't return and we're getting a bit nervous."

"I noticed that when they didn't show up for the meals."

"I don't like that. Donny never stayed out that long, not even after his cousin arrived. He might stay out one night, but he'd be home for breakfast. The little stinker wouldn't miss it for the world. You know how he enjoys his meals," Bunky smiled at the thought, then his expression clouded again. "And his father left without giving a second thought to his son!"

"Now, that's not fair, Erastus!" Maria was the only person who called Bunky by his Christian name. "You know how concerned with Cristina he was. And we haven't heard from her yet, remember? I saw him when Alcina and I went to milk the cows, before he left. He said he'd been to both Donny and Annie's rooms and they were not there. He was not worried, because Donny has stayed out sometimes, as you yourself just said," and she gave her husband a severe look.

Max joined the three.

"How's Desiree?" Bunky asked.

"I gave her something to calm her down, and she's in bed," he said and took a deep breath.

His wife had taken the long absence of the children very hard. Max knew Desiree never fully recovered from the loss of her parents and brother Ricky. She regained much of her balance when she met Max, whose sister was Ricky's fiancée, but the scar was there, latent, and never completely healed. Since learning of the children not returning, she had spiraled down, back to the days when, desperate, she sought oblivion in a wild, dissipated existence. Max was able to soothe her and, after giving her a mild sedative, stayed with her for a while, and only left when her regular breathing meant she was asleep.

"I say, this seems rather a storm in a teacup." And as Bunky turned a shocked face to him, Max elaborated, "Have you been to the neighboring farms?" And at the other's surprised look, he added, "I thought so. Let's send the hands to the farms. They can go on horseback and we can use the motorcars. If we divide up, we can cover a wide area more quickly."

They were about to put Max suggestions into practice when they saw Cristina's car being driven up to the garage. Following him was Aparício França's car.

"I guess Robert got news from Cristina," said Maria, naturally assuming it was Robert driving Cristina's car, and that he had not gone to Rio. "But what is Aparício doing here?"

"Probably snatching dinner—again!"

"Don't be like that," Maria told her husband and lightly elbowed him in the ribs.

The four stood there waiting for Robert, but it was the police chief who they saw walking out of the garage. Noticing Bunky, Maria, Alcina and Max standing together, Aparício walked to his car, and, telling Ezequiel to wait for him, went to join them.

"We thought it was Robert driving back from the airdrome," Maria told Aparício. "He must have gone to Rio too," a comment the police chief confirmed, and explained that Robert had done so with a friend who owned an airplane. "So, who's that, driving your car?"

"It's Ezequiel. Is something amiss?" Aparício asked her, noticing their tense expressions.

Maria told him their concern for the children's absence and the plan to search for them.

"I think it's a good idea. I'll get my car and we can split the farm between us. Did you talk to the hands already? No? I can drive to the field and tell them to start the search while you go your way."

And so, they started in different directions, anxious, in search of Donny and Annie.

CHAPTER FORTY-THREE

Tis said they're witches every one,
The women of the gipsy race;
And all men may too plainly see
That thou hast witchcraft in thy face.
—The Little Gipsy Girl in The Exemplary Novels of Miguel de Cervantes Saavedra. Translated from the Spanish by Walter Kelly. 1881.

U pon discovery of the missing rope, Annie went into a frenzy of screaming—first cursing the evil one who perpetrated the deed, then calling for help until she got hoarse. Donny tried, but unable to make her stop, let the crisis take its course. At the end of half an hour she fell asleep, exhausted. The pain in his shoulder was intense and kept the boy awake, but he finally dosed for a few hours. He woke up to a pitch-dark night. He was thirsty, but to reach the canteen he would have to disturb his cousin, and he did not want to wake her up. He fell into a light sleep, but thirst woke him up again. Day light was filtering through the well. He looked at his watch, but it had stopped, broken when he fell. Trying not to disturb Annie, he reached for the canteen, but a stab in his shoulder made him moan in pain.

The girl sat up, groggy with sleep. She rubbed her eyes and, looking around wide awake, remembered where they were.

"No one will find us," she moaned.

"Of course they will! Someone might come over to change the flowers. They do that all the time."

"You know that isn't true. The padre is gone to Pelotas to visit a sick relative, and there won't be mass this Sunday. Today is Tuesday. No one will know where we are. We'll be dead from thirst and starvation when they find us." She reached for the canteen and shook it. "Nothing left. I poured water in the kerchief when I tried to wake you."

"You couldn't know someone would remove the rope. You were very brave coming down without help, just to see if I was alive."

"I'm not a baby! And I'm not afraid!" An incongruent statement, considering how she fell into a crying and screaming fit just a few hours prior.

Donny made no comment, realizing nothing would be gained by starting an argument. He knew her assessment was correct, but he refused to give in to despair. Something would happen!

Annie opened her haversack and turned it upside down, letting the contents spread on the ground. It was a mishmash of items: a little roll of string, some marbles, a pocket-knife, a rumpled little handkerchief, a mismatched sock; a chunk of cheese, another of ham wrapped in brown paper and a little bag with leftover sunflower seeds; coins; one small fork; a couple of candle stubs and a half-full matchbox; a tiny metal compact that opened when it fell from the bag, revealing a Richard Hudnut vanity containing rouge, powder and a lipstick tube with mirror.

"What? Cosmetics! Were you expecting to meet your boyfriend?" he teased her and got an evil look in response. "Does aunt Desiree know you keep makeup in your bag?" And that comment the girl ignored.

The last thing to come tumbling down was a well-worn book.

"So, that's where it is," said Donny, holding his copy of the Hardy Boys' The Tower Treasure, and looking at the girl askance.

"I was not going to steal it! If I was, it wouldn't be in my haversack, would it?" she said, making a face, then sticking her tongue out at him.

"And what did you plan to do with one sock?"

"Obviously I lost the other, Sherlock!"

Suddenly raising a finger to his lips, Donny bade his cousin still. "Listen," he whispered.

In the silence that ensued they heard a cooing.

"Princesa!" Annie almost screamed, excited. "Call her, Donny!"

"What for? D'you want more company?"

"Just call her," the girl insisted. "I've got an idea, and I need her." That said she started to unzip the pockets from her haversack, until she found a little notebook with an attached pencil stub, which she handed to her cousin.

"What's this for? Do you think the pigeon can write?" he asked her, amused.

"'Course not, dummy! Just keep calling her."

Attracted by the boy's entreaties, Princesa approached the opening of the well. They could see her little head peeping down. Annie quickly emptied the little bag of seeds in the palm of her hand and, raising it, called the bird. "Here, Princesa, sunflower seeds!" she offered to no result. "Why doesn't she come down?"

"She speaks Portuguese, not English, dummy!" That said the boy proceeded to offer 'sementes de girasol' to the attentive pigeon and it was soon pecking on the girl's outstretched hand.

"Get the notebook and write this in Portuguese: Help! We fell in the well, in the chapel! And use exclamation marks—don't argue!"

Annie handed the bird to Donny. Taking the notebook from him, she tore the page where he wrote the message, and proceeded to fold it until it was a narrow, oblong piece. She cut a piece of string and, while Donny held the bird the girl dexterously wrapped the paper around its little leg, and tied it with the string, making sure it was secure.

"Let her go now."

They watched the bird fly up, go through the well opening and listened until the flapping of the wings could no longer be heard.

"Now let's hope someone on the farm sees the message." The girl heaved a sigh.

In the gypsy encampment the caravan was gone, but one cart stayed behind. That of Hilário and Dolores de Torres. Their four-year-old son, Inácio, was sick and they did not want to risk a relapse by taking the child on a long trip to the next campground camp. The shaking of the wagon might prove too much for the still frail boy. And so, they stayed behind, planning to join the rest of their people as soon as the child recovered.

Hilário had been especially restless; having none of his people around for several days, he missed their company—Romani, members of their caravan, who he had known since he was born. For Dolores it was different. She kept busy taking care of their son, cooking, washing. Bored, he went outside, sat down in front of the fire, added more wood and poked it with a stick. He turned his attention to cleaning his muzzleloader. It had served him well, as it did his father before him. He primed it and loaded the rifle. Then he decided to find something to shoot—perhaps a nice, juicy partridge. He knew Dolores fairy hands could turn it in to a delicious stew—Perdiz Ensopada.

Leaking his lips in hopes of a lavish dinner, he got up and started scanning his surroundings. Dolores joined him.

"Going to get some carqueja and camomila[46] for our boy. Whatcha doing with this weapon? Dontcha start shooting, 'cause you might hit me!"

"Go on wit ya, woman! Go get your herbs and go do your spells. Leave me be."

Suddenly a bird in the sky attracted his attention.

"What about a juicy pigeon, eh?" He smiled at his wife, then pointed the rifle and aimed.

The sound of the explosion mixed with that of Dolores scream. She had jumped at the gun and, slamming the barrel down, diverted the shot. The bullet missed the bird and hit a stone not too far from where they stood.

"Why didja do that for?" the enraged man asked her.

"But that pigeon belongs to the lady Cristina!" She saw him blanch at that statement. "Can you imagine if you kilt it? Every year these nice people let us stay here as long as we wants." She was trembling. The tragedy averted, her legs felt weak and she had to sit down on one of the large stones encircling the fire, that served as stools.

Hilário dropped down next to his wife, unable to speak. He looked up. The pigeon was just a tiny white smudge in the horizon. He thanked God for no mean blessing.

---

[46] Respectively *Baccharis trimera* and *Matricaria chamomilla*.

CHAPTER FORTY-FOUR

Prayer is innocence's friend; and willingly flieth incessant
'Twist the earth and the sky, the carrier-pigeon of heaven.
—The Children of the Lord's Supper, Esaias Tegnér, 1820.

Uncle Benê sat by the open door of his house, enjoying his corn cob pipe, with half-closed eyes. The day was coming to a close and light was slowly fading. The old man never tired of watching the coxilhas, the undulating prairies with herbaceous and grassy vegetation. He had lived there his whole life and found the joy of watching his surroundings renewed every day. God had granted him the eyes to enjoy nature He created. Benedito felt he was a part of that perfect universe, a small grain of sand in the majesty of Creation.

Suddenly a ruffling of feathers to his right attracted his attention. A white pigeon had landed on the windowsill.

"Princesa," uncle Benê called and stretched his right arm, invitingly. "Come to me, my dear," and he made clucking sounds that were answered in the bird's own language.

He held the cooing bird on his hand and gently patted its little white head. The pigeon closed its little red eyes, gladly surrendering to his caresses. As he kissed its little head, he noticed something on Princesa's leg.

"What's this, Princesa?" and he proceeded to remove the note and read it out loud, "Help! We fell in the well in the chapel!" The old man thought for a few seconds, intrigued by what he had just read. Suddenly he realized it was a childish scrawling. "The children," he told himself, alarmed. "A well in the chapel... May God keep the kids until we can get to them." He turned to his pet, "Good job, my dear. Now, let's go to the house and tell them about this message."

In his haste, he quickly emptied the spent pipe, getting up as fast as his old body allowed him. Then, with the pigeon sitting on his shoulder, he lumbered to the big house. The place was in darkness. He knocked at the kitchen door and waited. No answer. Where would everyone be? He tried the door handle, which he knew would be unlocked.

Before entering the kitchen, he sent the pigeon away. "Go to the coop, Princesa. It's time you be sleeping."

He watched the bird fly away then entered the kitchen, turned the light on and checked the stove. He revived the cinders and prepared some coffee, then sat on the old rocking chair to wait. Time passed slowly. His coffee finished he filled the bowl of his pipe. His tamper had been left behind, so he pressed the tobacco with his thumb, repeating the process until the pipe was two thirds full. He gave it a few test puffs to make sure air would flow freely. He struck a match, waited for the sulfur to burn off, then applied it to the bowl, while gently drawing. He sat back, slowly rocking the chair, and took little puffs of smoke, savoring the flavor of the tobacco. The crackling of the fire was soothing and not long afterwards, the pipe again spent, he fell asleep.

Uncle Benê woke up with a start, to the sound of cars parking near the kitchen, and car doors being slammed; people's voices. He got up from the chair with difficulty—his joints were especially painful at night, with the higher humidity. Peering through the window he could see several people; in the darkness they were just silhouettes, but he recognized their approaching shapes—the huge one was Bunky, then the much shorter ones were Maria and Alcina; a slim shape must be the British gent. Two others were unknown to him, until he realized it was Aparício and one of his henchmen.

Having seen light in the kitchen they burst in, Max being the first, the others following on his heels. Their excitement immediately gave way to dismay when they saw that, instead of the children, it was Uncle Benê. They had been so worried and tense, none of them thought it unusual to find Benedito in the kitchen. Before he could convey the message from the little note Princesa had brought, Desiree burst into the room, coming from the bedroom upstairs. Her bleary eyes told of the efficacy of the sleeping draught Max had given her earlier. Not seeing the children with the adults, she wailed, "Where's my daughter?"

To the old man there was no need to translate her words into Portuguese. Her question was obvious. Max held her in his arms and started to whisper calming words.

"Miss Cina," the old man addressed Alcina, "Princesa brought a message earlier. It was wrapped in her little leg. I didn't know where everyone was, but from the message I reckoned you'd be searching for the young'uns." At this point he realized they did not understand the meaning of his words. "You better read this, Miss Cina. You'll understand and'll be able to explain in them for'ner's tongue." He handed the little crumpled strip of paper to the young woman. Then gently patted her face and smiled, adding, "Everythink will be fine. Tell that to little Miss Annie's mama," and he turned to indicate Desiree, "that her li'l 'un is fine—them both are fine. Go with the blessings of our Savior." That saying, he left.

With trembling fingers Alcina handed the message to Maria and asked her to translate it and the old man's assurances to the benefit of Desiree, Max, and Bunky. Desiree started crying, thanking the Heavens. She wanted to run after the old man to thank him, to find the pigeon and lavish the little animal with caresses, but she could only cry with joy.

CHAPTER FORTY-FIVE

Most Americanists, however, emphasize the gaucho's mestizo heritage—a racial
and cultural blending of Indian and Spanish components on the pampean frontier.
  —Gauchos and the Vanishing Frontier, Richard W. Slatta. 1983.

There was a frenzy to see who could get to the door first, but Desiree's motherly instincts gave her wings and she burst out, running ahead of everyone. It was all Max could do to stop her from jumping into the police chief's car and taking off.

"This is Aparício's car, m'dear," he told her while holding her, then almost running along with her to the garage, to where the farm's car was parked.

"I am driving!" she anxiously told her husband. "Let's go, for God's sake, let's not dally here any longer!"

"Let Bunky drive. No, listen," he turned her to face him, holding her by the shoulders, "he knows the farm better than you and can get there faster in the twilight. And we want to find them as quickly as possible, isn't that so?"

Desiree took a deep breath. She assented with her head in agreement and silently joined her husband in the back seat of the car.

"I'll stay here. It will be too crowded in the car, with the kids," Alcina told them.

She stepped back. The police chief joined her and stayed also, in the eventuality that the message was a hoax and the children showed up. Together with Ezequiel, the two watched the car drive away.

199

There was still some light on the horizon—a long, inflamed red scar inflicted on the last vestiges of faded blue while darkness started to very slowly take over. The headlights shone through the low, furry grass, revealing the landscape. There was just a dirt track to follow, and the rough terrain made the going slower than they wished. Conversation was made impossible as they were jolted against one another—not that any of them felt like communicating their anguish.

Holding the wheel, his knuckles white, was Bunky. Unconsciously he was aware of the tense silence of the other occupants. Maria was at his side, Bacon sitting at her feet; the dog had sneaked into the car and he growled menacingly and showed his white, sharp fangs at any attempt to remove him. On the back sat Max and Desiree.

Bunky focused on the rough path ahead. He inwardly cursed the geography of the place; the absence of lamp posts; the liberty children were so naturally awarded in a farm environment. But he, who had instantly fallen in love with the farm, could understand how the very nature of the place was even more inviting to children, as it was to adults. The wide landscape of gently succeeding hills ended at the horizon, far away. It had a wild beauty: the flat grassy areas sparingly dotted with clusters of trees; the little rivulets that cut the lush pastures where grazed horses, cows, and sheep; the wild animals that inhabited the Pampas—jaguatiricas, anteaters, rheas, deer, armadillos, and joão-de-barro, the bird that lived in clay houses it built—all so different from what he had known. Yet he loved it as if he was a child of that rugged land. He felt integrated, a part of it; it was his home now and it would be forever.

But none of this came to his mind while he crossed the coxilhas as fast as the irregularities of the terrain would allow and the car could run. It was darker now and after a nerve-wracking twenty-minute driving, the little hill where stood the chapel became visible. A sob was heard coming from the back of the car.

"We are almost there, dear," Maria turned back and patted Desiree's hand, trying to comfort her. "They will be fine. You understood what Uncle Benê said, didn't you?" And at the other's agreement, she continued, "He has never erred. Have faith."

The car laboriously drove up the hill to the front of the chapel. It was in the dark and the door was closed. Desiree jumped out of the car even before it stopped. Following in her footsteps was Bacon, pricked ears, a dog clearly on a mission. In a frenzy Desiree opened the chapel's door and, not waiting for anyone else, ran inside the dark building. The dog darted pass her and disappeared in the darkness. Her footsteps echoed in the silence and she stopped, uncertain.

"Annie, Donny!" she screamed, sobbing, while tears ran down her face. That was followed by Bacon's fierce barking.

"Aunt Desiree, stop! Don't move!" That was Donny's voice coming from the front of the chapel, where the altar was located. "There is a hole in the floor, you might fall!"

"Stop, mommy!" cried Annie. "We're lighting our flashlight. Can you see it?"

By now the others had entered the chapel. Maria, hearing the children's warning, took a stern hold of Desiree's arm, fearing that she would take off despite the children's cautioning. "I can see a weak beam of light coming from the altar. From the floor, it seems," Maria said, confused, then, turning to her husband, "Erastus, throw some light ahead of us. It's coming from near the altar," she repeated for his benefit.

Bunky waved the flashlight around. The small sanctuary seemed so much bigger; the walls concealed in darkness contributed to the illusion. He focused the beam on the floor and started to slowly walk forward. Now they could discern Bacon, a light smudge ahead. The dog was standing on the left side of the altar—which seemed unusually off-centered—looking down on the floor. He turned to them, then to whatever he saw on the floor, jumping up and down repeatedly, while barking.

"Oh, my God!" whispered Desiree, horrified, when they got to the altar and looked down from the edge of a wide opening—a hole.

She stood grounded to the floor. She was quickly joined by the others and they beheld the scene, dumbfounded. Several feet down, their little faces turned up, hands protecting the eyes from the light beam from Bunky's flashlight, where Donny and Annie.

"Are you all right?"

Bunky's baritone voice cut the silence that had momentarily fallen so sharply, making Maria and Alcina jump, "Are you all right, children?"

"We're fine," the boy answered. "I just dislocated my shoulder. But we're fine," he added quickly.

Desiree's legs gave way and she dropped to her knees, while emitting a deep sigh of relief, almost a sob. Bacon restarted barking and, suddenly, everyone was speaking at the same time. The tension that held them since they left the farm, suddenly dissolved—a damn washed away by the relief they all felt. The adults repeatedly asked if the children were well; the two little explorers tried to convey their woes; and Bacon emitted low growls and squeals, pacing around the edge of the well, as if calculating the feasibility of covering the distance between him and the children.

"Silence," boomed Bunky. Having attained the result he wanted, he asked the children, "How did you get down there?"

"There's a rope up there," Annie answered. "We used it to get down here."

Bunky shone the light in several directions, but saw no rope, which he conveyed to the children.

"There is one," the girl countered on the verge of tears. "At least there was one yesterday, until someone pulled it away..."

"Pulled it away?" Bunky was shocked. "Why should anyone do that? Never mind," he added, and clenching his fist, "I'll find the bast—I mean, the culprit later. Right now, we need a long rope."

"Should you go back to the farm to get one?" Max asked.

"No," Bunky answered after briefly hesitating. "We passed the house of Policarpo Rodriguez on the way here. He's Alpídio's grandad," he explained. "I'll drive there. He's bound to have a rope." And without waiting for an answer, he ran out of the chapel.

The sound of the car motor echoed inside the chapel, and then it was gone. The silence was so complete it felt oppressive after the tumult of a few minutes ago. Unnerved, Desiree started asking questions to the children.

"What possessed you to move this?" she pointed at the stone that had been moved to reveal the opening on the chapel's floor. And although the children were down several feet and could not see at what she was pointing, they knew exactly what she meant.

"Oh, mom, not now," Annie moaned. "It's a long story. Can we tell you tomorrow?" the girl pleaded.

"We have time right now: Bunky went to procure a cord, so go ahead and start your story," was her father's answer.

This time Annie merely nudged her cousin, implying that it was his turn to talk.

"We wanted to find the treasure," he said, sheepishly.

The startled adults stared at each other, uncomprehendingly.

"Treasure? What treasure?" asked the bemused Desiree. "What are you talking about?"

CHAPTER FORTY-SIX

*Boleadeiras: [Adapt. from Span. Plat. boleadoras] N. f. pl. Braz., RS. device
used by gaúchos to lasso animals, or as a weapon of war, consisting of three balls (of
iron, stone or ivory) wrapped in thick leather and linked together by leather ropes,
two of which are of equal size, the third being smaller, called manica or manicia, is
the one the boleador wields to handle the set.*
—Novo Dicionário Aurélio da Língua Portuguesa. Editora Nova
Fronteira. 1986.

"Can we have some water first, dad? We're parched."

"Of course, darling," Desiree answered and, turning to her husband, instructed him to get the vase from the altar, throw away the dried-out flowers, and bring water from the river. "And make sure you wash it well before you fill it with water." And since he did not move, but just looked at her amused, she asked, "What are you waiting for?"

"How are we supposed to get that vase down to them, old gal?"

She took a few seconds to answer. "When they come out of that hole, we better have water for them, so, off you go!"

Even before he got out of the car, Bunky could hear the radio blasting music. Old Policarpo Rodriguez, whose hearing had been failing lately, was enjoying a transmission from his native Uruguay. Tango music came to him directly from Montevideo's Grand Splendid Theatre, via the Rádio El Día. For years Policarpo had dreamed of owning a radio. He had saved every penny he could spare, and, with the help of Alpídio, his grandson, had amassed a considerable sum. But it would be a few years before he had the necessary amount. Learning of the old man's yearning, Robert offered to help. Policarpo thanked him, but said he could not accept. Robert gave it some thought and made a proposition. Knowing the old farmhand was also an expert cobbler, he suggested he paid his debt by fixing the farmhands' gear and boots. The old man accepted. Fond of Donny, Policarpo had taught him how to make rawhide ropes, and even how to mend his little boots.

Bunky had to bang on the door several times until the radio was turned off. He heard the old man's shuffling steps while he muttered at the tardiness of the hour and the lack of consideration of some folk, who came banging at the door of honest people's homes. The door was thrown open and the old man stood there, a scowl on his face—until he recognized Bunky's massive stature.

"Good evenin', Mr. Bunky! Come in, come in, please. I'm just enjoying some music from my country."

When anxious, Bunky was prone to have difficulty expressing himself in Portuguese, and at that moment, when he most needed, he had drawn an absolute blank. He stood there, sweat pouring from his bald pate down his temples, anxiously trying to convey it in Portuguese, but, unable to remember the word, kept repeating, "Rope, rope!"

Frightened by that odd behavior, the poor old man started to slowly back up into the house, trying to close the door. But Bunky put his foot down, holding it open, and mimicked throwing a rope.

"Oh, I see! You want my boleadeiras," and Policarpo opened a toothless smile and pointed at the wall behind him.

From a hook hung, coiled, a long rope made of braided rawhide straps with three rounded stones bound at one end. The rope had been changed innumerous times, but the stones were original. They had passed to the next generations by Policarpo's grandfather, Karai, a Pampeano Indian who was originally from the region that later fragmented into the countries of Uruguay and Argentina. Karai's grandson had inherited his tall stature and athletic bearing; the characteristic high cheekbones, aquiline nose, and prominent chin, as well as the dark eyes, and straight bristle hair of that almost extinct race.

"No, no," said Bunky, now in desperation. And that was when the word miraculously popped into his mind, "Corda!" And the relief he felt at having remembered the word in Portuguese was perfectly expressed in the way he vocalized that single word: rope.

A few minutes later he was driving back with a couple of coils of sturdy rope, leaving behind a bemused Policarpo.

"For'ners," the old man mused, scratching his head. "Looking for ropes in the dark of night." As he started to close the door, a terrible thought occurred to him: what if the man wanted the rope to hang himself? He looked pretty desperate. Well, if that was the case, it was too late now. And shrugging his shoulders he went back to his radio. Nothing like a good tango to clear the mind.

In record time—less than fifteen minutes—Bunky had gone and returned from his errand. He burst into the chapel carrying the coils of rope on his shoulders.

"Finally! Hurry, please!" Desiree begged, barely able to contain herself.

Bunky set to work. He made a large loop on one end of one rope; he tested it and decided it was strong enough to hold the light weight of the children. He then lowered it and explained to Donny and Annie how to use the rope.

"Put it around you as if it were a swing, d'you understand? And hold tight while we pull you up. On the way up you'll have to push your feet against the walls, to keep you away from it so you won't get scratched."

When the rope reached the children, an argument started, to decide who would go up first. Annie insisted that, since he was hurt, Donny should be first. He argued that, since she was a girl, she should be the first to be lifted. At the end a decision was arrived by playing rock-paper-scissor. Donny's paper wrapped a very annoyed Annie's rock. She grudgingly got the rope and followed Bunky's instructions. She held the rope tight, both hands above her head.

"I'm ready, uncle Bunky."

He looked down and saw Annie's little face turned up, illuminated by the flash light. He prayed the girl would hold tight.

Max rushed in with the water and, leaving it on the floor nearby, went to help Bunky.

"We're starting to pull now," Bunky warned the girl. "Just hold tight and make sure you use your feet to stay away from the wall, OK?"

Upon her assenting he and Max started to slowly work the rope. Desiree's hand was too shaky, so Maria held the flashlight. They could hear the girl's shoes scraping the surface of the well, until her head appeared on the surface and Desiree, grabbing the child under her arms, pulled her out, holding her so tight the girl protested.

"You're suffocating me, mommy!"

"And I should be spanking you, instead of hugging." Desiree's face was washed with tears. She smiled and cried alternately.

Bacon, happy at seeing his playmate again, covered her with dog kisses.

Because of his dislocated shoulder, Donny was a more difficult enterprise. Still, he was able to use the rope the way his cousin did, but had only one hand to hold it. Stifling moans of pain, he finally made to the top of the well, where Maria and Desiree helped him out, and Bacon howled and jumped around joyfully.

The adults decided that it would be wiser to question the children about their escapade when they got home. But by the time the car stopped near the kitchen door, the two treasure hunters were deep asleep. They told their story the following day, omitting the finding of the Templar ring; that, they had decided during the night, would be their secret.

CHAPTER FORTY-SEVEN

And on his brest a bloudie Crosse he bore,
The deare remembrance of his dying Lord,
For whose sweete sake that glorious badge he wore,
And dead as living ever him ador'd:
Upon his shield the like was also scor'd,
For soveraine hope, which in his helpe he had:
Right faithfull true he was in deede and word,
But of his cheere did seeme too solemne sad;
Yet nothing did he dread, but ever was ydrad.
—The Faerie Queene: Book I, Canto I, The Legend of the Knight
of the Red Crosse, Edmund Spenser, 1590.

Friday, October 13 of 1307. Jacques de Molay was arrested by order of the French king, Phillipe IV. His coffers almost empty, the king turned covetous eyes to that order's rich possessions. A few years later, in 1312, the order of the Poor Fellow-Soldiers of Christ and of the Temple of Solomon, known as the Knights Templars, was suppressed and Phillipe appropriated their riches on French soil. Throughout Europe hundreds of Templars were accused of the worse vices and abominations, humiliated, tortured, then executed or burned alive. Jacques de Molay remained in a Parisian dungeon, under harsh conditions, until 1314. He was a broken old man, probably in his seventies, when Phillipe IV decided his fate: he was to be burned alive. The Templars were created to protect vulnerable pilgrims visiting the Holy Land; they were destroyed by the cupidity of powerful men.

Portugal, Lisbon. It was the seventh day of July in the year of 1385 of Our Lord. On the crowded Rua Nova, parallel to the Tejo River, was the dwelling of the Troyes family. It was a sultry day and not even the proximity of the river helped alleviate the heat. Through the opened windows permeated heat, humidity, mingled with the scent of the tide and the noise from the street. Pedro de Troyes had just received word from the Mosteiro de São Dinis, in Odivelas, where his father, Sulpice de Troyes, was dying. He immediately commandeered horses and went to change. Madalena, his wife, was in the kitchen. She heated a stone and, protecting her hand with a thick cloth, started to quickly press out the wrinkles on his shirt.

"Thank the Virgin the whites were washed this week!"

A devout of the Mother of Christ, according to her, all benefits were always bestowed by that Lady. She came into the room where her husband was making his ablutions and laid the immaculate shirt on the bed to cool down. Madalena was proud of having made the shirt from 'five yards of good linen!'

The barber had been called with great haste and was shaving Pedro. As he finished, it was just a matter of a few minutes to don hose—his favorite, for special events, of soft wool with one leg blue the other yellow—then Madalena quickly helped him ease into the shirt. Over it went a black velvet kirtle, long, touching his knee—a gift from his father on his last birthday. He affixed the money pouch under the kirtle and tied the richly embroidered ankle boots. (He had refused to wear the purple silk, fashionable poulaine, despite Madalena pleadings—she had new moss mixed with rosemary stuffed into the poulaine's long, pointy toes—arguing that boots were easier for him to move around!) In less than one hour he and his page were riding north.

Over fifteen miles to the monastery—at a trot, with resting and watering the horses, almost three hours—breathing the dust from the road, under a scorching, blinding sun, that made your eyes water. The sweat streamed down Pedro's forehead, slid down his neck to soak his shirt and design dark stains on the kirtle. The blinding light did not relent. The scent of the hot saddle against the horse blanket penetrated his nostrils and he felt nauseated. His hands inside kid gloves were sweaty, but he held the reins tight. His tongue felt like rough leather against his palate. Thirst. Heat. Ride faster.

Ninety-one years ago, in the year 1294, Sulpice de Troyes was born in the north-east of France, in the city of Troyes. There is where the Council of Troyes met in the year 1129. The council was summoned by Bernard de Clairvaux—Saint Bernard—to hear the petition of Hugues de Payens on behalf of the Templars. In his youth Sulpice had been squire to Friar Chaplain Pietro da Bologna, one of the defenders of the Knights Templar during their trial in France. Now he was old, his body weakened, but his mind was still lucid. And it had been his wish to die in the monastery at Odivelas. It was not just the desire to get away from the noisy house near the river, but to be near his dear king and, after dead, also be buried in that monastery. The body of Dom Dinis rested in a beautifully ornate tomb that stood in the central nave of the church, in front of the chancel. Upon arrival Sulpice's chair had been brought there so he could pay his respects to the king and pray for his soul.

He closed his eyes, exhausted. Such a long life… There was no longer place for the healing of the body; now, it was the healing of the soul that counted. Sulpice did penance and was absolved. The priest anointed his forehead, chin, cheeks, hands, nostrils, and breast, and proceeded with the Viaticum. Having attained a state of grace, his mind dwelled in the past, back to France, in the days when King Philippe had commanded the apprehension of the Knights Templar…

Fra Pietro da Bologna, Templar, had escaped from the Parigian dungeons in early May of 1310, two years prior to the dissolution of the order. Pietro went back to his native Bologna, where he joined the Hospitallers of Saint John of Jerusalem. He and Sulpice were separated during their scape and would never see each other again. Fra Pietro died in the year 1329. On the fourth day of May of that year he was buried in the church of Santa Maria. His tomb read: 'Pietro Rota - Here the intrepid defender of Christ rests, beloved, in the bosom of the Order.'

Other lucky Templars who evaded the mass slaughter that took place in Europe, cut their beards, got rid of their impedimenta, and fled to Portugal and Spain. Sulpice de Troyes, then a sixteen-year-old stripling, decided to try his luck in Portugal, where, he had heard, King Dinis was friendly to the Knights of the Cross. There he joined the Genovese Emanuele Pessagno, who became the king's Royal Fleet commander in 1317.

Sulpice lived a long, fruitful life. He married three times, and fathered ten children—of which nine died of the pestilence[47] and only one survived: the youngest, Pedro—named in honor of Sulpice's Bolognese master. And there he was, his dearest Pedro. His beautiful brown eyes shadowed by sadness, unshed tears welling up, nesting on his eyelashes like crystal drops. With trembling fingers, the old man pulled a chain from within his sweaty gown. Dangling from it was a ring, which he proceeded to hand to Pedro. This bauble was not made of gold or precious stones, but, it was said, from a nail from the cross of Christ.

"Keep it. Always against your heart." His voice was a mere whisper and Pedro had to approach his ear to his father's lips to be able to hear. Sulpice continued, now in Galician Portuguese, "Ai flores ai flores do verde pino se saberes novas do meu amigo…" Here the old man's voice failed and the last words of King Dinis love poem went unsung. Sulpice de Troyes was dead.

"Ai Deus, e u é? Ai flores, ai flores do verde ramo, se sabedes novas do meu amado? Ai Deus e u é?[48]," Pedro finished reciting. He kissed his father's cold lips, made the sign of the cross, and got up from the kneeling position.

He looked at the small metal object in the palm of his hand and hung it on his neck. The metal felt cold against his chest. He had seen it many times, hanging from his father's neck, yet had never held it; it was his now. A ring, octagonal, with an inscription on the flat surface: Ἰάκωβος, the Greek name Iakobos. It was the ring of Jacques de Molay, the last grand master of the Knights Templar.

---

[47] The Black Death.
[48] See Appendix for translation.

CHAPTER FORTY-EIGHT

In France, where such news arrived (the tragic end of Duclerc's expedition), a company of reprisal and revenge was prepared. René Duguay-Trouin, bringing together elements of merchants and the State, armed 16 ships of the royal navy, four private ships, with crew and soldiers for disembarkation, in total more than five thousand men and on September 12, 1711, he turned up, hidden by the fog, and already inside the Guanabara Bay.
—As Expedições de Duclerc e de Duguay-Trouin ao Rio de Janeiro (1710-1711), Eduardo Brazão. 1940.

Like his father, Pedro de Troyes lived a long life. And like him, he also begot a large family. With the passing of time his last name evolved to the Portuguese spelling and became de Tróia—as in Troy, the legendary city of Helen. The de Tróia family were actively present in Portugal's maritime enterprises. Two brothers, Felipe and Augusto de Tróia, were with that nobleman, Captain Pedro Álvares Cabral when, on March 9 of 1500 they sailed with the intent to reach the coast of India. Fifteen hundred men—doctors, apothecaries, priests, caulkers, soldiers—distributed in thirteen ships, travelled for forty-four-days, at the end of which, in the afternoon of the twenty-second day of April of that same year, Cabral discovered Brazil. When the Captain returned to Portugal—with only five hundred survivors—Augusto stayed in the New World. Unlike the two convicts who were left behind with no choice, his decision was not of force majeure, but the desire to unveil the wonders of that new, savage land. But there was also love: he had married a beautiful Tupinambá maiden, Jaciara, whose name meant born of the moon. She was slim; her body shone like polished copper and she walked with the grace and lightness of the jaguar; her long hair was like the starless nightly sky and covered her in more splendor than the silks and brocades wore by the noblewomen of Augusto's Portugal. She had eyes the color of liquid honey, and her smile was akin to a sunny day. And the young Portuguese, enrapture by so much beauty, fell in love with the young woman.

Adventurous descendants of Augusto and Jaciara joined the bandeirante[49] Antônio Dias de Oliveira, who in the late 1600s found a rich vein of gold in the region of Minas Gerais. The fever of gold took hold of them and they braved the wild jungles of Brazil, populated by jaguars and snakes, in search of that mineral, precious stones, and slaves. Some died of fever, others of accidents, some were killed in ambushes or duels, or by wild animals; in the skirmishes and wars between the Portuguese, Paulistas, and Emboabas[50]. Then the ones who survived moved to Paraty, a city in the state of Rio de Janeiro, near its homonymous capital. There the gold they subverted from the Portuguese Crown was lavishly spent. Slowly the years passed. The family, their fortune drained by their profligate lifestyle, started to move south in search of new riches.

In seventeen sixty, right after the expulsion of the Jesuits by the Marques of Pombal, the stonemason Alfredo de Tróia, together with his wife Clotilde and daughter Arminda, moved to the newly incorporated southernmost territory, the future state of Rio Grande do Sul. In that wild land of vast silent extents, home of the Pampeano Indians, they settled. There he erected their house—little more than a hut, four mud walls covered with a thatched roof—on top of one of the hills. Near their abode Alfredo dug a rustic well. Pure water was abundant at first, but soon the source dried. The well was abandoned and they had to turn to the creek that skirted the base of the hill for their source of water.

---

[49] Bandeiras: armed expeditions that, generally leaving from the captaincy of São Vicente, explored the backlands in order to capture the natives or find gold. Novo Dicionário Aurélio da Língua Portuguesa. 1995.

[50] Paulista: from the city or state of São Paulo. Emboaba: [from the Tupi language] in colonial Brazil, a nickname that Paulistas gave to Portuguese, Brazilians or any foreigner who entered the jungles in search of gold and precious stones. Novo Dicionário Aurélio da Língua Portuguesa. 1995.

Little Arminda, a lively child of eleven, quickly made friends with the children of the only family who lived half a mile from them. These neighbors, Domingos and Jacinta da Cruz, had three children: Onésimo, Fortunata and Sebastião, aged twelve, ten and seven. The four became inseparable and with their similar coloration and build, anyone would have thought them siblings. The children's friendship influenced the parents, who also became fast friends. The Cruz children's father was a talented carpenter who was born in the city of Rio de Janeiro, where he lived until marrying and moving to the south of Brazil.

During the cooler summer nights, they sat around a bonfire, and the children would invariably request and be told stories of their parents' youth. In their childhood, both Alfredo and Onésimo heard tales of French pirates raiding Brazil, and specially the cities of Rio de Janeiro, and the nearby Paraty—the main port for the gold coming from the mines of Minas Gerais, that was shipped to the Portuguese crown. And these stories they now repeated to the wide-eyed children. Onésimo told them the tale of the botched attack to Rio in the year seventeen ten by Jean-François Duclerc, who was captured and later murdered in prison; of the following year's successful raid of that town by René Duguay-Trouin, who caused its citizens to part with a large ransom in order to have their city back. Alfredo would keep his audience spell-bound with stories of the Knights Templars. His childhood had been full of accounts of their heroic deeds—and their cowardly demise, orchestrated by the king of France. On such occasions he would proudly show the children the ring that belonged to Jacques de Molay, the knights' last grand master, that he always carried on a leather cord hanging around his neck.

The children drank the words that spelled 'adventure,' dreaming of travels and dangers, of knights, pirates, and treasures, and at the end of these stories bombarded their fathers with questions. Excited, they only kept the swashbuckler, romantic aspect of their stories, discarding their tragic side. At the children's pleading, Onésimo built them a small, rustic trunk that they planned to use to hide a treasure—the Templars' treasure. Inside it they put a jumble of pieces of wood and small fabrics rolled and tied to emulate ancient parchments, and a few polished stones they found in the nearby stream—these, to them, as precious as diamonds and gold.

"The well," Arminda suggested after they had given much thought to the location where the treasure should be hidden.

And Alfredo and Onésimo, who could not resist their offspring's plea, were given the task of building steps so the children could reach the bottom of the dried out well. Pieces of wood were securely hammered to the walls and strategically placed. Excited, the four children went down the well, dug a tiny cave and reinforced it with stones from the river. That accomplished, the trunk was taken down to the well and stored inside the little cave-like opening. Then with the help of their parents, they conceived a riddle to guide future adventurers to the correct location of their treasure. After much deliberation, Alfredo was entrusted with the task of inscribing the following text on a piece of flat stone: 'Full it gave life./ Empty it became dangerous./ Deep inside, within the darkness,/ Lies the treasure of the Templars.' The stone was buried near the creek, at the foot of the hill, beside a large stone they called Sugar Loaf, for its similarity with the homonymous mountain in Rio de Janeiro. As the little companions grew older, their treasure was forgotten, other sort of entertainment having been found. A few years later Onésimo da Cruz and his family moved away. The well, abandoned, had become an unnoticed gap, taken for granted as it stood there for so long, covered by a few wooden planks—that rotted with the passing of time. Concealed by the undergrowth, it became part of the scenery.

One moonless winter night, Alfredo left in search of Acuab, the old Indian healer who lived nearby. Clotilde, his wife, was delirious, and he hoped the shaman would have the herbs he needed to abate the fever. Hours, then days passed, but he did not return. Arminda stood at her mother's side, day and night, rarely budging and barely eating, until she was healed. When Clotilde was strong enough, she and her daughter went in search of Alfredo. But after a few days of fruitless wondering, they abandoned the enterprise.

It was a cold night. The Minuano wind, blowing hard, whistled through the cracks of windows and doors, and winter frosted the world outside, when, many years later, Alfredo appeared to his daughter in a dream. He told her where to find his body and that a chapel should be built over the place. The next morning, Arminda and her mother walked to the abandoned well. It was surrounded by thick, wild vegetation. They had to remove some of the overgrown vegetation to be able to approach the opening. Looking down, they backed away in horror: they saw the skeletal remains of what was once Alfredo de Tróia. Soil was poured down on the well and slowly the remains were concealed. A priest came from the distant village of Rio Grande de São Pedro to bless the unlucky man's resting place. A stone slab, naturally flat and smooth, was pulled over the opening. Around it, Arminda and her mother slowly built a small chapel, using stones and clay, then whitewashed the outside walls. On the top of the small bell tower, they placed a wooden cross.

In seventeen eighty-nine her mother dead, Arminda, the last of her lineage, decided to enter the cloister. She chose to join the order of the Clarisses, and entered the convent of Nossa Senhora da Conceição da Ajuda, in the city of Rio de Janeiro. She sold the land to Ubaldo Freitas, but before she left for Rio, she visited the chapel one last time. There, after making her prayers, she took the wooden image of the Virgin Mary from its niche, detached a little piece of wood from its back that served as a lid, exposing a small hollow. She then inserted a little folded note inside the gap. The note read: 'Beneath the place of worship/ The treasure was hidden./ There lies a good man/ And the dreams of four children.'

Arminda closed the hollow, kissed the hands of the statue before replacing it and, making the sign of the cross, left with a serene smile. Before going up to the chapel, Arminda buried a metal cookie box beside the stone where she and her little friends, years ago, had buried her father's inscribed stone. The box contained a piece of paper. On it she wrote 'Inside the sacred image/ Lies the key to a treasure./ At the third quadrant plus one/ Find the shadow of the cross.' She did not believe anyone would ever find these childish clues, but it pleased her to repeat the same gestures of so long ago, when she was an innocent child, and, with her playmates, roamed the wide-open spaces of that beloved land. But in the eventuality of anyone finding these mementos, would they understand the meaning of the words? Would they find the treasure of her youth?

CHAPTER FORTY-NINE

During the late repair of the Temple Church, a. d. 1830, the workmen discovered an antient seal of the order of the Hospital, which was carried away, and appears to have got into the hands of strangers. On one side of it is represented the holy sepulchre of Jerusalem, with the Saviour in his tomb. At his head is an elevated cross, and above is a tabernacle or chapel, from the roof of which depend two incense pots. Around the seal is the inscription, "Fr—— Berengarii Custos Pauperum Hospitalis Jherusalem." On the reverse a holy man is represented on his knees in the attitude of prayer before a patriarchal cross, on either side of which are the letters Alpha and Omega. Under the first letter is a star. These particulars have been furnished me by Mr. Savage, the architect.
—The History of the Knights Templar, the Temple Church, and the Temple, Charles G. Addison. 1842.

Robert and Cristina had been back from Rio for a couple of weeks when John and Helena Laughton returned from the month they spent travelling through Uruguay and Argentina. "Oh, I wish you had been with us," Helena told her daughter. "Buenos Aires is such a wonderful city. All those cafés and night clubs. You two," she said, looking at Robert, "would have looked gorgeous dancing the tango, I'm sure."

"No way, I wouldn't," Robert protested, and was promptly elbowed in the ribs by his wife. "Watch out, little one," he warned her, and successfully avoided being elbowed again. "Have pity on my delicate constitution." Then, turning to Helena, "Do you see how your daughter treats me, Countess? I have bruises all over my body. I won't be able to wear my new bathing suit."

"Don't be a bore. Go play outside while I talk with my mother."

"I might go to the Police Station and file a charge of spousal abuse," he said, then left, but not before stealing a kiss from his wife.

"We also went to the Teatro Colón—magnificent. I felt I was back in Europe," Helena continued. "We watched a race at the Jockey Club. Such elegant ladies! I wish you could have seen the dresses. And the hats! Then we went to Tigre by boat and stayed at the Club de Regatas la Marina. We were invited by a friend of John's. Such a beautiful neoclassic building, right by the Paraná River. We had dinner one night at the Club Canottieri Italiani; they have a wonderful restaurant and the food was absolutely divine."

"And did you get any inamoratos again?" Cristina asked her mother, referring to years ago when, while they were staying in the city of Rio Grande, her mother dined in an Italian restaurant and was fawned over by the owner, manager and servers, all Italian.

Both Cristina and her mother laughed and that is how John Laughton found them. The smile died on his lips as soon as he learned the reason for the ladies' hilarity. He did not have a happy memory of that dinner. That evening he did not enjoy watching the woman he loved being wooed by what he called a bunch of mustachioed, unctuous idiots. It was more like watching a fortress being assaulted by overwhelming enemy forces. Understanding the reason for his irritation, Cristina and her mother teased John Laughton until, annoyed, he left them.

"Now, I heard that your Apolo brought his sun chariot to this farm recently," Helena said with a mischievous look. "Ce chevalier sans peur et sans reproche," and she gave her daughter a mischievous look.

Helena's saying was about Pierre Terrail, Seigneur de Bayard, a Frenchman who lived in the Twenty-Fifth Century and who, by his prowess, was idealized a 'knight without fear or reproach'.

"My Apolo," Cristina repeated, intrigued, trying to understand her mother's riddle. "Fearless and faultless knight. Mmm… Who do you mean?"

"Who else, but that gorgeous Rafael Souza, child?" And she patted her daughter's blushing cheek. "I knew he couldn't resist any longer. So, he came to see you, didn't he?" She chuckled, giving Cristina a meaningful look.

"Stop that, mother!" she riposted, annoyed. "He's always been very correct. And he did not come here to see me!"

"Yes, the perfect gentleman—he loves in secret. Hides his feelings, how romantic," Helena joked.

"This is absurd! He's just a good friend. I don't know where you get these kinds of ideas."

"From the expression of his green eyes when he sees you, my lovely, naïve daughter. I wonder that Robert doesn't mind his presence. John would have been furious."

"Robert is not the jealous type."

"Aha! So, you do admit that if he were, we'd have cause for jealousy!"

"No! I said no such thing! You're putting words in my mouth," Cristina looked at her mother, annoyed. "I can't believe you even think that of me, mother! And I, a married woman, with three children—remember?"

"'Course you are, my sweet. But you aren't dead—nor dense," and Helena winked at her daughter, teasingly. "Come to think of it, it seems to me this lady protests a bit too much…"

Cristina ignored the inference. "If Rafael was, well, as you say, why doesn't he come visiting often?"

Helena shook her head in disbelief at her daughter's naïveté. "Because, my sweet heart, love sometimes can cause pain."

Classes had started and Donny and Annie went their separate ways. He went to Colégio Nossa Senhora Auxiliadora, and his cousin to Colégio Franciscano Espirito Santo. They spent their first free Sunday in the company of their parents—Max and Desiree having decided to stay a couple more months. They went to the theater and to an ice cream parlor, after attending mess in town, at the Saint Sebastian Cathedral. At the end of the day, they were taken back to their respective schools, without being able to talk unobserved.

On Tuesday of that week Donny got a letter in the mail. The sender was his cousin. Anxious to get in touch with him, the girl had decided to use the Postal services. It was written using a code they had devised—

merely splitting the alphabet in half and replacing each letter in the message with its opposite. He read:

'Sbhaq gur ghary! Vg vf abg zlgu, vg rkvfgf! V knyxrq nyy gur jnl sez urer gb lbhe fpubby ynfg avtug. V xabj jurer gur npprff sebz lbhe fpubby vf. Arkg Fhaqnl jvyy gryy lbh ubj gb svaq vg.'

Quickly he worked it and came up with the following message—of which grammar mistakes were corrected to facilitate a smooth reading:

Found the tunnel! It is not myth, it exists! I walked all the way from here to your school last night. I know where the access from your school is. Next Sunday will tell you how to find it.

So, it was true, he thought, excited. The underground tunnel connecting the two schools did exist.

After his cousin's momentous revelation, the days lagged, and Donny could barely wait for the Sunday when he would be privy to the secret passage that linked the two schools—which was vehemently denied by both priests and nuns.

It was a couple of weekends later when Donny and Annie were finally able to steal a few minutes for a private conversation while the adults were not paying attention. They planned to meet in the underground the following night, Monday, when everyone would be asleep, because on Sundays, with all the excitement of the time spent out of school, the students usually defied the retiring hour and kept exchanging confidences and talking about the day's events until late.

Monday dragged endlessly and both cousins were reprimanded by their teachers for their lack of attention to the classes they attended. Much later, at night, both in their respective dormitories waited until the regular breathing of the surrounding beds told of their companions being deep asleep. Leaving their slippers behind, not daring to wear them for fear of making noise, each child, at the appointed hour, tiptoed barefoot to the secret entrance to the passage—which will not be disclosed here for obvious reasons—carrying a candle stub and plenty of matches.

As previously agreed, Donny and Annie only lit their candles when already inside the passage. It was a long walk and the still air carried the heavy scent of mold. The little candle did not illuminate much farther and the darkness ahead seemed that of the very path that led to the Styx River. Their soft footfalls, augmented by the vaulted, narrow construction, echoed so loudly through the stones they feared they would be heard outside. Especially for Donny, whose first time was in that place of mystery, the path felt endless; he kept walking, the candlelight inefficiently illuminating the darkness ahead that seemed to keep forever receding, the end never approaching.

Suddenly he thought he saw a tiny point of light in the distance. Yes, there it was—and getting stronger at each step he took. Soon, he could identify his cousin's silhouette in the distance, until the details of her face were made clear by the halo of wavering light that preceded her.

"Boy, I thought this was never gonna end," he complained.

"It's a bit long," the girl granted.

"And dark," Donny stated the obvious again.

"Yes, and humid, and silent like the grave, et cetera," the girl added, annoyed. "Now that we've got it all listed, can we talk about what we're here for, please?"

The boy's answer was to shrug his shoulders and frown at his cousin.

"You have the ring?"

Donny pulled a chain from inside his pajama top from which hung the ring they found in the farm's little chapel.

"We need to decide who'll keep it."

"I found it, so it's mine," he retorted.

"That's not fair! We were together looking for the treasure! And talking about treasure, we need to plan our search for it next vacation."

"We should go back to that well and dig. I bet there's where the treasure is!"

Annie agreed and after some arguing they decided to share the ring. Each would keep it for one month. Making the exchange would be difficult when around the adults, so they decided to meet in the tunnel at appointed dates. The search for the Templar treasure would start again during their winter break, at the end of May. In their excitement, they did not realize that the weather, with rain, cold and wind, would not be very conducive to being outside for long extents of time, treasure hunting.

Yet the future would bring them great disappointment, as there was no hidden Templar treasure. But as Scottish poet Robert Burns so cleverly put, suspense is worse than disappointment.

CHAPTER FIFTY

Do not lay up for yourselves treasures on earth, where moth and rust destroy and where thieves break in and steal.
—Matthew 6:19

Terri Kramer and her cousin Harry had returned to the little rented house in the Cajú Beach they occupied since they arrived in Brazil. It was not very far from where the hydroplanes landed, at Ponta do Cajú. The faultless blue sky announced yet another hot day ahead. After his morning swim, taking advantage of the still cool breeze coming from the sea, Harry laid in a hammock wearing a terrycloth beach robe, his wet hair disheveled. He was holding a letter, but not reading it; he was looking straight ahead, his eyes not focused on anything. It was from his friend and college pal George Harding. They met when both studied at the University of Leipzig and became very good friends. George had fallen head over heels for Terri, who was also at Leipzig at the time, but the girl's independent spirit had kept him at arms' length.

Coming from the beach, Terri stood over her cousin and shook her head, causing drops of water to fall on him.

"Watch out! Can't you see I'm holding a letter?"

"Who from?"

"George Harding."

Terri laid in the other hammock, and adjusted the folds of her beach pajamas of peach silk. It was the latest fashion, the top a kimono with short sleeves and embroidered chinoiserie portraying female figures, butterflies and floral motifs, and the draw string pants with wide, flowing legs.

"Am I supposed to know him?"

"We called him Redhead Georgie in college." She still did not recall, so he added, "That fella who had a crush on you when we're at Leipzig."

"Which one of them?" she winked, teasing him.

"The American, you conceited piece of work! Rotkopf Georgie!"

"That prig? Gott im Himmel! How could I ever forget him?"

"Oh, that's not fair," he complained. "Georgie's a good fella, Terri."

"Yeah, I'm sure he's changed. Well? What of him?"

"As I told you, I've got this letter from him in the mail today. You've got to hear what he writes."

"Give me a fag, will ya, Harry? If I'm to endure his rigmarole, I need one, otherwise you must land me your razor."

"Whatever for?" her perplexed cousin asked.

"To cut my wrists and escape the horrors of Georgie's drivel!"

"Oh, don't be silly, Terri! And did you already forget that I quit smoking? Looks like your source of free cigarettes is over, old girl. And it's not like you don't have jack! Aunt Terri gives you a nice, fat allowance."

"Mater got mad at me 'cause I didn't get rid of Robert Laughton for her. She said she's going to disinherit me—but I doubt. Who'll she leave her money to?"

"Maybe I'll be her beneficiary," Harry said, excited at the idea.

"Ha! You hope so, my boy. She's probably going to hire someone to do the job then come to terms with me. Come to think of it, I must write to Cristina to warn them," she said, pensively.

"I still don't understand why the Laughtons didn't throw you in jail. You almost killed her. I would if I were him!"

"'Course you would. You're really stuck on Mrs. Laughton, aren't you?"

"She's marvelous. Her beauty is unparalleled. She is graceful and sweet, and all that is wonderful!" He took a deep breath and, entranced, started reciting Lord Byron's poem, "She walks in beauty, like the night of cloudless climes and starry skies; and all that's best of dark and bright meet in her aspect and her eyes—"

"Oh, stop the booshwash, Harry," Terri interrupted her cousin. "C'mon. Let's have this letter, if you must."

"You never had an ear for poetry," the disappointed young man accused his cousin. "Oh, well, let's see," and he turned his attention to the sheet of paper in his hand. "Georgie's been doing research at the Bibliotheca Albertina. About the Knights Templar."

"Knights Templar?" Terri asked, surprised.

"Your hearing apparatus is in perfect order, cousin. Now, listen to this. Let's see." He read through quickly. "Ah, here," he found the passage he was looking for and started reading it out loud.

'Old man, there's a story (supposed to be a myth, but I don't care!)…'

Here Terri snorted, and got a dirty look from her cousin, who then resumed reading where he was interrupted:

'…about some Templar—or maybe it's more than one?—going to Brazil during the age of discovery—you know, 1500's and all that, but there's much criticism among scholars, whoever they are. Well, old man, I've been doing all kinds of research and I'm pretty sure it's true. I found heaps of sources from European authors, but it was all superficial research, since none actually believe it. Well, except for one. A Brazilian author wrote a book years ago about it. Perhaps you can find the book since you're in Brazil? The author is Elisete da Silva Costa and her book is Templarios na America do Sul—hope I spelled it right. So, find the book and read it, old man. I know you'll agree with me. And I want to find this treasure! If you're game, I'm coming to meet you and we can search together."

Harry interrupted the reading, since next were a couple of paragraphs related to Terri, where Georgie gave way to his romantic nature and mentioned his undying love for her and the hope to meet her while in Brazil. Harry looked at his cousin searchingly. With the exception of that extemporaneous snort, she had listened in absolute silence, her face a blank, her eyes focused on the ground, not giving any hint of her thoughts.

"So?" he asked, tentatively. "Whatcha think?"

225

"Treasure hunting?" she turned an excited face to him. "Heinrich, my boy," she slapped him on the shoulder, "count me in. When do we start?"

"Mr. Souza's here to see you," Alice Christensen told her son.

"I ain't home," Claes mumbled, upset at the interruption. Then, suddenly, alarmed, he tore his eyes away from the book he was reading—instead of doing his homework—and shrieked, "Doncha' let him in, mother!" He had a strange feeling about Rafael, and the last thing the boy wanted was to be in that man's presence.

"Don't yell at me, boy! What's with you lately? All jumpy and always stuck in this bedroom."

"I'll handle him, Mrs. Christensen," said a voice behind her and Rafael Souza materialized. He looked at the boy sternly and saw him pale. "C'mon," he motioned with his head and the boy followed him without argument.

They left the house under the surprised eye of Mrs. Christensen, who wondered if her son, Alcino, was right after all—that a man's strong presence might curb Claes impetuous nature. She feared he was losing her adored son, the image of her dead husband. Maybe Mr. Souza's offer… She wondered what Claes would do.

Rafael and Claes walked to the entrance gate, the two handsome and tall; the blond one a fresh promise of future perfection; the dark one in the prime of physical strength and beauty. On either side of the gate were rustic benches facing each other, a mere couple of rough boards, the wood mellowed by the passage of time. Above it stood a frail wooden arch twined with Japanese honeysuckle and roses that provided a most welcome shade that late afternoon. The boy sat down on one bench and resumed sulking. Rafael stood in the shade, removed his hat and fanned himself for a few moments, while observing Claes. He sat down and faced the boy.

"I know everything. *Everything*," he stressed the word, but getting no reaction, added, "Including the car accident." At that the boy turned a suspicious countenance to him. "I know it was your doing. Don't," he cut short the denial he knew was coming. "I grant that the car—it would have been impossible to identify you. Except that I found and kept the wrench you used." He had omitted to hand the wrench to Robert, having turned to him only the lug nuts he found when they had searched the garage. "I matched the fingerprints in that with the ones I got from your lure." He saw the boy's surprise and explained, "Yes, that day, when you were fishing, you dropped a lure. And I have both—lure and wrench—in a secure place."

In his profession, Rafael was wont to encounter all kinds of misdeeds, and deal with crooked, immoral characters. After a few years, he started to become inured to these human flaws, much as a baker when confronted with one loaf of bread that did not properly rise: something of little consequence. While he felt indifference toward the culprits, at the same time their wrongdoings exerted a kind of fascination upon him. And that paradox turned to be an asset in the course of his investigations, for crime did not particularly affect or revolt him. Devoid of emotion, he had a purely academic interest in crime. He enjoyed studying its intricacies, although not vowed to dissect its motivations. But in this instance, there was a factor that differed from his usual detection work, and, although not clouding his judgment, forced him to see things in a different perspective: he was emotionally involved. Deeply.

"Now, the well," Rafael shook his head, disapprovingly. "Tsk, tsk, tsk. Your footprints are unmistakable, Claes. I just don't understand how no one saw it."

The boy's face looked haggard. He turned stormy eyes to his foot. That damned deformity, that curse!

"No one else saw," continued Rafael. "I was there the next day and trod on the few that were left. I obliterated the footprints." The boy's eyes turned to him, now clear of trouble. "I know what you're thinking. No doing, my boy. Who do you think the police would believe if I were to report what I saw? You or me?" Claes knew the answer, no need to say anything. "She sees you as a child, don't you realize?" No answer. "You stupid boy!" Rafael's voice rose, taking an aggressive intonation. "If any harm had come to her husband or her son, she would suffer—don't you see?"

Claes turned a troubled face to him, Rafael's words having sunk in. For the first time he realized the harm his actions would have caused, how much they would have affected Cristina.

Rafael watched these thoughts going through the boy's mind. "I guess you get my point."

The boy nodded in agreement and lowered his head, defeated.

"This must be stopped, Claes," he urged, sternly. "And I know how. I have a proposal to make."

His proposal or the pokey, were Rafael's terms. And so it was that less than two months after this conversation young Claes Christensen left the Brazilian countryside for the cosmopolitan New York. There he would live under Rafael tutelage, and attend school while working in the detective agency. He was promised his foot, the biggest disadvantage and constant weight on the boy's mind, would be cleverly disguised by Rafael's skilled boot maker, after a visit to a famous bone specialist. Rafael hoped that his and his father's strong influence and example might divert Claes' from the crooked path he would unavoidably follow if his tendencies were not curbed. And Rafael's mother, who constantly hinted of her wish for a grandchild, he knew, would quickly take to Claes. The fact that she was Brazilian, he hoped, would help the boy not feel so much as a fish out of water.

EPILOGUE

Awake! for Morning in the Bowl of Night
Has flung the Stone that puts the Stars to Flight:
And Lo! the Hunter of the East has caught
The Sultan's Turret in a Noose of Light.
—Rubaiyat of Omar Khayyam. Translated by Edward FitzGerald,
1859.

Familiarity breeds contempt—and children.
—Mark Twain's Notebook. 1935.

The sun had just begun its slow ascend over the hills and started blushing the pale sky with a myriad of shades. From her bed Cristina could see the first, shy rows of pink preceding the sunlight, framed through the open window. Robert turned in his bed, opened somnolent, bleary eyes and smiled at her. He swung his long legs to the floor and, stretching his arms, gave a might yawn, then vigorously scratched his head, messing up his hair.

"Good morning, lazy thing. What? Gonna skip your daily devotional today?"

She languidly stretched herself, still laying down, taking time to answer. "Not sure. I think for the next few months I'll let you bring me breakfast in bed." She gave him a mischievous look.

He stared, not sure of her meaning. "What are you up to, young lady?" She did not answer, so he decided to use a threat he knew always worked, "Do I have to tickle it out of you, girl?"

"No!" she almost yelled, sitting up in bed and warding him with stretched arms. "Don't you dare! I'll start screaming if you get closer!" She then giggled and laid down again with a satisfied air. "Just know I'll feel lazy from now on…"

Her mischievous expression puzzled Robert. He watched her for a few seconds, then shrugged his shoulders.

"You know I'm not good at riddles. So, either tell me your meaning, madam, or it'll be tickling," and he started to get up, menacingly flexing his fingers at her.

"No, no, you brute!" she recoiled in bed, "Don't you do it or I'll really scream!" But he kept coming and she finally pleaded, "Can't you recognize the symptoms?"

He froze, then, a wide smile illuminated his face. "A baby?" And as she said nothing but only beamed at him, he scooped her from the bed and kissed her face, her eyes, her lips, while she giggled and tried to stop him. "This is wonderful! I must tell everyone," and he carefully lowered her back to bed.

"What are you doing?" she stopped him as he opened the bedroom door to leave. "Come back! It's too early. They're all sleeping."

He obeyed her and meekly sat beside her on her bed. Suddenly an idea occurred to him. "Remember that trip to Egypt I've been promising you and we never go?" Without waiting for an answer, he continued, excited, "We must do it. Immediately! Before it's too late. It's a good time to visit that blasted place, ain't it? I believe you told me late October to March—so we still have time if we start soon. We'll stay at the Mena House so you can wake up in the morning to the view of those derelict piles of stone—what taste you have, love, well, except for me, of course!" and he kissed her smiling lips. "And when we go to Luxor, we'll stay at the Summer Palace."

"Winter Palace," she corrected.

"As I said, Winter Palace. And I'll hire a dragoman—the best one in Egypt—and he'll run before our carriage with a torch when we visit the pyramids at night! During the day I'll drop you at the Egyptian Museum with a lunch box. Then I'll go to that bazaar, er, what's the name again?"

"Khan el Kahlili," his diverted wife answered.

"Yes, that's it. I'll sit in the El Fishawy Café," he said, proud to remember the café's name, "enjoying a terribly sweet mint tea, smoking some Turkish cigarettes. And you'll bathe in the sacred lake at the temple. . . What's the name of the temple?"

"Karnak," she helped him. "But Karnak is almost five hundred miles from Cairo. You're in the bazaar with your tea and cigarettes, remember?" she teased him. "And the water of the lake is rotten!"

"Ingrate female, who disavow my efforts to please her! Anyway, we'll get a dahabeah and sail up and down the Nile until you're sick of all that old junk and…"

"Silly," she interrupted him and sat up. Holding his face with both hands, she looked into his eyes. There was no better place to be in the whole world, hers told him. Then she squeezed his cheeks and pointed at the door, "Now, stop this badinage, go to the kitchen and get me some breakfast. I'm starving!"

He made a formal bow and started to leave, but a sudden thought made him stop as he was going through the door. Turning a troubled expression to his wife, he asked, "Promise you won't land us with another pair of brats like Dr. Jekyll and Miss Hyde, will ya? I couldn't survive that much excitement in my old age…"

A well-aimed pillow hit him while he tried to sneak out through the door. He was able to avoid another projectile making its way to him.

FINIS

Emilia Rosa

De tudo, ao meu amor serei atento
Antes, e com tal zelo, e sempre, e tanto
Que mesmo em face do maior encanto
Dele se encante mais meu pensamento.
Soneto de Fidelidade, in Poemas, Sonetos e Baladas, Vinicius de
Moraes. 1946.

Above all, to my love I'll be attentive
First, with so much zeal, and always
That even under the greatest enchantment
By love be more enchanted my thoughts.
(The author's attempt to translate the untranslatable.)

FINDING CRISTINA: TREASURES ON EARTH

DRAMATIS PERSONAE

Many of the characters in this list appear but briefly or are just mentioned. Do not get daunted with their number!

- Cristina Laughton (née Abramov, but not exactly), the reason for the story and Robert's wife.
- Robert John Laughton, he who loves the reason for the story, and her husband.
- Donny (Donald John Laughton), Robert and Cristina's first born; a practiced trouble-maker.
- Loulou and Alexi (Alexander and Anne Louise) Cristina's double gift to Robert and trouble-makers on the making. Their loving father nicknamed them Dr. Jekyll and Miss Hyde.
- Bacon, Donny's faithful companion; a discerning dog.

- John Albert Laughton, Robert's father.
- Helena Laughton, Cristina's real mother, an ex-Countess (with a long story really worth telling—who knows the future?), married to John Laughton.

- Maria Petronila Griffith (née Specht), married to Bunky Griffith. She worked for the Abramovs (Cristina's putative parents), helped raise Cristina, and is more a family member than anything else.
- Bunky (Erastus Magnus Griffith), tough hombre with a big mustach, 6'5" of pure muscle, and a heart of gold—or so Maria says. He raised Robert, for only he could have done it! Enjoys playing the butler for the Laughtons.

- Desiree, Lady Walston-Armstrong (née Laughton), who in her salad days was styled "Little Scourge of God" by her uncharitable cousin, Robert.
- Max (Maximillian Oscar Walston-Armstrong, Earl of Bembrock), husband to Desiree and Robert's friend.
- Annie (Anne-Marie), their daughter. A little girl who keeps a journal and does not take 'no' for an answer!

- Rafael Souza, a private detective whose heart is taken by Cristina. He could have posed for Myron's forever lost bronze Discobolus!

- Alcina Christensen, tall and fair, works for the Laughtons, and lives in their house.
- Alcino Christensen, Alcina's twin and physical opposite; also works at the farm, but lives with his mother. He is infatuated with Cristina.
- Claes Christense, their thirteen-year-old brother, also infatuated with Cristina. A troubled youth, endowed with beauty, but an attitude— for a good reason, some might argue.
- Alice Christensen, widowed mother of the above three.

- Uncle Benê (Benedito), who was once a slave and loves telling a good story.

- Farmhands: Mercúrio (whose name no one knows), João Silvano, Lobo (Sétimo Filho do Nascimento), Alpídio Rodriguez, Policarpo Rodriguez (Alpídio's grandfather), Belo (Adonis Bello), Dionisio Bello (Adonis brother), Fulgencio Ribas.

- Gildo (Hermenegildo Rosa), who was born in Bagé in 1918 and is the author's father. A real gaúcho! - Emilia Rosa, a lady who could ride. Gildo's grandmother, who raised him after his mother died in childbirth. The author's great-grandmother.

- The Polack (Bogdan Zietarski), a real character. Manager of a prince's stud farm. He was never in Brazil and never met Cristina, nor— and be happy for him—Robert.
- Carl Raswan (nee Carl Reinhard Schmidt), also a real person. A German globetrotter who lived with the Bedouin and was an authority on Arabian horses. He did travel with Zietarski, but was never in Brazil.

- Fafá (Fátima Kalil), another fictional character. Sinuous beauty, daughter of Salim Kalil (a real person), and heiress of her father's haberdashery empire.

- Marcelino Paranhos, Colonel and owner of Cavalo de Ouro, a large horse farm.
- Maricota Paranhos (Maria), wife to Marcelino, who might snort when she laughs.
- Sérgio Paranhos, their son. A pretentious egocentric, who has amorous inclinations toward the beautiful Alcina Christensen.
- Onélia da Silva (né Paranhos), their daughter. She married the wrong man and is the apple of Aparício França's eye. Mother of Antonia and Virgílio.

- Aparício França, police chief, great friend of Robert. A nice man with a nice moustache. Onélia da Silva is the apple of his eye. Godfather of Virgílio da Silva.
- Divina (Diva Maria França), his sister.

- Fidêncio Enildo de Araujo Valentim, a wealthy farmer and long-suffering husband.
- Quininha Valentim (Joaquina Perpétua da Silva Gama Valentim), his wife. A tiny woman with a haughty disposition and well-connected—to a Baron, no less.
- Jô Valentim (Joaquim Feliciano de Araujo Valentim), their offspring. Not the sharpest knife in the drawer according to Robert. He carries a torch for Alcina Christensen, going against his mamma's expectations.
- Father Valentim (José Luiz de Araujo Valentim), Fidêncio Valentim's brother. Beloved pater of the Catholic community.

- Terri Kramer (né Teresa Lucrecia Griffith), Bunky's troublesome cousin and the reason of the young Bunky escaping Huron, his hometown in Ohio. Apparently still causing trouble.
- Terri (Karola Teresa Kramer), a feisty, modern young woman, whose mother has a grudge against the Laughtons—absolutely groundless, by the way.
- Harry (Heinrich Jürgen Kramer), her cousin, who falls for Cristina.

- Quirino Robaina, a friend of Aparício França and airplane aficionado who owns several planes, and takes Robert for a flight.

- Dr. Anatoly Orlov, a doctor who came from Russia. A bear-looking, grumpy man.
- Denise Krause (nurse at Orlov's clinic), a beauty of Florence Nightingale's call. Cristina hoped she would capture Rafael Souza's heart.

- Germanito (Father Roberto Germano), a real character and one of the founders or Colégio Nossa Senhora Auxiliadora. A Salesian priest born in Uruguay, he arrived in Bagé in 1904, staying there until 1972.

- Hilário and Dolores de Torres, and Inácio, their son. Gypsies who are granted stay at the Laughtons farm. And almost cause a catastrophe.

- Ubaldo Freitas, first owner of Fazenda Minuano, built in 1790.
- Héloïse Freitas (née Jacquet), wife to Ubaldo, depicted in a beautiful paining on the library wall. She left France just in time to escape the Reign of Terror.
- Bernardo Freitas, their descendant.
- Teresa Freitas, his wife.
- Vitória Freitas (Uncle Benê's Miss Toria), their daughter, last of the family. Sold Fazenda Minuano to the Laughtons and became an Italian countess.
- Francine Jacquet, or The French Connection. She was related to the Freitas by way of the lovely Héloïse.

- Sulpice de Troyes, a Frenchman and squire to Pietro da Bologna, a Knight Templar. Escaped from France to Portugal during the persecution of the Templars. Father of ten children, but left with only one.
- Pedro de Tróia (originally de Troyes), Sulpice's only surviving son.
- Madalena de Troyes, Pedro's wife, who bore him many children.
- Felipe and Augusto de Tróia, descendants of Pedro. Travelled with the discoverer of Brazil, Pedro Álvares Cabral.
- Jaciara, a beautiful Tupinambá India, Augusto's wife.

- Alfredo de Tróia, stonemason. Descendant of Augusto and Jaciara. He built a well—and should have left well alone.
- Clotilde de Tróia, Alfredo's wife. - Arminda de Tróia, their very imaginative eleven-year-old daughter.

- Domingos (carpenter) and Jacinta da Cruz, a couple. Neighbors of Alfredo and Clotilde de Tróia. Their children—Onésimo, Fortunata and Sebastião—were friends of Arminda.

- Acuab, an old Pampeano Indian healer who was never found.

- Pietro da Bologna (Friar Chaplain), an historical character who lived in the Fourteenth Century. Knight Templar who escaped France's annihilation of his order. He went back to Bologna and joined the Knights Hospitallers. He is interred in the church of Santa Maria.

- Farm animals: Mr. Valentino (a disgruntled rooster who needs an alarm clock); Leonidas (a... rat?); Bucyrus (Donny's horse); Simoom (Robert's horse); Peludo (a unique fox); Demosthenes (a duckling who trusts a fox!); Princesa (the queen of the dovecot); Mr. Felix (a farm cat who dreams of roast pigeons).

Emilia Rosa

FINDING CRISTINA: TREASURES ON EARTH

PRAISE FOR THE AUTHOR

Emilia Rosa envelopes the reader in an evocative setting. Her prose is rich, and her characters have life and purpose.
> —Jeffrey Hatcher, author, playwright and screenwriter.

Rosa excels in writing historical fiction, absorbing herself and the reader into the period with her nuanced, intelligent detailing that threads through every aspect of dialogue, dress, and setting.
> —Rose Auburn, author of Cobwebs of Youth

ALSO BY EMILIA ROSA

Finding Cristina (2021)
Finding Cristina: A New Life (2022)

CONTACT

Facebook, Instagram, Goodreads, X (EmiliaURosa1)

APENDIX

On page 143 of this book I mentioned Manjar Branco, also called Manjar de Coco (Coconut Pudding). Below you will find a recipe similar to the one we made in my home in Brazil, when I was a child.

This pudding has a mild, delicate taste, with a subtle hint of coconut. The syrup takes it to another level.

Give it a try; I think you will like it!

MANJAR BRANCO

PUDDING:
8 to 10 tablespoons cornstarch
3 cups milk, divided
400 ml coconut milk (not coconut water)
1 cup sugar
SYRUP:
300 g prunes (seedless)
2.5 cups water
¾ cup sugar
1 cinnamon stick

PUDDING: Dissolve cornstarch in 1 cup milk; reserve. In a medium saucepan, add coconut milk, 2 cups milk and the sugar. When it starts to boil, slowly pour in the reserved milk. Cook over medium heat, stirring constantly until thickened, about 3 minutes. Don't let the cream thicken too much or it will become lumpy. Pour it into a round 7-inch tube pan (similar to a bundt pan), that has been very lightly coated with oil. Let it cool completely. Refrigerate for at least four hours, or until the pudding is firm. SYRUP: In a small saucepan, add sugar, water and prunes. Heat over medium heat until it starts to boil; immediately turn temperature to low. Cook for ten minutes, or until prunes are soft. Add the cinnamon and cook five more minutes, until you get a slightly thick syrup. Let it cool and refrigerate. Unmold the pudding on a plate. (You might need to run a knife around the pudding.) Drizzle with the syrup and arrange the prunes around it. Keep refrigerated.

For a stronger taste of coconut, replace ½ cup milk with ½ cup coconut milk for the pudding. You can also add ½ cup unsweetened grated coconut to the pudding. Or even use a few drops of coconut flavoring.

From King Denis' Cantigas de Amigo (note 48, page 211).

Ai flores, ai flores do verde pino,
se sabedes novas do meu amigo?
Ai Deus, e u é?

Ai flores, ai flores do verde ramo,
se sabedes novas do meu amado?
Ai Deus, e u é?

Oh flowers, oh flowers of the green pines,
Have you any news of my friend?
Oh, God, where can he be?

Oh flowers, oh flowers of the green branch,
Have you any news of my beloved?
Oh, God, where can he be?

www.ingramcontent.com/pod-product-compliance
Lightning Source LLC
Chambersburg PA
CBHW050340030726
47503CB00008B/2534